MONDAY'S
LIE

ALSO BY JAMIE MASON

Three Graves Full

MONDAY'S
LIE

JAMIE MASON

GALLERY BOOKS

NEW YORK   LONDON   TORONTO   SYDNEY   NEW DELHI

Gallery Books
A Division of Simon & Schuster, Inc.
1230 Avenue of the Americas
New York, NY 10020

First Gallery Books hardcover edition February 2015

GALLERY BOOKS and colophon are registered trademarks of Simon & Schuster, Inc.

For information about special discounts for bulk purchases, please contact Simon & Schuster Special Sales at 1-866-506-1949 or business@simonandschuster.com.

The Simon & Schuster Speakers Bureau can bring authors to your live event. For more information or to book an event, contact the Simon & Schuster Speakers Bureau at 1-866-248-3049 or visit our website at www.simonspeakers.com.

Manufactured in the United States of America

10 9 8 7 6 5 4 3 2 1

Library of Congress Cataloging-in-Publication Data is available.

ISBN 978-1-4767-7445-9
ISBN 978-1-4767-7447-3 (ebook)

How could this be for anyone other than my mother,
Jeanne Miller-Mason?
It couldn't. I love you.

The future destiny of the child is always the work of the mother.
—Napoléon I

MONDAY'S
LIE

I t's funny what you remember about terrible things.

The scattered shards were far more beautiful than the crystal lamp they'd been an hour before. The clearest night sky had nothing on the flicker and shine strewn across the black canvas bag that lay at the foot of the stairs. The industrious back-and-forth of the man's shadow tricked the shimmer into life with his every pass.

If I'm ever a ghost, this will be one place they'll see me—the translucent drenched girl in pajama pants and soggy sweatshirt, hovering and shivering in the foyer. Part of me never left. I can see everything about that night if I care to rewind my memory back that far, but I remember nothing so vividly as the broken glass.

I was never formally introduced to the special ops agent who had come for my mother. Technically, his was a welcome invasion of our home. He was helping her, but from what and into what, I didn't know. I was a child and willfully so. I could easily have been older than my thirteen years, but I wouldn't do it. Not then. Not yet. It gave her too much permission to leave me.

The first time I saw him, earlier in that night, he was only a shadowy blur bustling through the dark of our house, speaking urgently in a low voice to my mother. Then she sent me out into the darkness, dragging my eight-year-old brother, Simon, through the rain on a nonsense errand. I was savvy enough to know that she'd sent us out for our own protection. In fairness, I think even Simon knew.

Now, in the blazing light of every bulb in the house, the man was a bustling blur again, only in living color, gathering up my mother's few things as she packed them. He still droned urgently, but in a louder voice and speaking into the telephone this time, talking about ETAs and protocols and rendezvous points.

I breathed, and what should have been an automatic thing was now a trick of measuring air—not too much, not too little. My head threatened to swoon away each time I got the dose wrong. I listened to them getting things done while I couldn't, anchored in place, useless, staring transfixed into the glass that sparkled in the bursts of light between the eclipses of his shadow. He paced over the floor and back again, past a platter-size hole in the previously unmarred plaster of our foyer wall.

He never stood still long enough for me to get a fix on his face, and since the light show off the wreckage on his duffel bag was one of the few things not flitting around the room, dialing up the anxiety, that's where I pinned my gaze. Otherwise I might have been tempted to watch my mother prying Simon from around her waist, shushing him with tears in her voice, assuring him that everything was fine and that she'd be back soon.

My heart crashed tremors through my body. I squeezed my hands into fists and tucked them under my crossed arms to keep the trembling a private thing. I waited off to one side and out of the way, feeling around the edges of my blank mind for a fingerhold, for some train of thought I could tip over, or any good idea that I could wedge in, force open a gap, and fight my way past this wall in my mind so that I could be there with them. Really be there, with an unclenched throat and an argument made of something—anything—that couldn't lose.

A sob coiled in the roof of my mouth, pressing against my tongue. If I looked at them, I'd howl. My small family—a good, stable tripod when we stood together, faltered out of sync now, nerve-strung and scattered, the three of us wide-awake in the middle of a night that had been just like any other night when we'd all gone to bed a few hours earlier.

I was afraid to see on their faces what I heard in their voices. It would surely rattle me right out of the stranglehold I had on my self-control. The glittering kept my eyes busy enough to hold off the tears. They'd still be there, both the tears and the shattered mess on the floor, when this was over. I saved the crying for later. It would go well with the chore of sweeping up the foyer.

I tried to watch my mother in the final minutes before she left, to save a last image of her to hold in my head for when she wouldn't be there. My heartbeat hammered *soon, soon, soon* in my chest and I looked away.

My attention slid off the practiced last steps of her leaving dance, her head bent over the wallet in her hands in a quick accounting of the sheaf of cash that padded the length of it, and the brisk, casual grace in the sweep of her arm as she reached for the keys on the hall table. I pointedly didn't want to see her face or my brother's, or whoever the man was with the ready-when-you-are tone in his voice and his hand on the doorknob.

But we're programmed from birth to find faces everywhere, as if the pattern of the human mask is some sort of touchstone for reality. We seek its layout in wood grain and in clouds, in every indistinct thing. We find eyes looking back at us over noses and mouths in the scorch patterns on toast and in the craggy stacks of mountains. So I couldn't resist the pull of the man's ID tag. It had twisted around on its plastic tether on the glass-covered bag, landing upside down to show me an inverted photo of the efficient young man with the soldier's posture who had woken us out of the sweet summer storm, the man who had for the last hour or so been treading the boards of our home with unearned privilege. Special Agent Brian Menary.

My concentration tunneled a path out of the room, away from the merry twinkling of the broken bits of lamp on the black fabric, away from my mother's departing instructions and the unexplained disarray of our usually tidy front rooms. I stared at the picture on the tag and burrowed my focus into the man's upside-down eyes, as if I could stamp the blank, official expression on this stranger's face over the panic that clogged up my throat.

My mother pulled me away from the study of his identification badge. I couldn't say anything to her at first as she gripped my shoulders, squeezing fear into me when she meant to telegraph strength.

"Dee, Paul's outside. He'll stay until Marie gets here."

Aunt Marie was my mother's sister. Paul was my mother's boss, but also a fixture in our lives.

"We don't need a babysitter. I can do it," I said. I'd be going into the eighth grade in just over a month. I could certainly manage the TV's remote control and a few peanut-butter sandwiches for Simon.

"Of course you can. But, Plucky, it's going to be a few days at least."

"Mama, what happened while we were outside? Why did you send us out there?" I pointed back behind us without taking my eyes off her. I could smell flight in the air. Fight had obviously already happened.

Avoidance sounded the same as reassurances and grocery lists from her. "A chunk got knocked out of the wall. I'll fix it when I get back."

"Mom." I rarely called her Mom. She was always Mama. I didn't usually trust any application of hard edges, even in sounds, to my mother. I never tested whether she would break against them or ricochet off. Either way she'd be gone.

"I don't have time to work out how to explain this to you, Plucky. And I won't do a half-baked job of it or do you the disservice of lying about what happened tonight. I'll tell you this, though. You're completely safe. I have to go away for a few days to straighten this out, but I'm safe and you're safe."

"Mama! No! What—"

Simon was crying again.

"I know, sweetheart."

Stubborn felt better than wild, so I grabbed for it. "Don't go. You don't have to. Just tell this guy to go away. He doesn't need to be here. Everything is okay. You said that we're safe, so, I believe you. Right? We're fine. Just tell Paul you won't do it. This is crazy. Why won't you tell me what happened?"

"Oh, Dee. There are parts of this motherhood thing I'm just not very good at. Saying the right things that make everything fine is one of them. I'm so sorry. You deserve better, both of you."

"No, that's not true!" I wailed, wounded in that irrational, bruised yard of soul that's cordoned off for love of the mother who loves you. "You're the best mother ever!"

"If you really think so, then there's not a thing left in this world that scares me. And if I'm not scared, Plucky, I promise you—you don't need to be either."

Within ten minutes she was gone and we wouldn't see her for more than seven months.

I would set up my mother's house for her return as soon as the taillights of the SUV swept out of sight in the turn at the end of our street. Before I stretched out on my bed to stare at the ceiling until the first faint light of the morning brightened my bedroom, I'd cleared away the glass and straightened out all that had gone crooked and sideways in the foyer in the night.

I made sure that the entire time she was gone the hole in the wall would be the only flaw left to hint at the night's disruption. My aunt Marie, tucked in under a blanket on the sofa, would be its plus one. I'd been overruled on that. She stayed. We would all wake up after not really sleeping, to Day One of the Long Trip.

Breath held. Everything in its place as it should be. Everything but my mother.

Later, and for years after, the thing that twisted me into a restless tangle in my sheets was the certainty that every normal night was on a hair trigger, leaning in at the ready to explode into something else entirely.

In the end, I did everything my mother asked, but as for her telling me the story of what happened that night? She never did.

But a story is a house, a home for something that happened. The truth lives there forever, along with its cousins, the half-truths, and also with everyone's servants—the lies. And no house has only one door. There's always another way in.

I

Friday

It's Friday, but Monday's lie made today what it is. I don't quite recognize myself this afternoon. But no matter what happens today, at least I'll always know it went down on a Friday.

I don't know why I even think of things this way, but I always do. Milestones of varying weight have always been marked in my mind with the day of the week. I broke my wrist when Danny Gardner pulled my chair out from under me on a Tuesday in the second grade. When we were both just twenty-two years old, Patrick proposed to me on a Wednesday, which was weird. I had always thought those kinds of things happened only on Saturdays. My mother left for more than seven months in the middle of one Friday night, just after my thirteenth birthday. She came home on a Friday as well. And years later, she died on a Sunday.

Tabbing events with the day of the week is an utterly useless filing system, but my brain has always done it that way. I can't seem to make it stop.

So even though today is Friday, Monday was the day to mark. On Monday I knew for certain that my marriage was—at the very least—over. And at the very most it was . . . Well, I'd soon find out.

I'm driving to a place I've never been, to talk to a man I've never met, and all of it to put an end to what I've almost worked out is wrong with my life.

My mother always said never to keep a man for more years than you could count on your fingers. Of course, that was a faster-paced game for her than for most people. She'd lost two of her fingers in completely separate escapades. Her long, abbreviated left hand and the mischief glittering in her eyes made the joke all the richer. Everyone's scars are interesting, but my mother's always hinted at epic.

She was the reincarnation of Errol Flynn, which meant that she would've had to steal his soul well before his death, but that would have been just like her. She wasn't as beautiful as much as she was dashing, more pirate than princess, an excess of Robin Hood to put the breeches on Maid Marian. I know that she worked for the government at intervals.

Most people never knew a thing about my mother or her work and never realized the spectacular lack of specifics. She could talk all around it in lively stories without ever revealing a single thing about the true nature of her business. To this day, even I know very little of her global worth. But there was always something. Her gravity bent light like a neutron star. She breathed in the mundane and exhaled ozone. She baked cookies the other PTA mothers were reluctant to eat without being able to say exactly why.

Someone with the authority to do so called her away twice while we were growing up—the longest stretch being for that seven months when I was thirteen. But for the longest time she was mostly just our mother and was as competent at that as she was at everything else. If suburban ease chafed at all, she never let on, and for the majority of our growing up, it was just the three of us—my mother, my little brother, Simon, and me. Occasionally there was an extra jacket, leather or sometimes tweed, on the hall tree for a season, or a thick-banded diver's watch next to her delicate bracelet one on the dresser.

Her men never left in tears. But they always left.

Mine, however, was still around, and I was fast running out of fingers to count the years on.

Friday

You can buy more advantage with audacity than you can with a million bucks. Hello, Mama. I can hear her in my mind's ear now as clearly as if she were right beside me, as if she hasn't been dead for more than three years. I spur down the gas pedal, launching my car down a road that matches an unfamiliar blue line scrolling out on the GPS screen toward Carlisle Inc., a company that, among other things, builds aluminum storage and warehouse facilities. It's almost four o'clock, and if the workweek ends, so do my chances. I need to get there before they all go home.

I'm looking for a man, or more generally for a blue sedan that has been menacing me in its mild insistence on turning up too often in my rearview mirror of late. If I find the car, I find the man. Then I find out what the hell is going on.

I let urgency trump my fear and let boldness chew my common sense to silence. If I can put a gag on anything that feels like wisdom, I'm hoping that all I'll have left is courage.

The address I've entered puts my destination in an old industrial park out past the county line. I've never been out this way. It will take most of an hour to get there, and I think there's a good chance my mother and I will talk in my head the whole way. It's the conversation I always assumed she'd wanted, the one where I ask how I can be more like her. But in the answers I sense waiting for me over the ridge and the next one and the one after that, in the responses I'm assigning to her, I realize it's not that at all. It never had been. She'd only wanted me to know her.

I couldn't have the dates and times and places of so much of her life. Those were classified. But in her games and in her axioms, she'd been more candid with her soul than anyone else I'd ever known. She'd been so generous with who she *really* was that she is somehow still with me, even now, reminding me of what I learned from her and advising me on what I am about to do next.

I don't believe my mother, Annette Vess, thought that mothering and training were the same thing exactly, but a blurred line stitched the two ideas into our security blankets from infancy. In the end, I did feel loved, but also more than a little automated.

It had been a game with her when we were little. She'd give us points for noticing things. We'd stand in the checkout line at the supermarket, and on the way to the car she might say, "Okay, Plucky and Sixes"—Simon was "Sixes" by virtue of his extraordinary penchant for rolling them in dice games—"heads up! We're playing. Five points: What was the man two places behind us in line wearing?"

"A tan sweater," I'd say.

"Black shoes with tassels," Simon would crow.

"Five bonus points for each item in his basket you can name."

"Vanilla ice cream."

"Itch ointment."

"Baked beans."

"Three cans of tuna. Do I get fifteen points for that one?"

Whoever had earned the most points at the end of whatever period she'd set would get signed out of school on some random afternoon for a trip to the ice-cream parlor or the zoo. She could keep an accurate scoreboard in her head for weeks.

As we grew older, the games advanced in their cunning. It was fun at the time, bonding the three of us together against an unnamed Them. But it was impossible to unlearn.

As for where the games came from and her hobby that was more like a mission to polish our instincts and reaction times, it all started with Paul Rowland. How she got snagged into this web in the first place was one of his favorite stories. Ultimately my mother made a career of, from all I could tell, nothing but sticky intrigue, knowing looks, and heavy, unfinished sentences between her and Paul. I remember hearing the story for the first time once when we had company over.

As usual, they were people I didn't know and likely wouldn't see again. My mother was unreadable, leaning back into the sofa cushions, watching Paul sidelong as he recounted to the group the first time he'd met her. Her eyes flashed onto mine. I was eight years old and all elbows and knees when it came to stealth. I'd crammed myself into a corner of the front hallway for its acoustics, half-turned away, miming devotion to my toys. I watched my mother measure the angle from Paul's vantage point to my hideaway, but I had already calculated it. Even when he leaned in to tap the ash from his cigarette, I still fell outside his field of vision.

My mother tracked from my eyes to the doll in my hands, a ruin-haired thing I hadn't touched in a year. We locked eyes again, but she drifted her attention to her guests with the pretense that she hadn't really seen me. She let me stay, but more important, she made sure that I knew she'd let me stay. The transaction tingled at the base of my skull.

Paul was too beefy for me to consider nice looking. I had only just begun to check men for handsomeness, and at the time, it was always how they stacked up against my music teacher. Mr. Noakes was narrow, with longish, dark blond hair that swept his collar. He waved like seaweed in the ocean, eyes closed over a sweet, crooked smile, when he set us playing on our recorders, woodblocks, and maracas. I had decided I was one of his favorites since I'd scored a coveted assignment to the ranks of the new xylophones the school had just acquired to Mr. Noakes's pride and delight.

Ever on the lookout to shrink Paul in my opinion, I saw him as the anti–Mr. Noakes: too thick even if he was nowhere near fat; too old-fashioned with dark, tightly trimmed hair held down with a sheen of styling wax; and I was sure that Paul would only ever sway in an earthquake. He was solid when he stood, feet planted in line with his broad shoulders, and he went just shy of clumping when he walked.

Because of Paul Rowland, for the entirety of my life I never met a mustache I liked.

"So I get to the door," Paul said, "and there's this skinny little girl with wet-noodle posture, droopy hair, and not a damned thing going on behind her eyes. So, I ask this kid, I say, 'I'm with the Veterans of Foreign Wars membership committee, and I'm looking for Carl Cowling.' And she says . . ." Paul laughed into his pause. "Go on, Annette. I can't do the accent like you did."

My mother let her face fall slack and somehow snuffed the lasers out of her eyes. "Uncle Carl ain't here. I ain't seen 'im in a coon's age."

I would have sworn on a stack of Bibles that such a sound could never have come from my mother, but it slid up and out of her throat with the casual music of mountain mine country, utterly natural and pleasant in the way that things can be only when they fit just right.

Paul sniffled over his mirth. "Oh, she played me, I tell you. She had me going with this story of how there'd been somebody else poking around for her uncle earlier that very same day, which, of course, got my radar buzzing. I mean, who the hell else was hot on Carl Cowling besides me? I had to know. I was half on my way to giving her my name, rank, and serial number while Cowling slipped out the back and right off into the sunset, while this one"—Paul cocked his thumb at my mother—"led me around by the nose.

"Then she finally drops the accent and the dim stare and right before my eyes turns all hard and *real* pretty like some damned magic trick and says, 'Look, Carl lit out of here half a minute after you rang the bell, G-man. He said he'd give me five dollars if I kept you busy. He said you were a debt collector. Then *you* say you're from the VFW. Nobody tells me anything.'

"'G-man? Why do you think I work for the government?'" Paul said he'd asked her.

"'Well, you're not a cop.'

"'Who says?'

"'I do. You asked me if the men who had already been here were cops. If you were a cop, you would know.'

"'Not necessarily.'"

Paul crowed with laughter ahead of his own, or, more accurately, my mother's own, punch line. "This one, she just laughed at me. Right in my face, she did.

"'Bingo,' she says. 'And if I didn't know that you weren't a cop before, I surely know it now. *Not necessarily.* Jeez, mister. So that leaves mob or government, and pardon me for saying so, but you're not dressed nice enough to be mob.'

"'You shouldn't believe everything you see in the movies, kid.'

"'Words to live by, I'm sure. Thanks for the tip.'

"That's what she says to me! 'Thanks for the tip,'" Paul wheezed.

"Anyway." He swatted the air after catching up with his own amusement. "That whole Cowling business turned out not to be the leg up and big promotion I had hoped it would be, but discovering the smartest skirt this side of the Berlin Wall? That took all the sting right out of losing that little fish."

"It only took you three more years to bring me into the fold," my mother replied.

"It was worth the wait. Best damned liar I ever met."

Later, when they had all left, I braved the subject that had kept my mind stuck in the afternoon's eavesdropping. "Mama, why does Uncle Paul think it's good to lie?"

The question dog-eared the moment in time. A thrill sped through me. I'd never asked her anything important before. I'd never pitted her against my private opinion of Paul.

She had always been open and matter-of-fact about everything, never fatigued by any endless volley of curiosity that my brother and I had pummeled her with. But this question seemed even bolder out loud than it had sounded in my head. It hung in the air between us, and for the first time I knew that pricking someone with a question could be more important than whatever answer they might come up with. For the first time, I knew I might have nudged her onto her back foot.

She watched me balance up the weight of the moment. "Five points for you, Plucky. That's a very smart question." She turned to the mirror and swiped a dollop of cold cream over each eye. It looked like white frosting going on, but darkened to gray sludge with each swirling pass of her fingertips. "You know how they say, 'Honesty is the best policy'?"

I nodded.

She continued to massage her mascara into the cream. "If you're still there, Plucky, I can't hear your brains rattling. Speak up!" She laughed as she groped for a tissue.

"Yes, I'm here." I slid the box of Kleenex under her searching hand and knew for sure that she wasn't put off by my question. And then it was another first for me to find that, as relieved as I was that she wasn't mad at me, I wasn't entirely pleased at my inability to rattle her.

"Well, for a change, the great nameless, faceless *they* is absolutely right." She wiped her eyes bright. What she lost in wattage without her makeup, she gained in youth. "Honesty is most certainly the best policy."

Then she turned and took my hands. From the corner of my eye, I could see our profiles in the mirror, her bending down to me, the towel turban making her taller than ever.

"But *they* make it sound so simple. And the biggest, meanest trick in all the world is how complicated *they* have made things. They know, even as they say it, that the best policy doesn't always get the job done. Honesty is like your best shoes." This was especially relevant, as she well knew, because I kept trying to convince my mother to let me wear my white, patent leather Mary Janes with everything, most recently my bathing suit. "Your best shoes make you feel good and they make you look good, but there are some jobs that just aren't suited to them."

"Mama, do you lie to do your job?"

Not a ripple in her composure, she smiled into my eyes. "Sometimes."

The sapling of my eight-year-old integrity quivered. "Do you lie to me?"

"Not ever if I can help it."

"But they say you shouldn't lie!"

"Ahhh. There *they* go again, huh?" My mother kissed the backs of my hands. "Tell me. Do *they* know your favorite color?"

I shook my head.

"Do *they* know that you like the side and bottom crusts cut off your sandwiches, but that you like me to leave the top one on?"

"No."

"Do they love you as much as I do?"

"No, Mama."

"Do *they* build the world you live in?"

I froze.

Finally, a flinch from her; from somewhere deep in her eyes it shuddered and drew tears in its wake. "Two points for you, my darling, for stopping to think on that one." But she did not tremble. Her hands were calm and she took my face between their warmth. She pressed her lips hard against my forehead. She hugged me to her, and the blue chenille smelled of Chanel No. 5. "You're such a bright girl, Plucky," she whispered into my hair.

She pulled back. "*They* do indeed build the world. So do listen when they say things. Hear what they say and weigh it carefully. But when you hear *me*, remember that I *never* told you *not* to lie, baby girl." She checked to see that it had sunk in. "I'll only warn you to hate it."

2

Growing up, we'd wanted for nothing. We lived in a plain, saltbox house on a plain, saltboxy cul-de-sac, but my mother always had her clothes, even her blue jeans, tailored. That's how I knew for certain we weren't like other people. My little brother was oblivious and never thought that it was odd that he had only to whine for a new football, baseball glove, or hockey stick and somehow "Uncle Paul" would, like a magician with his rabbit, pull it out of nowhere on his next visit. I'd get a bag of coconut Neapolitans and a bauble or a book. I could feel the oily purpose, like a film, on those gifts—*Keep 'em distracted and they won't ask any questions.* My mother would get a fat manila envelope or locked briefcase and a courtly kiss on the cheek.

I hated Uncle Paul. He'd take us out to dinner or to the movies, so I liked his visits well enough, and the coconut candies fed my rabid sweet tooth, but the air crackled whenever he came around. My stomach would go tight and heavy without ever answering to my brain for its unease. As I got older, I'd feel my hair bristle and my skin crimp into goose bumps, only to turn and find Uncle Paul watching me, a little knowing smile playing under his mustache.

"Annette, you're tuning them up. You sure that's wise?" I'd heard him say after one of our little standoffs. I turned the corner and held my breath to eavesdrop, but my mother only laughed.

Whether Paul Rowland approved of them or not, my mother's games put her eyes on me. Or perhaps more accurately to the way it really felt, the games were a sure chance to put me in her sights. I was the target, my mind a solid bull's-eye for her aim. I never felt more real, and she never felt more anchored to me, than when she worked a lesson of what could be known from the quick scanning of a deserted park trail or how much could be read in the postures of the people on a busy street corner.

My mother's attention had a clamping quality, and somehow I'd been born feeling full of helium, as if I'd sail away into oblivion if I weren't nailed down. She was all mine, the paperweight to my flutter, when I would work under her instruction, mastering whatever trick we were honing at the moment.

For me, that's what the games were for—for seeing her and for being truly seen. Simon, on the other hand, thought the games gave him superpowers.

From time to time, Simon took his fledgling knack for observation and deduction for a test-drive with varying degrees of success and the occasional punch in the nose.

He'd solved the case of our missing outdoor shoes when he was nine. First, my mother's left garden clog went missing. Then Simon's flip-flops and one of his soccer cleats disappeared. I straightaway brought in all my shoes from the back porch at the first sign of trouble and lost nothing. It turned out that our neighbors two streets over had a dog, and this dog had a neurotic affection for shoes with a sidecar mental disorder, a hoarding complex.

Simon staked out the clues and worked it all back to the dog's impressive stash of ancient-to-almost-brand-new footwear. Seven full pair in all, plus nineteen singleton shoes, left ones only, were squirreled away in the crook of an old planter and a hose box behind the neighbor's house. If only Simon could have figured out why the crazy hound always took the lefties first, I would have called the mission a complete victory. As it was, no one wanted the chewed-up, spider-infested things back, but Simon was pleased with himself, and to me at least, the world is always righter with one less mystery in it. My mother gave him twenty-five points for his persistence.

From that proud moment on, he was completely hooked on sleuthing.

Then when the middle-school band trip was in jeopardy from the theft of the fund-raiser candy, Simon put an eye on his class-mates and an ear to the ground. His blood was up—in equal parts righteous indignation against crime in general and also that he'd been fizzing for months with barely hidden glee for the chance to play the saxophone in a big auditorium and take his own picture of the famous arch in St. Louis.

With a speed and precision that startled even our mother, Simon called out Brendan Corrigan and his buddies for nicking Red Cross badges from inside the blood-drive vans that had been out to the school, then selling the fund-raiser chocolate bars in the guise of volunteers, all on their own, for mad money. A couple of afternoons hitting up the far neighborhoods with red crosses pinned to their lapels, and suddenly Brendan Corrigan and his crew were pumping tokens into the arcade games all afternoon in flashy new sneakers.

But by the end of the week, both my brother and Brendan Cor-rigan were in the nurse's office with ice packs on their faces, and my mother was in the principal's conference room letting his canned speech slide right over her. I heard the whole thing from my chair, waiting just outside.

"Mrs. Vess, we're going to have to assign Simon a week's worth of after-school detention for fighting." Mr. Campbell paused in the expectation of protest.

He got none. "I understand," said my mother. "And I'm sure Simon does, too."

"While we very much appreciate Simon's efforts to get the band fund-raiser back on track, I'm sure we can all agree that it would have been better if he'd simply brought the information to us and let us handle it. The tensions over tattling—"

"They didn't fight over the candy situation."

"Pardon me?"

"You talked to them, yes?"

"I did," said Campbell.

"Then you know it was all posturing. Chest beating." She got no reply and presumably a blank look from Mr. Campbell. "A pissing contest? Once the Corrigan kid couldn't get a rise out of Simon by calling him names for getting him in trouble, he switched up tactics and called me a dyke." I could see in my mind the curl of amusement bending her mouth and sending the words out sideways, letting them hit with just the right thump. Not too hard. Not too soft. The Goldilocks of confrontation.

Mr. Campbell coughed in discomfort, and even from the other side of the wall I could tell he didn't realize he'd done it. He would have been surprised to hear a taped playback of his automatic rumble of unease at considering my formidable mother in sexual terms of any sort.

I bit down on the corner of my lip to keep from smiling, wondering if she was, too. I was nearly seventeen, wavering on the line just past giddy blushing at anything in the same zip code as innuendo, past most of that sort of silliness, but not yet at peace with the idea that all kinds of things made the world go round, but nothing so much as sex and the near constant calculations over what to do about it.

Mr. Campbell cleared his throat. "Well, yes. I'm sorry you had to hear that. I'll have Mr. Corrigan write up an apology for baiting Simon like that and bringing you into it with an insult."

"It's not an insult," my mother said in her best peppermint voice.

More coughing from Campbell. "No! Of course not. I just meant—"

"It's fine. And it's all beside the point, too. It had nothing to do with me. 'Your mama' jokes never do. It's all about escalation. It's what boys do."

"Of course, of course. And I'm sure you don't need your son to defend you, Mrs. Vess."

"Now why would you say that?" Voice a little warmer. Buttermints now. "You don't know me, Mr. Campbell, I could very well be emotionally delicate."

Campbell's giggle-cough put him just where my mother liked him, liked all of them: talking freely. That's how she got things done.

The principal cleared his throat again, an obvious tic, not an allergy. "Now, the boys do have an option to replace detention with a joint presentation, of their own devising, to the Health and Development classes on why violence is never the answer to a conflict. They would work up a ten-to-fifteen-minute talk with slides or some kind of visual aids, and then they would lead a discussion. They'd get out of the detention and get extra credit for the project. We like to think of it as turning a negative into a positive."

"Simon will take his detention."

"Well, shouldn't we at least ask him if—"

"No."

"Okay," Mr. Campbell said, blunted to uncomfortable silence. She'd shut him down, withdrawn the light, rescinded the invitation to stand on the same step.

"Mr. Campbell, I know you mean well, but you'll strip every bit of lesson from this dustup if you or I or anyone else digs into their business any deeper. We don't need to turn this into anything in particular for them, positive or negative. Let the boys weigh the pain in their faces that they feel today and the nice afternoons that they're going to lose to detention next week against whether or not it was worth it to push it that far or, on the other hand, to push back to make it stop."

"Mrs. Vess, you can't want Simon to think anything's ever settled by force."

"Of course not," she said, all velvet bludgeon. "Except for the things that are. Life is choices, Mr. Campbell. And sometimes other people's choices even more than your own."

3

Friday

I'm headed straight west and the sun is preheating this damned oven of a car. I'll be cooked by the time I get there. But even though it's way too hot in here, I roll down the windows instead of turning on the air. I'm already not blinking enough as it is, staring wide to take in all of this road that I've never seen before, making sure I don't miss anything. That's how I do it when I'm caught out of my routine. I can take the shine off anything new faster than anyone I know. I scour down every novelty with lathered-up concentration until it feels normal.

So I'm studying this countryside hard, eyes scanning, cataloging the roll of the road and the different shades of green at the borders. The few sections of as-yet-undeveloped fields are flagged with ruins, the silvered barns in the near distance looking set there as leaning markers to the time when this was probably all one vast farm. I don't want cold air pouring into my face from the vents and drying out my eyes any more than they already are. If it did, then I'd blink. Then I'd miss something. Then I'd doubt. And when I doubt, I freeze. And when I freeze, I convince myself that maybe it's not so bad—it's familiar, it's safe, it's normal, I guess I'll just stay here. . . .

So instead, I'll use the windows and be too hot.

My mother would laugh at me, overthinking my eyeballs along with everything else. But she's not here. No matter how hard I wish she were. So I laugh at me for her, out loud. The sound is startling and out of place and I like it. I definitely don't recognize myself today.

My alpha error, it seems, was seeded in me sometime shortly after Santa Claus was exposed for a fraud. I've somehow thought that I needed to figure out my mother in order to figure out myself. For the longest time, I've been adamant that her contradictions are not mine, that gentleness and warmth don't come in the same package as danger and cunning. If they appear to, then one of the elements has to be a lie, or at the very least, it has to be less true than all the others. Except I won't admit that I know well—too well, even— that sometimes it works out to be just exactly that way.

That mistake has taken me so far around the long way in life, in a detour on the way to myself, that skimming over these unfamiliar roads right now is also something that feels exactly right. It's time. I have no idea where I'm going. But I know what I'll find when I get there. I'll find me.

Contradictions, and even polar opposites, coexist in the same skin. Of course they do. I have to know that and admit it now, because a nice set of contradictions lived—and still does—in me, if not comfortably then at least functionally. Right from the beginning, I was always both fascinated and mortified by the stories of my mother's escapades, simultaneously pulled and repelled by imagining her doing these crazy things that were nothing like what she did every day at home where I could see her.

One of her more elegant gifts was for narrative without handholds. Her stories rang like swordplay and sparked with every humor that glinted off the sharper edges of the tale. But when she was done and the laughter had faded and the dishes were drying in the rack, only then would you realize that you'd never be able to point to a spot on a map or a box on the calendar to make any more of it than what she'd given you. You could think on it all day, or all of your days even, and never work so much as one extra deduction from putting her various twos and twos together, or come to any conclusion that she hadn't spoon-fed you.

And for all the years afterward, you could only ever retell the story the way she did, or less so. Those were your choices. She'd left no clue as to where it fit into her heart or her résumé. It was just a fable, not a link to the how or why she'd been in place to see such a marvel, never a hint as to what she had been doing.

I was impressed with her, but afraid I didn't know her. My mother was kind; she was devoted. And she was also an asskicker.

In the overlap of our lifetimes, I'd heard her tell one story a hundred times, and it never delivered any clarity on how much she might have mourned her first professional injury and the resulting scar it left, but the story of how it happened never got old. I had already eavesdropped it into my memory by the time I could tie my shoes, as it spooled out again and again to uniformed or plainclothes company, but I loved it even more, with wide-eyed dismay, when it was told just for me, for the first time when I was eleven years old. Being trusted with it, counted old enough to be part of the conversation, her dark eyes steady on mine, it was better than the cherry on top of my prize ice-cream sundae.

My mother lost the little finger on her left hand in a knife fight, in a prison, in an undisclosed South American country. By today's standards, she wouldn't have been old enough to drink.

She had been called back into the field in the middle of the night. More accurately, as she always groused, Paul Rowland had summoned her from the dead center of a hard-earned sleep. She said she'd gone to bed at eleven and had ordered a wake-up call for six in the morning. She remembered vividly that the phone had rung at 3:32.

Fresh off a job well done and following the buzz-killing (and hours-long) debrief of what she'd accomplished, she had snuck off and checked into a hotel under an assumed name as a reward to herself. Her story always hinted at one of two motivations (or possibly a smidge from column A and a dose from column B) for good ol' Paul.

There was the irritable point driven home that she was always findable, and then there was his pride. The stories of my mother's earlier adventures always hinted at a possessiveness that Paul felt for her and for the work that she did under his direction. He couldn't wait to trot out his best triumph, his finest trick pony.

Literally couldn't wait, not even for dawn. She saw the sunrise from the tarmac of an airport runway, where the plane's touch-and-go stop would pluck her from her furlough.

That the prescribed errand had been cobbled together without enough information and foresight was readily apparent once my mother found herself relieved of her passport, a tad too thoroughly searched, and shackled at the wrists and ankles on a bench in a mossy cinder-block hut—and all of this before lunchtime.

Even more than coming home minus one digit, my mother had always seemed especially outraged that these things had happened after she'd been arrested under verifiable diplomatic immunity. She refused to leave out that tidbit of bureaucratic insight when she told this story, although most of her others steered around any mention at all of her employers.

She took care to describe the catalyst for the day's disaster— a filthy oscillating fan that blew humidity, but not much relief, around the room. Stirring away at the heavy air, it had also sent strands of her vacant-eyed benchmate's long, frazzled hair into my mother's face with each rusty pass of the blades, as the two of them waited for processing.

My mother's finger wasn't severed by the fan, but ultimately it was still sort of the fan's fault. The woman on the bench next to her had dozed off, chin on impressive chest, a shiny thread of drool feeding a growing wet spot on the forehead of the sunny smiley face that beamed up from her ragged T-shirt.

In the last important turn of the fan's slow circuit, the tepid whoosh plucked up its usual hank of hair from the woman's shoulder and twisted it through the air and, most unfortunately this time, through the drool. When the sodden strands connected with my mother's cheek, it put paid to the last of her patience.

When she swatted away the one offense, she accidentally lit the fuse on a new one. The chain on my mother's handcuffs snagged the full wisp of hair and plucked it, roots and all, straight out of Sleeping Beauty's head.

Where a dozy beast had been napping, in a flurry of cursing and rattling chains the Devil herself woke up. My mother managed to pin down the woman's thrashing arms, but took a volley of stout kicks to the shins and ankles until she had her wrapped, huffing and spitting, in the tangle of my mother's trained reach. She crooned soothing words and apologies in Spanish, well at odds with her iron grip, until the woman relaxed and relented. Mother let her go.

"Illuminada!" The guard came hustling from around his desk as Illuminada wrenched herself to the other end of the bench, to the full length of her shackles, and smoldered pure hatred back at my mother from as far away as she could get.

"Vaca estúpida!" *Stupid cow.* He laughed as he unlocked her feet and swatted her on the back of the head. He yanked her off her seat and taunted her with more barnyard insults as he relocated her to the opposite side of the room where there was no bench. He locked her hands to a low ring buried in the wall. The chain was too short to let her stand in even a parody of dignity, so she slumped defeated on the mildewed concrete floor.

My mother said that she stewed there for more than two hours after they had hauled Illuminada away, so it was less than a welcomed surprise to find them penned together again, unshackled, in a more general holding area later that same afternoon.

My mother said Illuminada had a light mustache that bristled with the sobriety that had bloomed in the intervening hours. The guards formed up around them in a jeering circle when the strung-out slab of a creature took up their quarrel with renewed vigor and an audience. The jumble of prisoners and jailers gasped and shuffled bets in colorful paper currency once the she-Hulk pulled the blade.

The looky-loos crowded in on the pair, dialing the arena down to a tight dance floor. Her opponent lunged, but stumbled, still a little woozy from whatever had mellowed her earlier. In the misstep, my mother lost out to a gift from dumb luck to the generally luck-less Illuminada. It put her in place to catch my mother stranded off her position by a few inches and directly in front of someone clearly rooting for the home team, or at least for the novelty of some blood-shed.

My mother never saw who owned the strong hands that shoved her toward her attacker. Illuminada flailed in surprise more than she could ever be accused of finessing the knife. In the collision, my mother's pinkie was sheared off clean at the third knuckle. Cackling and taking all of the credit for a trick of fate and physics, Illuminada snatched the severed finger from the floor, gave it a prissy little kiss on the nail, and shoved it into the pocket of her baggy pants.

As the victor aped for the crowd, grinning and pumping her fists in the air, my bloodied mother crawled toward her on her hands and knees. The guards, not anxious to end the show, let her come on. At the last moment, Illuminada spied my mother's progress from the corner of her eye. The expression of stunned alarm bloomed to re-solve on her rough face, lit by an ember of defiance from somewhere deep in Illuminada's wounded pride. She'd go another round. My mother saw that she'd go another ten rounds if need be to salvage her status as Queen Colossus of the Usual Suspects.

A fair fight wasn't to be had.

So my mother stopped, grinned, and shrugged a sheepish you-caught-me. Then, in the pause, she reached out and yanked down Illuminada's loose cotton trousers. All of the action stopped in a moment of slack-jawed tempo change before everyone, including the bare-butted and dangerously offended Illuminada and my own mother, burst out laughing at the slapstick turn.

Still laughing, my mother rose up into a crouch and took out Illuminada's knee with a sideways elbow. She snatched the shiv from where it had fallen on the floor during the grand tumble, and with her mangled hand, she pressed the blade to her unreliably vanquished foe's throat. With the other hand, and a pinning foot, she ripped the gory pocket from the pants that had puddled around the other woman's ankles.

My mother's knife hand rained blood from around her grip, but she stood up, smoothed back her hair with her cleaner hand, and demanded to be taken to a hospital.

Unfortunately, jungle climate being what it is and banana-republic jailers being notorious for their lack of empathy, it was too late to re-attach her finger by the time she was finally seen by a doctor.

So it went—stories of daring stunts in exotic backwaters and then, twenty minutes later, my mother helping me with my algebra. There were packages delivered by moonlight, English melting over the doormat into the rapid, gorgeous rhythms of other continents. There were the strictest warnings on never touching the phone in the den or any of the sealed envelopes and boxes on her desk. And then, all of a sudden as you do, it was movie night, or homemade soup when we were sick.

I had closed my fists around every trace of her that I could catch after she'd come home from the Long Trip. Sometimes I got nothing but smoke between my fingers, and sometimes I latched onto strings I could pull a little bit, to tug her off her purpose, if I dared.

She'd slept for two days straight and had a shower that lasted half the next morning. After that she was almost the same again, her crisp linen self. But I was different. I gritted my teeth down over anger and a sadness, ground them into a routine of headaches and upset stomachs that got my hair petted for hours over her first months back. Payback for her leaving me was my sulking head in her lap, her fingertips dragging chills over my scalp. I loved that she couldn't go to the sink to do the dishes or read a book, make a phone call or run an errand, pinned as she was under my malady. She was patient, though. We didn't talk, just the two of us, but she stroked her amends into my hair.

She'd set the rhythm back into our days as the first order of business. There wasn't much unpacking to do as she'd left with almost nothing and had come home with even less than that, wearing unfamiliar, travel-creased clothes that smelled of foreign, strong cigarettes. She would cover the phone and pull funny faces at us between repeatedly telling Paul to piss off whenever he'd call the house in those first few weeks.

We silently agreed that the Long Trip was a black hole in our little suburban opera. It dragged at the usual brightness all around us, and we fought its gravity together until the three of us pulled free of it as one. We reknit our relationships, even if I now trusted that my life not only could be, but *would* be, tipped over by chaos if I ever let my guard down against the odd and the offbeat.

We never talked about the gash in the wall, which was fixed in her first week back. It's as if we knew, in a way that shimmered of almost posthypnotic suggestion, that we were not to bring up those first dark hours of the day she left.

My mother went back to work after a rest and an extended hide-and-chase with Paul that lasted through blatant rebuff, not-so-sly telephone tag, and two episodes of playing possum when he dropped by our house unannounced. Simon and I lay on her bed with her, the curtains pulled over the windows, all of us with a hand clapped over our mouth, holding in the giggles and going red in the face while Paul hung on the bell until the uselessness of cooling his heels on our welcome mat outraced his pointless ambition to speak to my mother when she didn't wish to be spoken to.

I fed and watered the hope that she'd hold out against him forever. But Paul's aim didn't need to be perfect when he never ran out of ammunition. He took out her resistance and her resolve over a series of growling arguments behind the closed den door, and then our life got back to what it had been, more *and* less, with the cup full of something extra that kept it from being normal.

There had always been random visits from black Bentleys in the middle of the night, delivering men with accents and poise to our door, or on the other hand, cars so plain vanilla they fairly shouted their undercover importance, but eventually and inevitably, I'd had enough.

I had never liked strangers popping in and annexing our living room for a makeshift boardroom. Everything would be in order, a quiet and perfectly normal Sunday, and suddenly I'd be evicted from the sofa to go read elsewhere when some fat cat in an Armani suit would congeal out of thin air and ring the doorbell. He (or very occasionally, she) would wait pointedly on my exit, all false patience, pursed lips, and pompous scowling brow.

But with age comes sass. When I came home from the senior prom to find four stocky men in camouflage and jackboots laughing and drinking Scotch with my mother, the sass bloomed like Vesuvius.

"Don't even tell me you all fit in that Beetle." I jerked my thumb over my shoulder toward the door and the toy car parked in the driveway beyond. The absurdity shone in high contrast: a princess in apricot satin taffeta glaring down an entire olive-drab, off-the-record powwow in the living room.

"Plucky, don't worry. They were just leaving." My mother's voice was mellow with her customary confidence, but her eyes shone soft with sympathy.

"Like I even care." I stomped a dramatic exit, but my inexperienced ankles wobbled on the spiky heels. I stumbled at the foot of the stairs, then hurled my corsage into the foyer as an exclamation point and pounded the rest of the way to my room in a blushing fury.

I'd only just flung myself across the bed when a subdued, all-business murmur drifted up from the front hall, just ahead of the closing of the door. The dead bolt clicked into place, then the insufficient car rattled to life and faded down the street. I could hear glasses clinking as my mother cleared them, knowing full well that her puttering was engineered to give my steam some time to blow itself out. Finally, the stairs creaked her intent to set us right.

I'd left the bedroom door ajar. I always did. Somehow, I never had the courage to shut her out completely. It seemed too big a bluff, one I always feared her self-assurance would call.

I lay on my side in a rumpled T-shirt and gym shorts, still the hair-sprayed and lipsticked debutante from the neck up. From deep in a force field of glower, I kept my smoldering face to the wall, my arms crossed against any conversation, while she rescued my gown from the closet floor and hung it on the rod. But I lost my battle with the knot in my throat as her weight pulled a valley into the mattress.

"Plucky." She rubbed apologetic circles on my back.

"It's okay," I croaked. My mother curled around me, stroking the heat from my cheek with her cool hand as I sobbed.

The slow unclutching of the apron strings began that night. I never told her that the worst part was in feeling forgiveness when I couldn't really pin a name on the fault in the first place.

4

Simon didn't remember our childhood as I did. It was a big deal to him to drive home the point whenever he could that our mother *wasn't* a big deal in the business, although it kind of left the question of why no one ever said what, exactly, the Business was. In fact, he loudly doubted that her government work had ever been anything other than low-level translation services, even if the occasional action-hero story could be embellished out of the memory of one of her back-in-the-day trips abroad. According to Simon, she was a good storyteller and that was all; an entertainer when she wasn't being slightly edgier than all the other work-from-home mothers we knew.

The Long Trip was an anomaly Simon couldn't diagram away. He didn't even try. He simply canceled it out, willing his eyes not to roll at me, with the overly patient certainty that whatever it was, they wouldn't let James Bond live on a tree-bordered cul-de-sac, with all the international secrets tucked in with the banana-bread recipes.

I said he was being naïve. He said I was being dramatic. She was fluent in four languages, proficient in another three. It explained away most everything. What remained was dismissed as either paranoid fantasy or just "her way." It didn't, however, go very far in accounting for Uncle Paul.

We always knew that Paul Rowland was no relation to us. He was just our mother's boss for nearly her entire life, a man who was, and had always been, around often enough that he insisted on tagging himself more familiarly than was warranted. He said that "Mr. Rowland" was what everyone called his father, and that he would never stand on any ceremony that made him feel old. He was, however, more than happy to stand on a ceremony that made us address him as part of the family when we didn't want to. As we crested into adulthood, Simon was never keen on talking about Paul's influence on our mother and on the way our lives had spooled out. And it only got worse.

The Big Argument was on a Saturday. If I ever needed to account for why I tagged things with the days of the week, it could have been that it was a reflex, a hand-in-hand natural tendency to go with our family's quirk of naming certain scenes in our shared history, using shorthand for referencing events that we didn't want to discuss in detail. The Big Argument would take its place on the shelf with the Long Trip and the Business.

Simon was right out of the army, commended and discharged. We'd already had our welcome-home event with the neighbors and his friends, and this would have been our first dinner together, just the three of us, in my mother's backyard at the cast-iron table that was nestled into the patio circle of dogwoods and irises, next to a lattice arch of climbing roses in new bloom. She called it the chapel. Dinner in the chapel was sacrosanct. No backing out. No balling up the plans.

Paul's car was in the driveway. My teeth clenched automatically, but the scoffing sound at the back of my throat was something I'd practiced.

I heard their voices, indistinct but loud, through the open living-room window when I shut off my car's engine. I slithered out of a tiny wedge of open angle, all that Paul had left me if I didn't want to ding his door with mine. Paul's ego, and the Cadillac he toted it around in, took up the whole middle of the driveway as if he owned the place. Their angry words rang clear through to the lower half of the street once I got out of my car.

Simon had already yelled his voice rough. "I've done *every*thing you've ever asked me to do, you asshole."

"I did you a favor," said Paul. "And you'll come to see that."

"Paul," my mother cut in. "You had no right. What were you thinking? Why would you even do such a thing? It wasn't your place and you know it."

I'd made it to the front door just as Paul made it to the other side. I pushed it open ahead of his reaching for the handle so that he looked about to shake my hand as the door swung wide. I could have sworn in court only that he was utterly composed, but you could feel a tremor of blood pressure in the air around him, a fury that hummed in his aura that his face didn't do justice to, even if his color had gone over to rare-steak red in the jowls.

"Annette, whatever our arrangement has been, you'd do well to remember that I still don't ask your permission or your forgiveness for the things I do. I know you know that in private, and I don't appreciate you posing like you don't know it right here standing in front of your son."

He brushed past me with a tight nod. "Dee."

"What the hell was that?" I asked.

It turned out to be the fallout from Paul's cashing in on some sort of official favor to scuttle my brother's application to the FBI.

In some ways, Simon had admired Paul, almost as a father he didn't love but looked to for the occasional bit of good guidance. He certainly cared for Paul more than I ever had. The betrayal burned bright and long, Simon railing against Paul at every opportunity until even Simon got tired of hearing it. In this massive falling-out they didn't speak for ages.

For years afterward, all the way up to her funeral, they avoided run-ins by simply following a rigid schedule of never visiting my mother at the same time. She was a wall, not just between the two of them, but between the specifics of their clash and me. There was no cajoling her into gossip. I never once got her to diagram the collision for me, but since the result gave me more Simon and less Paul, I stopped wondering about it as much as approving of the results.

5

Friday

The crossroads are looming less frequently now; each unfamiliar bend in the lane and unknown street sign is tugging at my attention more than ever for how rare they're becoming along this wheeling spool of pavement. It just goes on and on. The last sign loomed up and passed, but it left its mark more than the others have, and now my heartbeat is booming into my eyes. Bowers Road. I don't know Bowers Road. I've never been out here past the last of the industrial office parks, the rows of low, brick buildings that line up for acres, each with one strip of parking spaces and plain signage advertising a host of services less sought out by your average joe. Having never needed custom-stamped sheet metal or specialty bolts and screws, I've never given this sketched-in edge of the town a second thought.

Some spiritual people say there is no such thing as coincidence, and I guess I can't know if it's the chicken or the egg for my lack of spirituality, but I do believe in coincidence. I believe in it very much. I see it everywhere. I have to. Otherwise, I'd start to believe that the universe is adversarial. And I don't need another opponent right now.

My husband's name is Patrick Bowers Aldrich and of course it doesn't mean anything that Bowers Road just crossed my path like a black cat. My mother-in-law, whose forebears have been all over this area for ages, ran through quite a number of remote family surnames to give each of her six children a unique middle name, so I suppose it's possible that this Bowers and Patrick's own *Bowers* are historically linked, but it doesn't mean anything today. It doesn't. Even if I am preoccupied with my husband more in fear than affection on this drive to Carlisle Inc.

But now I know I'll see the road sign in my head, landmarked forever. It took less than a second to pass it, but the spindly reach of the crepe myrtle's shadow at the corner of the crossroads, and the exclamation-point pattern of the fuzzy cattail weeds skirting around the signpost, have all been snapshotted into my memory against my will. I will remember this scene. I'll remember the sign. I'm sure of it. And I don't like that thought. The free association links up again, kicked off by the coincidence of Bowers Road—Patrick Bowers Aldrich, then Carlisle Inc., then the blue sedan, then the strange things that have been happening. The burglary at the yoga studio. Our house tossed over so stealthily that only I could tell. The insurance.

A cool, gray tentacle of premonition strokes the back of my neck.

Patrick Bowers Aldrich edges past my mother in my thoughts, nudges her back into the past, the only place she can be now. A pet saying of hers rings in the hollows of her absence: *If clues waved flags and blew trumpets, baby girl, we'd all be Sherlock Holmes.*

Something is not right and hasn't been for some time. I miss her sorely. More than ever in this moment, I feel the leading edge of the storm in some inarticulate place in my gut. And I'm afraid I'm going to have to white-knuckle this one alone. No one knows I'm out here. I boarded up the windows without telling a soul, long before I knew for certain that my husband wasn't what I'd always insisted that he was.

• • •

Everyone rebels against their upbringing, either honestly, right out in the open, or deep in their hearts while they pay lip service to their splendid childhoods. The midwife may cut the cord, but each child has to walk away to become her own. Me? My choice of husband was my ultimate defiance.

Patrick Aldrich and I married straight out of college. Unless there was a Williams in the room (or once, there was a Zambrano, who played his heritage like a mob-movie joke—silk suits with pocket squares in high school, no less), my last name, Vess, had me at the end of every alphabetized queue. Right from freshman orientation, I noticed Patrick up front with the *A*s and *B*s, well scrubbed and well liked, but not too much of either.

I stalked him through the campus, learned his schedule, and then I pointedly crossed my path with his patterns to be seen when I wished to be seen. I asked him to be my date for the homecoming dance after only two engineered encounters—one in the library and one in the dining hall.

Patrick was good-looking in an apple-cheeked sort of way. Just by his alert struggle against slouching I knew there would be parties, but that they would end short of wild. His mildness made me bold. He looked to me like a smooth groove in a bumpy road. In his company, there was no need to fear the shadowed trails branching off the good path, those dangerous tangents that distracted the less vigilant people off their true courses and into weird lives. With Patrick, the sum of the parts meant there would be no toothy surprises lurking in the comfort of Grandma's flannels.

We were an easily matched set. All throughout school our grade point averages hovered within a small decimal's reach of the other's, and we were both attractive enough to take a handsome photo when the occasion called for it without the loaded burden of the kind of beauty that causes traffic jams.

Patrick had grown up on a street where nothing ever happened, and I had grown up on a street where *apparently* nothing ever happened, which is usually good enough for the neighbors.

I made the first move, and also the second, and by subtracting the fear of rejection from Patrick's world, I lit a fire in his ego.

He had two weaknesses that turned him mine so fast that it turned me his just as quickly for the adorable surprise of it all. I'd never known anyone so sweetly undone by a wink.

My mother had perfected the wink to an effortless one-note Morse code that could flash amusement, conspiracy, flirtation, or warning on her whim. I'd adopted a lower-volume version of it as a habit, but it hit Patrick in some sweet spot.

He'd pulled an instantly blushing double take when I reflexively winked on my way out of the library after our first conversation.

When I pulled away from our good-night kiss in the parking lot of my dorm after the homecoming formal, I guess I did it again.

"It kills me when you do that," he'd said.

"When I do what?"

"That wink thing."

"Oh, yeah?" I leaned in for another kiss and smiled against his straight, white teeth. "Why does it kill you?" I whispered onto his lips.

"I don't know," he murmured into our kiss, neither of us willing to back out of its tingle. "You look so sweet, and then you do that, and just for a second, you're like a badass."

I spluttered the heat out of the moment, giggling. My head dropped against his shoulder. "I'm a badass. Yeah, right."

"Maybe just a little." He laughed into my hair and I lifted my face against his cheek and discovered his second frailty when I kissed his ear. His low sigh sent a feathery chill down my neck.

I brushed my lips along the firm curve of his ear again, and his breath drew down to a soft moan. He pulled me over the armrest and we kissed to panting, twisting over the console at every need to breathe, hands in each other's hair, sliding and pulling over our fancy clothes, dragging for better reach of every unfamiliar curve.

I stopped us before campus security surely would have, but that was that. We were together.

He glowed. My lighthouse, safe and sound, shone out from the crop of boys who laughed louder or punched harder or studied more seriously in excess than he did. In his shy pleasure at my endorsement, I felt generous instead of gently scheming. I'd made him happy and I had got what I wanted out of it, too—cake and eating it if there had ever been a diagram of the saying. And our gratitude for the other felt like love. In the blur of new achievement and fun and youth and plans and small dramas stoked hot on the promise of making up, I'd never be tempted to jump out of the mellow frying pan.

My roommates played at catch and release with the ready crop of bad boys and all the rowdy, sweet ones who were on campus, or already at work in the low rungs of the town. They paid the toll in binge sobbing and regrettable revenge hookups when it didn't work out. Then they teased me for my single-mindedness and the Velcro hold I kept on the same guy from the start, but I insisted that the palette of love they thought was fanned out for all their choosing was an illusion. There were only two flavors: right and wrong.

I felt an advantage in my precocious wariness. I wasn't going to wait around to get tricked. I watched us, my friends and myself, set free by milestone birthdays or diplomas and then straightaway disillusioned with the daily routine. We'd long been indoctrinated by singing princesses and pink things to gauge life by its sparkle: the maiden's birthright. And while all that glitters is surely shiny, the business of spooling out twenty-four-hour days, 365 times each year, is a grind of many textures.

Today's maidens, by and large, take the sudden turn from all the twinkling in stride and get on with things. In the dullest part of the day, however, they keep the secret close—that they would trade their crisp independence in a hurry for a semi-tame rogue who would thrash a swath through their boredom.

That's how the daydream goes anyway, just like every other daydream—that unfocused longing to have something else. And it's hardly the domain of maidens at all. Everyone does it.

I was no different, in a different sort of way. I tended the same garden of endless, vague demand—that the next moment needn't be necessarily better, only that it be new. I wanted to be swept away, too—straight under a rug. Patrick was the best broom a girl like me could ask for.

We were still in our mortarboards and gowns when we picked up the invitations from the printer. Patrick's parents were thrilled. Young love with strings attached was an Aldrich family tradition. Pat's mother had dropped out of technical college to go full housewife at nineteen. Pat's older brother had his first child at twenty. And the four younger Aldrich sisters, each two years apart, spanned both a middle school and a high school and considered wedding planning no different from angling for the perfect prom, even if the dresses were hand-me-downs.

But they were happy, all of them. Or at least they were smiling, doing every regular thing and doing it well. Pat's mother taught me to make pie crust and bought us an electric skillet as a wedding present. I was at a loss at first, but the dull, square thing turned out to be tremendously useful. I used it a hell of a lot more than the crystal candy dish or the tablecloth that was simply too nice to go underneath supper.

Love is love when it's electrifying, but what is it when it's soothingly plain? As far as I could tell, it was ideal.

In our hearts, though, Patrick and I pulled out of rhythm. The edges of our wants didn't match up as neatly as they should have. I wanted to plant myself in the picture of his plain pedigree, in his family's pleasant, geraniums-in-the-flowerbox ordinariness. And he, unfortunately, was banking big deposits of hope that I had more of my mother in me than I let on. He was quite taken with her.

Ours being a college town, Patrick and I both lived at home and commuted to campus—Patrick to save money and I to be near her. I was always touching base, pinging home, perpetually nervous to spend too much time out of sight for fear of the rest of the proverb.

He and I did dinner and the movies. We studied and ate carry-out. We made out in the car. But after any time spent at my house with my mother, he'd grow pensive, staring into my eyes, searching, waiting, as if he'd thrown a stone down a well.

I ignored this because my brother said that Patrick was a boring dork who would build a picket fence, knock me up with 2.3 children, then buy a golden retriever. That sounded perfect to me.

My brother eventually got over not heading out to Quantico and falling into some urban FBI field office for thirty years and a gold watch. He became a cop at home. He stayed my best friend and my confidant. There's never been anyone else like Simon. He had always been my conscience and the only one I ever talked to about my problems with life. It was only natural to carry it into our lives as adults. Simon alone understood where we came from. He was always the only one who ever knew I wasn't crushingly normal. I told Simon everything automatically.

So there was a cold curiosity in feeling suddenly secretive in those months running up to our ruin.

6

Friday

I check the rearview mirror too much. I always have, but it's got a
lot worse in the last few months. Up until I was being followed, it
was just a by-product of my mother's instruction. I've always worn
the vigilance she taught us as nerves. She wore it as custom-fitted
armor.

I check the clock, then the mirror again. I'm making good time
and there's nothing behind me but a long tail of gray road stretched
to the horizon, empty. If I'm paranoid, I've come by it honestly.

She had worked on us so that she would feel we were safe, but
also in hopes that we would have bigger lives. She thought those
who, given the same amount of time, didn't dissect the moments as
they sped past were doomed to a hazy picture of the world, a plain
and normal sketch of it. But take a microscope to your small, diffuse
view and suddenly a sharp vastness was yours—even in the middle
of a parking lot or on the end of a lonely pier on the margin of a
lake.

But her magic spells had side effects. She knew that. When Patrick and I had just moved out of our newlywed apartment, bureau-

cratically now all grown up with a mortgage that would chain us to fifty-five-hour workweeks for the foreseeable future, my mother brought me flowers from her garden and warned me of recruitment.

"Don't be surprised if Paul tries to get you to come work for him one day," she'd said. "He's got his eye on you because of this crazy idea he has that there's some sort of premium pedigree for his shenanigans. He thinks that since he was looking for my uncle when he found me, it somehow works around, in his mind anyway, to believing that it's in the blood."

Paul had already approached me twice, once directly and once obliquely, but I'd ignored him both times all the way down to not even mentioning it to my mother.

"Nah, he wouldn't want me," I said. "I'm no good with languages."

She studied me with a tight smile. "Right. Though I don't recall you ever studying a language."

"I took Latin." I busied myself with straightening the salt and pepper shakers against the napkin holder.

"Right," she said again. "Latin."

"Besides, are you saying that I shouldn't follow in your footsteps? What's wrong with working for Paul? It seems to pay nicely, and no matter what happened, you were never in a serious hurry to leave it all behind." I risked a quick look up to see if the conversation was still on the lighter side.

"Paul and I had a deal. After the Long Trip, I said I'd stay and I stayed. High jinks ensued," she said with an admirably straight face. "Anyway, all I'm saying is that if you ever do go that way, don't let them make you think it was your idea if it wasn't. *That* you will resent. But don't ask me how I know that. Anyway, I suppose there's still plenty of time for you to learn some undead languages if you wanted to." She winked at me.

•   •   •

Our little Vess cabal had always danced over and around the notion of marital commitment. My mother enjoyed male companionship, always presenting it as a positive thing without confusing the issue by defining it as a necessary pillar of permanence in our lives. She dissolved her every partnership over the years with firm kindness, until Simon and I learned not to attach more than mild friendship to each carefully vetted man who came and would eventually go.

She teased us, and her suitors, that she could never get married again, obviously, since her left hand was down by two fingers and there wasn't any place to hang a ring. My resolve to persist with Patrick felt almost secessionist in my family's established patterns. Mother didn't. Simon didn't. Then I went and did.

I'd thought of it as a character flaw in her, a rare inability. I saw it, like her hand, as a forgivable deformity through some injury that maybe our father had dealt her. I wondered if perhaps in her travels there might have been some hurts I didn't know of, losses that had sentenced her romantic heart to solitary confinement.

I knew my mother didn't trust love.

She'd kept the last name Vess but unmoored her life (and ours) from the man himself, Jonas Vess, when Simon was still a baby. She explained, when I was old enough, that she'd delivered an ultimatum and that he had wasted little time in trampling all over the line she'd put in the sand.

The rift had to do with his drinking, which in turn had something to do with his poorly managed dissatisfaction over being occasionally left at home as a househusband in a time when that sort of thing was less than fashionable and more than odd. My mother traveled much less once we were born, but still more than could go without notice from the nosier neighbors. She had trusted her husband's discretion.

When she'd been confronted by the tipsy Tupperware lady at a block party with a smile and a nudge and a "What *have* you been up to, Mata Hari? Jonas says it's all very hush-hush," the match hit the kindling.

His intemperance was incompatible with her obligations, both her contractual need for control and her instinctive one. When she deemed me ready for the whole story, I took away a decidedly good-news/bad-news interpretation of the facts. My mother was extremely protective of us, and I basked in the safe perimeter of her fierce glow. On the other hand, I didn't know the word *intractable* at the time, but I did know what it looked like: my mother, dry-eyed, rescinding her love and closing the door in my father's defeated face. And never a tear shed over it, that I had ever seen.

We saw him only twice more before I started school and then nothing but the occasional letter after that. He did what divorced men did in those days. Starting over most often meant starting all the way over, as if the other life and the starter family hadn't happened. I knew several kids who saw their dads on weekends and maybe for a few weeks in the summer, but I knew just as many whose fathers were a birthday card with cash in it and a single present in the mail at Christmas.

Jonas Vess died of lung cancer before the surge of the Internet. The absence of his digital footprint made him seem less real to me than even the vagueness of my impressions of him: the cactus scratch of his bearded face against my cheek, the taste of red rope licorice that he bought for me in the grocery store, his pitch-perfect whistling in the garage, in the yard, in the kitchen . . .

When she had told me that she'd struck a deal with Paul Rowland to stay on as both his hammer and nail, I knew it had something to do with Aunt Marie. My mother had seemed resolved to be rid of Paul and his erratic, wall-dinging business when she first returned from the Long Trip. She avoided him when she could and firmly distanced herself with the coldest of shoulders when she couldn't. But I overheard hints of tears and snippets of conversation in her first weeks back, on the telephone or in the living room with her sister, until ultimately, my mother wedged herself between Marie and whatever had happened while my mother was away.

Paul and Marie played house during those months that my mother was gone, while Simon and I were quasi-in-her-care. At first, Paul had come over regularly to deliver messages from our mother. He brought news and assurances of her safety in the days that turned into weeks and months. Eventually, he sort of never left.

Aunt Marie was the pretty one. Annette was the younger sister and was certainly no mountain troll, but Marie had every physical gift that my mother owned, only slightly Snow White–er. At the crossroads of our need and her availability, when my mother was called away, Marie was divorced with a son in college, who had fallen estranged by the law of tough love.

My cousin, Justin, had found that he was even better at being the life of the party than he was at chemistry and biology. The funds for his tuition and books burned like straw in pursuit of beer to chug and white powder to whisk up his nose. And he was generous with his vices to an extra fault. His no-account friends warmed their party at the bonfire of Justin's money and good sense, and the situation went from a concern to a disaster in record time. Marie had cut him off financially, and he never called her except to wheedle her into a change of heart and *out of* some cash, only to break that heart with the vow to never call her again when she said no.

At the time of my mother's Long Trip, Marie was depressed and anxious—and also anxious over being depressed, because the most basic things in her life weren't getting done when she couldn't find a reason to get out of bed in the mornings. Her sick leave from work dried up, her checking-account balance fell to overdrawn, and her pantry was full of out-of-date condiments and not much to eat.

Then my mother needed her in a flurry of dramatic emergency and hasty exit, and Paul, the standard-bearer of my mother's much more glamorous troubles, was an intriguing distraction for Marie.

His attraction to her was both nuanced and obvious. Even at thirteen years old, I saw that Paul's control over my mother had its gaps, and that those unbridgeable ravines bothered him. If he looked at it sideways, sex and affection with Annette's look-alike could rough in a more complete illusion that he owned full jurisdiction over his protégé's kingdom.

And all of that might not have been a fair appraisal of Paul's motives and Marie's weaknesses, even though it was probably the state of things. Whatever else it was, it could still have been true love also.

Either way, my mother wasn't having it.

Aunt Marie had lived only a few miles away from our house. For the duration of my mother's trip, she stayed most of the nights with us, but she never technically moved in. She launched her workdays from her own place, getting ready for the office from her own shower and closet after seeing Simon and me off on the bus.

I knew that Paul had a key to Marie's house. He also had the good sense not to make a habit of being in my mother's bed when Simon and I woke up. But there were signs he'd stayed over, sneaking in after our bedtime and ducking out before dawn. There were double glasses in the sink, or too many cigarettes in the ashtray, and often a sheltered dry patch on the driveway that would have been dew-soaked if a car hadn't been parked there all night.

Marie lightened and brightened with purpose into the stretch of my mother's absence. I wanted not to know why, but two obedient and well-groomed children to roll out as evidence of her decency and capability went a far ways to soothe her fear that she couldn't do anything right. And a world-traveled lover to round out that picture, an image of achievement to cover over the hole of failure that she'd been staring into, was plenty reason enough to cradle the hope that it would last, if not forever, than for longer than the reach of her old melancholy. I'm sure Aunt Marie was relieved when we would get news of her sister that served as proof of life, but she wasn't on fire to have my mother back either.

Whatever final terms my mother put on the table when she learned of their relationship, Paul chose them over Marie, who, of course, never forgave my mother. Marie remarried within a year after a whirlwind romance, then relocated to the West Coast with her new husband, who was little more than a stranger to her, and died with him at her side behind the wheel in a drunken confrontation with a hundred-year-old oak tree without ever reconciling with her sister or her son.

With Paul, after Marie left, my mother's methods became both harder and more gentle. She teased him less, but thanked him more. The field had leveled in some way that made them more colleagues than what they had been before—more allies afterward than the conductor with his first-chair musician. For the rest of her life, Paul asked instead of ordered, and my mother briefed him in lieu of what had always been dutiful reporting.

When the call came in of Marie's accident, my mother laid her head on her crossed arms atop her desk. She was there, motionless and silent, for so long that Simon and I, knowing somehow not to ask her yet what had happened, slipped from the room in perplexed unease.

She was still there more than an hour later when I peeked in. I felt her awake in the room and tested the air for an invitation to talk, but there was none.

I busied myself in the kitchen, thawing out leftover soup and making grilled cheese for our supper. Simon and I were done eating when she finally came in. She had showered and dressed in pajamas. We never saw her that way except on the occasional lazy Sunday morning and Christmas.

She opened a bottle of wine and poured a half glass and, much to my teenaged surprise, set it front of me. Then she poured another, smaller serving for Simon, and another glass that she drank deeply from and topped off immediately.

I will tell you this, my darlings, the very worst regrets are the things you couldn't have handled any other way.

7

After graduation and our wedding, we had a quick year's lease in an argument-size apartment. Then Patrick and I bought a sweet whitewash-over-brick bungalow in a transitional tract of houses at the cheaper end of the trendy part of town. In that stretch of road you could get away with being anything you cared to be. American dream as-you-like-it, custom-tailored and eclectic. And all judgments were kept on the down-low, behind closed doors. We were all friendly on the street side of our thresholds.

Our neighbors on the left, one yard closer to the artsy West End bustle, were a middle-aged couple too gorgeous and sophisticated not to have been invented by a screenwriter. He drove an electric car. She bicycled everywhere she couldn't walk. They harvested rain in an artisanal-crafted barrel with a tree-of-life motif carved into its side. They watered their lawn from its bounty, and if we'd had enough weather and the barrel was full, they washed, too, their oversize roller skate with air bags and bucket seats. With sulfate-free soap, of course.

On the right we had a harried young couple with a cocker spaniel, a fat, smiling, squealing toddler, and another baby on the way. Down the street, one of the houses was painted purple. Across from the purple house was a gay couple, who played the best music. They ran it through their elaborate patio speakers loud enough that they might have drawn complaints if they hadn't been so talented with their mixes. Every sunny day was brighter for their ear, and rain was scored with the perfect melancholy.

Patrick and I set about being average until we decided which way to play it. We got settled in, assigned our sides of the bed, and got used to the background noise of the other. We were home. Patrick worked long hours, angling for a quick rise to account manager in the country's third-largest peddler of GPS technology. He pulled in nice bonuses and we spent them. Fun funds, we called it. I put bits of my good education to use in a midlevel position with a burgeoning firm that developed diet and fitness-management software. The bills were paid and we spent as we liked, sparing little thought to, and less action on, staking down what we already had.

"Want to go play house?" Patrick had said to me just after nudging the wedding band over my finger, smiling down at me. The minister had laughed. Everyone did. It sounded like a sitcom. The black lapels of his tuxedo lay smooth and crisp on his chest. He looked good. Very good. He'd rehearsed the line in the mirror. I could just imagine him doing it. He looked that day exactly as he'd decided a groom should look. The canned line was inorganic and scripted, but it was sweet, too. And it stuck.

Want to go play house? worked on many levels. It could be mumbled into the other's ear with an *ugh* plugged in up front as the signal to start making our way toward the door of an event that had lost its shine. On the phone, matter-of-factly, it was Friday afternoon's sign-off to the workweek. If it was said sadly with a sigh, we'd pack our swimsuits and shorts back into our suitcases and leave the beach for the real world.

Purred into the ear, it was surprising how sexy *Wanna go play house?* could sound. A silvery feather, warm breath and warm intent, would swirl a contrasting chill down my neck when Patrick would put the question on my skin. How could I say no? I always wanted to play house. I wanted that feather to tickle my mind quiet, only the sound of lips and sighs in the half-light, and murmurs of concentration completely divorced from thought.

But one day, it was a Saturday and raining, Patrick leaned in with a soft, intentioned mouth to give us something to do while we waited out the storm. He put his lips on the sweet spot at the turn of my jaw said, "Want to play house? I'll be the daddy, you be the mommy." I smirked into his kiss and found the tip of his tongue with mine. I didn't answer him but my pulse banged in my ears.

Afterward, I pretended to doze while Patrick actually did.

The next day, we were at my mother's. Patrick was cleaning her gutters. I was with her in the kitchen, layering berries over sponge cake in a trifle bowl.

"Hey." I waited until she was turned away, busied at the far counter. "Did you always want to have kids?"

I heard her turn toward me, knowing that I looked too intent on getting the berries stacked in at just the right depth. "Is that where the talk is going these days?"

A quick, one-shouldered shrug let me keep working.

"Well, I don't exactly know how to answer that. I wanted to have you, if that's what you mean. You were planned down to the last detail. I had even decided that I'd be swinging with you, whoever you were, in the hammock in July."

My birthday is July 19th.

My mother laughed. "I think I practically willed you into existence. Honestly, I don't even know how much Jonas had to do with it. You were made of pure design and insistence. Simon, on the other hand, was a complete surprise. And with absolutely terrible timing. But what an adventure he turned out to be, yeah?"

"But you always knew you would have kids," I said, instead of asking.

"I wouldn't say that, no. What's bothering you, Pluck?"

"Nothing."

"Dee, are you and Patrick thinking about having a baby?"

"Of course."

"I'll tell you this, baby girl. *Of course* is the worst reason ever to have a baby. Better it be an accident then *of course.*"

For the longest time, nothing unusual or subtly sinister happened, and I found it much easier to enjoy my mother's mysterious aura when I was well beyond its everyday reach. We grew close, she hemmed in as always by intrigue, and I in begonias and boxwood hedges, but we talked easily over our self-imposed fences.

A late-summer morning (it was a Sunday) in the month before Patrick's and my sixth wedding anniversary, the phone rang as I was settling in with a crossword puzzle and a plate of fruit and sweet rolls. Patrick had left at dawn, much more serious about god-awful plaid pants and eighteen holes in the ground than he was about sleeping in late on the weekends.

"Hello?"

"Hi, Plucky. Do you have some time for me this morning?"

"Absolutely. When were you thinking of coming over?" Most of our visits went down on my turf, which was just the way I liked it.

"As it just happens, I'm in your driveway right now."

I laughed and let her in. I didn't laugh again for a long time. My mother had cancer chewing through her bones and drawing black scrawls over her lungs and liver. The doctors had set the line at a year, at the most. My mother had reset the line at whenever she felt her dignity slipping. She wanted me to be sure of her intent along with the news.

I begged instantly, and somewhat to my own surprise (and she relented far more easily than I expected), for her to sell her house and move in with us. We tended each other on the way to the end. I made sure she had no chores, no to-do lists. She retold me every story she'd ever shared. We redid the life we'd already had, with the same parameters except that I brought her food instead of the other way around. Once more, for old times' sake, we traced over our steps, to put the memory of us closer to the front of the file. We rewound and fast-forwarded—mother and daughter, tale-teller and audience, teacher and student. And we included Patrick, almost always, brokenhearted and brave in the face of it as he tried to be.

She lasted eight months, four days. I held her dry, three-fingered hand in both of mine as she slipped away.

8

Friday

I'm watching the road, but I'm driving on autopilot. It's a bit crowded in my head just now. But it's not as if Patrick and my mother have never been juxtaposed in my thoughts before. They've sprung to mind at crossed purposes from the beginning, and in no small part by my own design. I loved my mother and I loved Patrick and both of them the better because they were as unalike as two people could be.

It turns out, though, that the joke is on me. The only thing they had in common was cause to hide in plain sight. It's been quite a lesson. Now I realize that everything you need for measuring a person can be found in the nature of what he chooses to hide from everyone else. That's all you need to know to gauge his goodness.

My mother's secrets were a professional necessity, kept close and tightly so, to let her work with any hope of success. But the secrets were also to safeguard our life together as separate and protected from her work.

My husband's secrets, or the biggest one anyway, is still ahead of me, just a few miles down the road.

•   •   •

Patrick had courted us both, my mother and me. It sounds awful—even perhaps perverse. But it was neither of those things, because I would only ever have had the choice between two kinds of people: those who wouldn't understand my mother and would be fine with that, and those who wouldn't understand her but would be helpless to resist trying. Patrick and I snuggled together in second category. All my favorite people were there.

She was a wonderful barometer. You could test the climate of a stranger just by his or her reaction to Annette Vess. She knew this, but somehow didn't mind being a tool for us to use. If her essential solitude was a curse, it didn't look like one. That was the hurdle I never managed to vault—it made me sad that her isolation didn't make *her* sad. That bit of tail-chasing irritated my brother, but Patrick alone seemed to understand the fragility of the anchor line that kept her from drifting away from me, from all of us. I loved him for loving her, and it certainly felt safer to adore my mother by proxy.

He chased the attention of those flashing black eyes and the reward of her laughter, the inherent approval of her casual conversation. I could hardly pretend I didn't understand that. She always checked my reaction to his incandescent performances with a steady, piercing look over a closed-lip smile, to see if I was okay with it. I always was. I didn't feel jealous of his efforts. His wit and charm bloomed in his bids to impress her. It was sweet, if a little manic, and Patrick was never better than when he was playing sweet. He was the very picture of all it should look like. I was proud that I drew out his calm, his *normal*, despite my upbringing. Without her, our regular days were long, but pleasant, a bustle of manageable to-do that faded into a routine of cuddle, drowse, and then deep, undisturbed sleep.

And if there was ever lightning and thunder in the dark, I'd pull his arm over me to pin me to my place and remind me that I need not venture out into it.

• • •

As much as he admired my mother, Patrick never understood what she'd done for Simon and me by all that she'd done *to* us with her games and with her outlook on life. He resented our oddness without the rest of the equation. He felt left out even though he knew the stories of origin. By the transitive property, he shouldn't have liked her since he didn't like her handiwork, but somehow he stubbornly never did that math. He wanted what he wanted of it, and to hell with the rest.

The first Tuesday of each month, Patrick had a standing work meeting downtown, which we'd steered into the habit of meeting for a monthly date night on restaurant row. One Tuesday I remember, I didn't recognize Patrick as I walked toward him. He sat at the table under the awning, two-thirds turned away from me, watching the course of people and traffic on Derby Street. I saw that it was him, of course. There were no surprises left in the way we looked to each other. I knew his face from every angle, the tilt of his shoulders, the certain blend of browns that made it only Patrick's hair. But I didn't recognize him.

Every now and again, I'd turn a corner—in my office, in my neighborhood, in the grocery store, or even sometimes in the mirror—and find myself pitched into the exact opposite of déjà vu. For a disorienting set of seconds, nothing rang true. Nothing looked right. None of it felt in any way mine.

This happened at the crosswalk behind Patrick. I knew the smell of cars idling in their own exhaust as they waited, tailpipe to grill, waiting to gain a few yards down the street only to stop and wait again, but the sensation felt more like catalog than actual memory— as if I'd been schooled in a laboratory to identify the throat-tickling fog of it rather than that I'd been steeped in it daily when I had worked downtown a few years earlier.

The leaves that spun on their stems in the storm-front wind looked painted on. The sun glowed hard white from behind the

cloud cover. Where I fit into this alien landscape, I couldn't feel—
and I couldn't recall when I'd lost track of it. The endless second of
lunatic doubt that I was possibly a figment of my own imagination
was an open space in my empty head, and the lightness of it was the
precursor to both fear and bliss.

In these short-circuited moments, pinned between outlander
and full-on Martian, I was compelled to run a full inventory of my
entire life in the span of a few heartbeats in order to reclaim reality.
It was Tuesday and Patrick was in the center of the picture, both in
fact and in practice.

The fence of my world drew its bold line around me again, my
husband at the hub. I remembered that I had made it so, and all of
it very much on purpose. Relief reattached itself to me as life came
back online.

I was always reborn after these little episodes, once I'd tightened
the straps back down and shoved the bundle of my life firmly into
its slot. All the colors were deeper, the blood in me keen and ready.
It was probably epilepsy's cousin, but it came with a dump of endor-
phins. I felt like Joan of Arc.

Patrick must have sensed me behind him, tickled with a psychic
flutter to feel me watching him. He straightened up and turned to
find me in the flow of early-evening hustle. He waved me over and
dragged the metal chair beside him away from the table in invitation. "Hey."

"Hi." I tucked my bag under the table and worked a horrible
metal scream out of getting the chair, and myself in it, wedged
under the table. "Simon is on his way. Hope that's okay. He was
supposed to be out of town for something, but he got back early. It's
his birthday. I thought we could buy him dinner."

"Yeah. Okay. That's good."

Simon didn't keep us waiting long.

The waitress set down a basket of bread and a plate of dipping oil
in the center of the table.

Simon caught my eye as she moved out of our street view and back into the restaurant. "Are you seeing this?"

"Yep," I answered.

"Seeing what?" asked Patrick.

"Those two people, across the street." I nodded that way, but didn't look over. "They're trying to get into that apartment building." I dragged a hunk of bread through the oil and kept my voice low to corral the information to just our table.

"So?" asked Patrick.

"Do they look like they belong in that particular apartment building to you?" said Simon.

I was glad Simon had gone there and not me.

Patrick replied, a step friendlier to Simon than what I would likely have got, "That's kind of harsh, don't you think?"

The young guy looked like a composite, like in one of those children's books that flipped in thirds to show you a tyrannosaur swinging a bat in a baseball jersey and cowboy boots. Turn the top segment and T. rex was an otter or a duck in the same getup.

The result here had a baseball theme, too, but only up top. The guy wore a billed cap with a team logo I didn't recognize, and his too-large golf shirt had a vivid newness. A dark block of tattooed letters to the left of his Adam's apple glowered against the prim baby blue of the collar, which sported a starchy perk that wouldn't stand up to even one laundering. I looked for dangling tags, but didn't find any. His pleated work pants weren't his own. The cuffs backed up in a short fabric jam at his ankles, and the worn bends in the knees were clearly from a taller set of joints than this guy boasted. His ragged high-tops suited him just fine, though.

The young girl with him was pale, with chapped lips and dark circles under her eyes, but at least her clothes were her own.

The front entrance of the building was around the corner and had a desk just inside an elaborately etched glass door with something more than a doorman and less than a security guard manning it. The deep portico rested on granite-tiled columns that projected out into the sidewalk to serve as both decoration and as a notice that this was where the money went when it didn't feel like driving to the suburbs for grass and fireflies.

The side entry that faced our vantage point from the bistro's out-door dining tables had a call-up access intercom and a code entry panel for residents. This pair of ragged not-quite-twentysomethings had parked themselves against the wall, fifteen feet from this side door directly across from us.

"Maybe they're waiting for someone who lives there," Patrick offered with a stubborn shrug. "Or maybe *they* live there."

"She's carrying stuff in a Walmart bag," I said into my plate.

Patrick's annoyance dialed up a notch for me. "Even rich people go shopping, Dee. Sometimes even at Walmart."

"It's not a new bag."

The bottom of the girl's plastic bag sagged and the sides bulged, but the total weight didn't strain overmuch against the loop handles. Clothing, unfolded, was my guess. The logo and printed slogan were heat-faded as if the bags had been closed up in a hot car for a time.

"And they're both jumpy as hell," Simon added.

Their tandem stiffness thrummed a sour note over the entire corner. They were blaring their attempt at invisibility. The boy in the ball cap was flipping a loose key through his fingers, rolling it surely over and through his knuckles in a sinuous wave of motion. The girl kept raking her long, dark blond hair down over her forehead, a limp curtain of anonymity.

"Well, maybe they get the feeling they're being watched and judged all the time," said Patrick.

So instead, we all watched and judged our appetites through the bread and the salads. The waitress refilled our water glasses.

"Ah!" I said.

"Yep," said Simon. "There he goes."

It was dinnertime and a battered hatchback with a pizza-delivery prism on its roof slid to the curb and set its flashers strobing. Ball-cap boy slipped in right behind him as he was buzzed into the building.

"Damnit," I said.

"Are you going over there?" asked Simon.

"What?" Patrick was nearly offended. "Why would she do that?"

"Look at her," I said. "What is she, seventeen? She's pitiful."

"What about him?" Simon asked me mildly, watching the girl, who had gone rigid with sentry duty. "Don't you feel bad for him?"

"What about him? He's toast. He's in there. He's doing it. Nobody can do anything about that now."

Patrick abandoned his fork with a clatter against his plate. "I mean, not to point out the obvious, but none of this is our business, you know."

"Well, it's kind of *my* business." Simon wiped his mouth and unclipped his phone and set it beside his plate. "I can't just ignore a possible burglary in progress."

"If that's what it is," said Patrick.

"True," said Simon.

"But she's stuck," I said. "If this is what it looks like it is, and if she's just waiting for him, she'll get caught up in the net."

"So you've decided she's completely innocent?" asked Patrick.

"I have no idea, but she's the one standing on the sidewalk while he's burglarizing some hotshot's apartment."

"You don't know that's what he's doing." It wasn't that Patrick didn't have a point. There were too many intangibles to explain over dinner why Simon and I saw what we did in the drama across the street.

"Maybe she drove him to it," said Simon, needling me.

"Oh, get real," I said.

"What, you don't think people can be driven to a life of crime?"

Patrick leaned out of our conversation, back into spectator stance in his cast-iron chair, both fascinated and horrified.

"I think everyone is responsible for his or her own actions," I said.

"Oh, boy. That'll come back to haunt you," said Simon.

"Simon, come on. What are you going to do?"

"What do you want me to do?"

"I want you to either go back in time and make us not know that this is happening or I want you to fix it."

"Great. Will do," he said. "And I'll tell the Easter bunny you said hi when the unicorn drops me off at home afterwards."

I sucked in my cheeks. "We really should do something."

"Then I'll knock it back over the net to you," Simon said. "What are *you* going to do about it, Sissy? If you go over there, I definitely have to call it in."

"I'm not going over there. That would be weird. And I know you're going to call it in anyway. I just think she should at least have a chance."

"What about him?"

"He went in. There's nothing that can be done about that. Clearly, she doesn't want to be here."

"Clearly." Simon smiled at me.

"Don't mock me. There's no way they could have known they'd be right in front of a cop."

"So I'm the bogeyman? How's that again? They were probably going to get caught one way or the other." He stared me down, daring and teasing. "Go fix it, Sissy. I'll give her a head start, if you can get her to take it."

"You're making fun of me. Our mother wouldn't do it. You know she wouldn't. We're not in the business of other people's business."

"Well," said Simon, "I kinda am."

"Right. But you're not going to scare off a material witness to a crime, so you don't count. And I don't know enough to go barging into this situation. Patrick's right."

Patrick nodded and uncrimped his scowl a little. "Thank you."

"But you still want to do something." Simon smirked at me and took his phone off the table. "If you're going to do it, whatever it is, it's gonna have to be now."

"Hang on," I said.

A street musician, a violinist, was setting up shop under a lamp-post just in front of the restaurant. His white shirt had ruffles and his jacket was cut modern, but out of purple velveteen, so I wasn't worried that he was shy.

I actually did the *pssst* thing and waved him over to the rope barrier of the café tables. "Hey. Hi. Can I ask a favor?" I rummaged through my bag for my wallet and pulled out a bill. "Will you take this to that girl across the street? She's in trouble."

He looked from the money in his hand to the girl. She was craning a long-range look down the street, gnawing on the cuticle of her thumb.

"Be a hero for me and I'll put some seed money in your case when you get back," I said. It was incentive enough. He shrugged and loped to the crosswalk.

"Twenty dollars?" asked Simon. "What is twenty dollars going to do?"

"It's not twenty dollars," I said, watching my proxy Good Samaritan.

Simon nodded his head. "I'm pretty sure it was twenty dollars."

Patrick also nodded at me in agreement. I was a rose between two head-bobbing thorns.

"Nope," I said. "What it is, much more than twenty dollars, is proof positive that she's being watched. Make your call, lawman. You do your thing. I'll do mine." I smiled at my brother. "Let's see what she does with this."

Simon dialed as the minstrel reached the tattered girl. Both of her feet cleared the ground in her startle as he touched her shoulder. He extended the money. She shook her head. A second's more conversation and she took the bill.

The girl looked up into his face, and I could read the question in her expression and posture even as it was washed vague by the distance between us. The violinist turned and the girl's gaze followed his finger pointing back to me. My heart reared up and pounded a wild drumroll. I looked away.

Simon whispered to me, "If she walks over here, do *not* tell her your name. Unless you'd like this to be the gift that never stops giving. Be the Lone Ranger, not her best friend. Got it?"

I swatted away the advice I didn't need. "She's not coming over here. Look." The girl was reining in her retreat to a rigid walk-trot that was way more obvious than if she'd just gone ahead and sprinted down the sidewalk. I thought at her hard not to run. *Just walk,* I said under my breath. The girl tripped up and stumbled, catching on to the brick wall at her right side to steady herself. Her head swiveled, scanning the crowd to see who saw her blunder. She looked back to me. It seemed our eyes met, but I couldn't be sure. She pulled the Walmart bag in front of her body, a sad, belated shielding of her crumpled dignity. But she pulled away from the wall and set off out of sight.

The waitress brought our dinners.

"Satisfied?" asked Simon.

"I guess I'll never know," I said.

"I meant are you satisfied with what you did? You can't control what she does with it."

"Yes. I think so." And I was. Mostly. I'd always do everything differently if I had the chance. "You okay with it?"

"Sure," he said. "No skin off my nose either way."

Patrick had been watching our tennis match, agape. "I don't even know what just happened."

"Me neither, really," I said. Patrick let me hold his hand. I squeezed. A beat too late, he squeezed back.

A patrol car rolled around the corner, and its roof lights lit up with a short whoop of the siren to clear the intersection. The officer lined up the car with the curb, and another cruiser followed in just behind it. One man stayed behind with the cars and an eye on the street while the other worked an officious stride through the deco-etched doors.

We all watched the stage being set for the intervention.

"Sorry your birthday dinner was ruined," I said to Simon.

"What ruined?" Simon scooted his chair around to set his back to the scene. "I'm eating. It's my birthday. If they want me, they know how to find me. Let's begin again, shall we?"

He stood up and shook Patrick's hand. Patrick gave over to smiling, his resistance and bother over what had just happened was helpless in the full shine of my brother's charm. "Patrick, my man! How's my favorite brother-in-law? Nice to see you. Thanks for tak-ing me out for my birthday."

9

Friday

That Tuesday at the sidewalk café when I tossed an unknown element into that girl's crisis to change the course of her day, the blue car that I'm on my way to find right now was still months away. Even then, though, its phantom engine was revving out there in the yet-to-be. If I'd known to cock an ear that evening, or even on the day I'd found the stash of bank statements, I might have heard it in the back of my mind where the future sows its seeds.

I never thought we were miserable. I really didn't. I kept careful watch that we were being normal, and every little spat and eye roll seemed to fit under that heading. In some small ways, even the squabbling felt like a triumph. We fought, but we stayed. I never asked him to change. I accepted him. I thought that was what I was supposed to do.

Then I looked up one day to find that the friendly, nearly conspiratorial glint in my husband's eye had transformed into the flat stare of a bored coworker. And of course it hadn't gone stale overnight. We'd made a project of it, the both of us plying the excuse of "I'm just tired" so often in our listlessness that it had turned into a secret code for the pointed exercise of neglecting each other. We had lost track of our alliance.

But Patrick still had his dimples and his hair, and if I skipped dessert four nights in a row, I could still fit into the blue jeans I had worn in college. In our careers, we'd both been the meat that was just this side of the fat, which had kept us both—more or less—off the corporate chopping block at the low swing of the economic cleaver. There weren't bonuses and overtime projects anymore, but we were employed.

Money had got tight, but we were doing okay.

So what did we have to complain about? Nothing. Everything. Just like everyone else. And being just like everyone else meant more to me than anything the blinders had blocked from my view.

"Why do you put up with this shit?" asked my brother after I'd discovered the first pebbles that would become an avalanche in my marriage.

Before the big things that were importantly disastrous, there were the slippery, subtle, little things. There were upsets and fusses, but of what I thought of as the normal, modern-day, first-world brand of problems. And those were, of course, the only sort I would ever entertain.

Patrick's hidden bank account, his secret stash of his-not-mine, was the first decoded clue. Half a year later, his second-tier flirting with Deirdre from the coffee kiosk in the grocery store nipped at our peace. It wasn't a big deal. They were just texts. Light innuendo among a steady stream of unnecessary details to be sharing with each other.

But each stone that tumbled from my fortress sent me running for the wine and a debrief with Simon. I hadn't confronted Patrick over the money or even asked about Deirdre, nor would I ever, but we were snarling at each other with exhausting regularity.

My brother safely held most of my secrets (and some of Patrick's as well) because he had simply never shown the inclination to do anything else with them. My brother was an angel. I looked at him now, sitting there growling at me in my own kitchen, tall and ox strong, his eyebrows bristling in irritation. But what I always saw first was the gallant little brother he'd always been.

I pulled back on the smile that might offend him. "Because it's normal. It sucks, but it happens sometimes." I poured the rest of the wine into his glass.

"That's shit, Dee. It's shit of you to believe it, and it's shit of you to just accept it if that's what you actually *do* believe."

"Couples fight. They bicker. They have a peek at the green grass over the fence, sometimes, right? That's all it was. He didn't actually *do* anything with her. Life goes on. You might even know that if you ever got out of the best-behavior phase with a girlfriend—even once. What's your record, like three months? A season and a half, maybe?"

"Yeah, your husband's a jerk because I'm single."

"No, but life doesn't happen in a vacuum is what I'm saying. There's stuff and sometimes stuff gets complicated. And depressing. That's why he's being—that's why he's *some*times being a jerk. He's depressed. He's stressed-out and he's making some mistakes." I took a sip from Simon's glass, as mine was empty.

He glared at me, then looked away through the kitchen window, disgusted.

I shrugged. "What? Should I just throw in the towel? This money thing is just how he grew up—always barely scraping by. It's a security blanket, I think. It makes sense. And now Patrick wants children. He's not wrong. We started talking about it ages ago. It's probably time. And it's normal. I know he can't very well be mad at me over it, but that it hasn't happened yet after all the articles we've read and with us counting the days for timing—"

"Yeah, yeah. I get it. Please." Simon warded off any more words with his palm in my face. "You're still my sister, and I really don't need to think about you and Patrick timing—things."

"Anyway, it's grating on him. His rational mind has agreed to schedule *things*, but maybe his ego hasn't. He just needs to feel, you know, potent. He wants to know that he's *still got it*." Neither Patrick nor Simon knew that I was swallowing birth control pills on the sly, every evening, just in case the timing of *things* actually worked. My mother never knew the chain of thought she'd kicked off with one comment about the merits of accidents over *of course*.

"Then he should go to therapy. Or get a dog. Or make bird-houses, for God's sake. Or how about he adjusts his nuts and acts like a grown man instead of sending flirty texts to the coffee-shop girl to distract himself? That's just obnoxious. *And* he's got the stones to si-phon money off the bank account? Just leaving you would be better than all that sneaking around if he can't cope with life. I'd respect him more."

"Well, there you go." I smiled mildly at my fuming brother. "Thanks for that. Your clarity is . . . what? Refreshing? I guess we should bury my marriage before it's even cold. And anyway, maybe that's what he's gearing up for. Maybe he will leave me someday. Then you'll respect him, and I'll, I don't know, I'll get a cat."

I hated saying it out loud, hated the slithery fear that floated up through my head. My hard grip on the image of how things should be was not, for all my willfulness, holding my world to its place. But my face didn't betray my slipping hold. My face, at least, I could still manage.

Simon slapped his palms on the tabletop, scaring the salt and pep-per shakers, but not me. "You're not even upset."

"It's not about being upset. It's just the way it is. I'm *trying* to handle it maturely. Like a normal person. And Patrick's still trying, you know. He is. He brought me flowers. See?" A mild bundle of dyed carnations and wilting Peruvian lilies staked out a little hopeful spot on the counter.

I didn't tell Simon that the floral department was right next to Deirdre's perch at the coffee kiosk. I wondered if Patrick had timed his flower buying for her absence.

"And we're going to the movies tonight," I added.

Simon remained unimpressed.

"I only wish I didn't know," I said. "I wish she hadn't programmed us—"

"Oh, here we go. God, Dee, give it a rest."

My mother would have understood. Whatever frost I felt when I hid my troubles from Simon's plain sight, there was also the tingle of alert that began heating up my blood. And I didn't hate it, but I hated that I didn't hate it.

In those early days, the signal was like the far wail of a siren. I could feel trouble in the near distance. But at turns, I'd reel with a swell of something less like concern and more like possibility. Then I'd have to reaffirm to myself that, no, damnit, I didn't want anything other than what I had chosen.

Then I'd look to Patrick and funnel my mood back to admiration of him—his long, rolling stride and easy laugh. Not too much; not too little. He'd catch me staring at him with a gleam of appreciation in my eyes, and he'd do that thing he sometimes did in a long look, like tossing a pebble down the well of my expression, waiting for the depths to echo back some inscrutable tone he so often seemed to expect, something that felt long overdue. But then I'd just wink, cutting the transaction short, reeling him in, and also myself, bypassing all the high-minded analysis in favor of a roll in the sheets.

But life is in the blood, whether it's warm or less so, and I had to admit to both life and blood pulling against my blue-ribbon stubbornness.

Keeping tepid had become a chore.

10

When *the penny drops, you've bought a dollar's worth of trouble.* It was one of my mother's little sayings, one of several she employed to warn us against carelessness—this one specifically for carelessness with secrets.

Everything changed for the first time on a Thursday. The memory of the whole scene is flagged THURSDAY in my mind, written in what I'd call Desperation Red. It really started on Wednesday, and had I known to break out the red highlighter for the calendar in my head, I guess that would be the tag, but I was clueless until Thursday evening.

On Wednesday, in the afternoon before the blowup, my more-or-less in-plain-sight hiding place betrayed me when Patrick went for my hairdryer, and I was accused and convicted in a single discovery.

The dominoes fell in this order: First (and painfully), an infant's crib mobile kicked off the day's calamity. Patrick had bought the plush, sweetly pastel thing as a gift for his coworker's baby shower. Then an overachieving bit of adhesive had welded the price sticker onto the package. The label wouldn't peel off with just his fingernails, and the soft plastic shell discouraged the use of a sharp scraper.

The last thing to fall, finally, once he realized he wasn't going to be able to wrap it up the way it was packaged, was the treat of a silver lining—the whole snag offered up an opportunity to deploy the recently mined Internet tip to hold a hairdryer's stream over any stubborn tags to remove them cleanly.

All for the want of a horseshoe nail . . .

Thursday's groceries were going into the pantry and I was singing as I worked. I hadn't seen Patrick all day. He'd left earlier than usual, while I was still showering. No good-bye peck. No coffee made. No returned call when I'd checked to see if he needed anything from the store.

I turned, and unlike on the last pass from the counter to the cupboards, the view through to the backyard was full of a grim-looking Patrick. My song yelped to a halt and my squawk rolled into a laugh as I caught up with my startle. "Hey! There you are. I thought you'd run off to join the cir—"

Patrick tossed a bubbled card onto the counter, and I had the reprieve of one breath, one last second of not feeling like a terrible person as I looked at the clattery foil and plastic that had been rendered completely unfamiliar by being so out of place. At first, I had no idea what I was looking at.

It stopped spinning on the granite, and the shame dragged down as the panic spiked up, holding me rigidly upright in the tug-of-war.

"What?" I flailed for just another plain white moment before what came next.

"I found these. Under the sink."

"Where did you even—? These must be ancient."

"Don't, Dee. Just don't. I found them yesterday. There's one more gone today."

And the day was tagged THURSDAY forever.

I'd sidestepped my regular ob-gyn for the prescription, which had worked out just fine for ages until the pharmacies began sharing drug information across the grid. After that little breakthrough of technology and intrusion, every doctor knew what every other doctor was prescribing to safeguard their patients (and their malpractice insurance premiums) against substance abuse and unpleasant-to-fatal chemical interactions.

"I thought you two were trying for a baby?" Dr. Wertz said at my next appointment. "When you were here last time, he was with you. I even wrote you a prescription for vitamins."

"We are," I said, bending the blindingly obvious into absurdity.

Dr. Wertz blinked at me.

"I mean, we will be. Soon."

"I remember he was a little worried that something was wrong since it hadn't happened yet. You have to tell him, Dee."

"I'm not going to take them for much longer."

"You know, the next thing would be testing you for ovulation if he wants to know why it's still not working. I don't know how we're going to get around that one, and I won't thank you for putting me in that position. It's going to come out anyway."

"I know. I'm just . . ." What was I just? *Reluctant* was too weak a word; *unwilling* was too strong. My reasons were there, just on the back of my tongue, trying to arrange themselves into something that sounded like sense, but Wertz was a gynecologist, not a shrink. I kept quiet, and his face showed that I looked more like a stubborn enigma than the woman he'd known for years.

He let it go with a sigh, and I trusted the net of patient confidentiality. The net held, but my tightrope didn't.

The birth control pills had been stashed away in an old box of hot-oil hair treatments that I had kept through two moves for no other reason than that I'd paid for them. They didn't work as advertised and left my hair a sad, limp mess, but by God they were mine, a fixture in the landscape of my toiletries. The skyline of boxes under the sink wouldn't look right without it. The carton had flipped over, spilling its secret across my bathroom cabinet's floor when Patrick rummaged for my hairdryer.

It was a completely traceable pain. I could step back through each casual choice I'd made, each assumption that I'd used to cover my tracks to keep it all a secret—my plan and my reasons to stall baby-making. It was so ridiculous that I hadn't thought it through better or even opted to be a better person in the first place, an honest person.

But I wasn't rejecting Patrick. I only wanted more time. And that would have spurred the inevitable question of what in my life needed more time. Then, the answer to that, sadly, meant acknowledging my decision to play to a picture of life instead of playing to the actual game of it as it came. All of which chased the tail of not rejecting Patrick. It was going to be hard to explain, so I figured I could wait it out until there wasn't anything to explain. I would get over my doubts, surely, or . . . or what? I didn't know. I'd never got all the way there. I'd always let distraction drag me away from getting to the heart of the "or what?"

If I'd only done this or only said that, then an errant snag of a hairdryer's cord could just have been a mild chore of putting my toiletries back in order instead of a full-on life derailment.

That Thursday, the fight was quieter than I would have guessed it would be, but there were tears of the worst kind. Patrick was humiliated. I had never seen him go more than red in the nose and shiny at the eyes at sad movies.

"Why would you do this? Why would you let me think—" Breathless, he stopped and heaved in a lungful of air past the tears in his throat. "What are we doing this for?"

I opened my mouth, knowing there were no words waiting, only mute dismay.

Patrick pushed away from the table and staggered out of the room toward our bedroom. He pushed the door shut without a slam. Something hit the wall with a leathery thump, heavy, but not too big. His day planner? A shoe?

Then he was quiet.

I was hollowed out, echoey. I could float away on any current, but the unbreathable air wouldn't move. It left me there at the table, knowing I should go into the bedroom to pad my apology with at least some effort to explain.

I don't know why I didn't insist on reeling in that moment. I didn't heed the warning of his embarrassment. Later, over and over, I would revisit the memory of his flushed face and my own hesitation and wonder if this hadn't been the moment I lost, the all-important one that got away.

But I was distracted from my guilt, my thoughts returning over and over to the unexpected restraint he'd shown in not confronting me the evening before when he had first found the pills. His quite-justifiable anger should have been in my face as soon as I walked through the door on Wednesday. That he'd waited to see if I was taking the pills was cleverer and cooler than I knew him to be. I'd thought it was in his DNA. He couldn't even wait a day to give a present if he'd shopped before an anniversary or birthday. It was one of the things I loved about him. I thought he was always direct with me. I thought I would never have to consider hide-and-seek to feel at home.

But we were both doing it, changing our ways and being coy about the adjustments. Patrick's little stash of money proved that he hadn't trusted the setup of our lives for some time. It wasn't all that different from the pharmaceutical trick I'd played to hedge my bets. Recognizing my own tactic in him tickled in the unease that had always been part of our background music.

"Can we try?" Patrick asked into the dark a week and a day later when he'd moved back into our bedroom. "Or is this it? Just you and me?"

I rolled onto my side toward him, my body stretched out along his, close enough to feel his heat, but not touching him. I was afraid to touch him, not knowing if he wanted me to. I was ashamed. And also still reluctant. I thought it might telegraph in contact.

"Yeah. We can try." I risked the reach, trailed my fingertips down his chest and heard his breath catch. I'd startled him. "But, Pat, no calendar, okay? Let's just see what happens and not push it."

"Why don't you want to have a baby?"

"I do. Or I don't know that I don't. It's just a lot of pressure." I scooted closer and kissed his bare shoulder, a peace token to steady the scales.

"How is it a lot of pressure? It's just what people do. They have kids. You always said you liked my family. You liked the way I grew up. But I grew up with brothers and sisters. It's so damned quiet around here."

"I know. But, Pat, you like the quiet. You say so all the time."

"I do like it. Or I did. But after almost ten years, I think we need more."

"More what?"

"More of everything. More life."

I tried not to be offended. More did sound good. He wasn't wrong.

"Look, I'm not saying I want a zoo around here, Dee. I had more than enough of that my whole life growing up. We don't have to have half a dozen, but even your mom had kids. Obviously."

"Well, if she's the example to follow, I'll need a new career. . . ."

"She was awesome. You could do worse."

"But could I do better? Or even half as well? It's a lot to think about. I just don't want to force it. We don't need to. There's plenty of time. Can we just see what happens?"

Patrick sighed. "You know what happens."

"Then I'll go with it."

"You will?" He didn't completely believe me; I heard a stubborn edge of a dare in his voice. A *Prove it* that went unsaid.

"I will."

The pills had never been to hurt him. Not then and not when I renewed the doses two months later after a short lull of détente. They would protect us both for just a little while longer. It was a cautious testing of the bridge, a bridge that, once crossed, would transform an abstract vow made at a church's altar into a very real baby in a pastel, converted guest room.

In my hope for a change in my own heart, I only hid the package better this time.

The memory of his confrontation in the kitchen mugged me now and again. I couldn't get the replay of it to leave me be. It jumped out of nowhere when I was having a sip of coffee or stepping out of the shower or fuzzing out of focus during a call at work. I could still hear the bright rattle of the pills against the foil and feel the same scalding fear that had burned through me when he'd thrown them down on the counter on that Thursday afternoon.

The whole plot with the pills had always been a hedge against my growing concern that I'd probably got it all wrong, from the very beginning. It was a common enough mistake, and that was somehow comforting.

I had chosen Patrick for what he represented, not for who he was. But he should have forgiven that, because I had forgiven him for it. We shared it as a common bond. It wasn't just my error. I had certainly disappointed his expectations of me, but I always would have. His forecast of who I would be was made of wishes, not evidence.

Because I had no blueprint for what I imagined normal should look like in the details, I knew now that I may have drawn it all cockeyed. In which case, unlike some mothers I knew, I would never put a cradle in the middle of a minefield.

As often as I cited her as the cause for my troubles, though, thoughts of my mother propped me up through the twitchy awkwardness of

reconciling with Patrick. Unlike me, I'm not sure she had been capable of feeling graceless. Merely remembering her made me stand
taller, and replaying the stories she told, and the way she told them,
it guided me to the right things to say. He thawed when I mimicked
her. So I mimicked her.

"Hey, Patrick," I said into the phone before he'd got through
his rapid-fire work greeting. "There will be daffodil gimlets on
the deck when you get home. So don't be late." I used my mother's
voice, which was more cadence than accent. "Today's the day, I'm
happy to say. But it's bullshit this year. We're going to have to wear
sweaters. It's not getting out of the fifties. Brrrrrr."

Patrick laughed, his younger-days, not-mad-at-me laugh that
had been on leave of absence for longer than I'd admit. "I'll be
there."

"Or you'll be square."

My mother celebrated the first bloom of daffodils with a vodka-
gimlet party. The challenge was to drink the exact amount of Grey
Goose and lime juice, and not a sip more, that would leave you as
sunny between the ears as the little green-sworded, lion-headed har-
bingers of spring looked on the lawn's border.

I smiled over our good-byes and sagged, both happy and sad,
back into my office chair. I'd win him over first, then tempt myself
back into line.

If I had reason to still doubt Patrick's devotion and to play it coy
with my brother after the pill debacle, it was rooted in guilt, as
many suspicions are. And not just my guilt either.

My brother understood what I'd done with the birth control and
my husband forgave me. Well, not forgave, perhaps, although that's
the word we used for a while. We moved on as a new couple afterward, relocated as it were, hand in hand, a little closer to the cliff's
edge than we had ever been before.

I watched Patrick and I watched myself, uterus on pause, as things grew calmer and somehow stranger. The peace felt insistent over natural, less happy than trying not to be mad. I sensed his impatience vibrating in the air, the expectation of return on the investment of ten years' time. I held on to the misgivings as they were transmitted down the tingling antennae of intuition. Vodka gimlets honoring the daffodils and extra effort celebrating the glow of reunion eventually gave way, as they must, to business as usual. Only it wasn't our *usual* usual.

Patrick didn't know that I realized he'd taken up a dark and distanced perch for an entirely new view of our lives, but I sensed it in every exchange. I felt it every time his shadow crossed mine, and I felt him try to hide it when we moved closer than that.

I folded down the unease to a portable, neatly hidden size. In the moonlit murk of our bedroom, listening to the rhythmic sigh of his sleep, those doubts grew paranoid flowers that, for the longest time, I pruned off in the rational light of day.

As Patrick drifted away, even before the frequent extended golf weekends and late nights at the office, my radar that I so hated pinged the truth time and again. I resisted snooping and calculating to the extent that I could, for as long as I could, soothing myself with the knowledge that national statistics bore out that at least four women on our street were flagging in the same quagmire I was. They just didn't know it. I steadfastly looked the other way and tried to suppress what was in my blood. I never hassled him over my discoveries, so he assumed I'd never made them.

His shortcomings breached the vows no more than I'd failed an unwritten clause in our agreement—to be interesting and to make babies. And I was just happy we weren't constantly, but casually, vigilant for a call on a special line in the den that hardly ever rang. No dedicated line, no stuffy diplomats dropping in with or without preamble, no hoodlums in military green skulking in for a conference under cover of night. The lack of it all meant that we'd got it right, according to me. I'd kept the parts of life that my mother had used only for set decoration, and I'd jettisoned the rest.

I bided and abided. I could change it if I chose to. I could start and he could stop and we could be what we'd set out to be. I felt guilty that my hyperprimed intuition was an unfair advantage over him.

But I always thought of my mother when a wedding anniversary loomed. I counted off on my full complement of fingers and smiled at her little saying. I'd kept my man already for more years than my mother had fingers. But now I was down to my last pinkie, and Patrick had drawn dark on me.

11

Friday

Well, I've had my first look at Carlisle Inc. The highway engineers cut in this road around these low hills in wide, skirting loops in the most level ground they could find. The view just opened up in the last left-hand sweep I took, and there it was: an eight-foot-high chain-link fence that pens up half of all the eye can see from this side of the hill. A baby-blue sign, with plain white, block letters announces the company's name and at the same time makes the point that there aren't all that many places to buy aluminum dome sheds. There wasn't any sense in paying for a fancy logo to set themselves apart.

I'm not ready to be there yet. I've had one glimpse of the place and already my heart is thudding in my temples. I pull in each next breath with greater effort, forcing the air down a narrowing path. The muscles in my arms are jumping under my skin.

I coast to the shoulder of the road and push the gear selector to park. For now, I'm still a good citizen. As such, I hit the button for the hazard lights, just as a good girl should; just as a normal person would. The rhythmic clicking jacks dread right up my spine. It sounds like panic and insanity marching in step. I slap it quiet.

I know why I'm here, and any reasonable person would say it's Patrick's fault. Or my own. And they're not wrong, but I'm not reasonable. Not right now. I stalk myself through the flashing memory of my life. Everything I'm upset about, everything I'm angry about, everything I don't have that I want and everything that I *don't* want and somehow still have, and everything I've always wanted to know, but wasn't told, they all have one thing, one source in common: Paul Rowland.

Patrick had just recently given up with his fascination with Deirdre, the girl at the coffee counter. He started buying his brew elsewhere, and I cleared his name as best I could with Simon. I'd forgiven Patrick without his asking, or indeed without his knowing, and was satisfied in my nobility, if not in our harmony.

Then Uncle Paul showed up unannounced one night after ten o'clock, soaked to the skin with a chill November rain. We hadn't seen him in a long time, not since my mother's funeral more than three years before, and it was hardly anything I'd peg as a welcomed intrusion.

"Sorry to drop in so late without calling," he said.

"I'm sure." I helped him drag the soggy coat off his shoulders. Paul had never got all the way to fat with age, but he had gone a bit walrusy in the shoulders, now heavy and rounded, somehow without losing height. He was always taller in person than he was in my memory. His hair and his mustache he'd let go a bit longer than he used to, lengthening his face to a slightly more glum version of himself. They were shot through with silver now.

"Where's my candy?" I demanded.

"God, you looked just like her when you said that." His smoker's laugh had grown thicker in the intervening years. Everyone in Paul's orbit smoked, even as it fell out of fashion.

"You couldn't see me. I was behind you."

"I can see with my ears as good as you can, Dee. And feel with my eyes, and hear with my fingers. Your mother learned her games from somewhere, you know."

"What can I do for you, Paul?" Any sort of banter with him was just land mines in the field of my relative tranquillity.

Paul sat Patrick and me down in our own living room and told us that we had a little money now. My mother had socked away savings for decades in a hidden, numbered offshore account. She had willed it to me and Simon in the event of her death, via Paul's administration over a lawyer's or accountant's. It had taken him, or more likely Them, a long while to secure the legitimacy of the funds and to follow the paper trail to a point of reassurance for everyone. But of course she'd done it right. Every i was dotted with visible ink and each t crossed with a verified flourish. The timing, though, stung.

I said, "Yeah, you know, this would have been really helpful last year. We had a pretty tight time and had to dip into the retirement funds to get by." I didn't offer Paul another beer even though his empty bottle had been sitting on the table since just after the pleasantries.

"Don't imagine I didn't think about that, Dee. Times are tight for everyone. I know how it is when you're counting on bonus money that doesn't come in. It can be a real bitch to the bottom line, not to mention the nerves. But at least you two kept your jobs. I just couldn't bring this up until we'd checked it all out. Money is gasoline and curiosity is matches."

I didn't ask him how he knew about our circumstances, and Patrick hadn't seemed to notice. Before any of our other troubles, my mother's death had wounded my husband. Our lack of a baby for all his reading up on it had frustrated him, then the added insult of canceled bonuses in the face of economic downturn, and the slowly mounting money shortage, had all stacked up to humiliate him more than he'd say out loud.

All these things he'd borne in blaring silence, his blood pressure playing ruddy in his skin. I had tried to see his playfulness with Deirdre as a bleeder valve for his frustration. The mortgage on his home and his childless wife were reminders of all that wasn't going well at the moment. His little side bank account bothered me more for its fundamental weight. If it was a petty-cash fund, it was un-called for. I didn't hassle him about spending. But if that money was the bare ribs of a lifeboat in the making, well . . .

I would have waited it out for the chance to talk these things through, but first of all I would have had to craft a work-around to explain how I knew about them in the first place. In the midst of that puzzle came the reveal of my little birth control stunt, which had done nothing positive for his mood. The only upside to it was that I'd been relieved of the need to straighten out the rest of the mess. So instead, I waived off the balance as a wash and set my eyes on the horizon. I tried to make a blank slate of it.

After a short swell of renewal, his temper had been riding an in-creasingly short fuse and his patience was a heavy burden he'd shrug off at our doormat, leaving me to tiptoe around his delicate sensibili-ties. He'd stopped bringing up the subject of babies altogether, and I wouldn't stoop to using it as a shortcut to sunnier conversations.

Paul had unwittingly rolled up just in time to miss the smoke end of the evening's fireworks. Dinner had ended with me scrambling for a way back from a long drop into an unfathomable argument.

"Want me to get his number for you?" Patrick had wiped the corners of his mouth on his napkin. The globed candles that used to light the tables of our favorite local restaurant had been replaced by battery votives that pretended to live like their flamed counterparts. The effect was almost the same until you caught the repetition in the flicker pattern.

Patrick was lit from below in the too-dark restaurant. He looked unfriendly, sinister even, all sharp jaw and glinty sparks where his eyes watched from deep caves of brow shadow. Historically, he'd never been the jealous type.

"Huh?" I said.

"The waiter. I can ask him for his number if you're too shy."

"Pat, what are you talking about?"

"You're tracking that guy all over the room. He's a little young for you, don't you think?"

"Oh, come on."

"Yeah, I'm imagining it." Patrick was simmering down from insult to pout. His complaint had lost momentum as soon as it was out loud in the air between us. It was ridiculous.

"Actually, I *was* just looking at him. I think he looks like Simon did when he was that age. I mean, if he had curly hair. Don't you think so?"

"Okay, that's not a little bit creepy."

"What? Ew. Don't do that. You're the one saying I have motives, so I'm explaining myself. I'm just trying to catch a look at him in the light. It's so damned dark in here. C'mon, Pat."

The money my mother had left us—almost $500,000, after the taxes were paid—was a balm to some of his hurts, but his moods still blinked off and on, not unlike the votives at our restaurant. I just hadn't picked up on the pattern yet. For certain, I saw him brighter in the brights and more grim in his lows, so I tread carefully, picking my way past his rise and fall, aiming for our old level ground. I reserved the right to hope the money would help us in more than just the finances.

Breathing room isn't the same thing as happiness, but money can surely buy it.

What goes up, though, swings back the other way eventually. And sometimes "eventually" doesn't take all that long to pounce. You've barely said your thank-yous for a little slice of good fortune and the rug's back out from under you before you've got even a quick feel of the nap of it between your toes.

We'd not taken in three of the plumper bank statements when the text came in from a number I didn't recognize. *Mrs. Aldrich— I need to speak to you.*

Of everything I ever resented about the way I was raised, the most persistent was the ghost of constant alert, the fixed cowering under a subtle pall of anticipation. From my mother's return from the Long Trip onward, it felt as if I never fully exhaled. Something was coming. Something could happen at any moment. Wait for it. Be ready.

Of everything that ever bewildered me about my mother, her warm acceptance of inevitability was the oddest. She embraced it. She wanted it. Let it be bad, but if it was a sure thing, she liked it better than a "maybe."

As sure as lies in church, baby girl. None of her adages purred out quite like that one. She reveled in announcing a certainty. Whether it was good news or bad, it was the starting gun to getting things done. And my mother was all about the getting done of things.

So it wasn't exactly surprise that burned through me as I read the text. It's hard to claim astonishment when you are forever poised for the jolt.

Who is this? I responded.

Rather talk in person. Meet me?

Last chance before I block this number, I typed with trembling fingers.

The trouble with pervasive, nonspecific alarm is that I never knew what or whom I was waiting for. Could be a winning sweepstakes notification, or it could be Dr. No.

As it happened, it was a woman named Angela.

My mother was not a dramatist even though dramatic things occasionally happened. Anything accomplished in preparation—for ant bites or apocalypse—was considered worthy. But in me, the call to readiness cultivated a certain yearning for the worst, if only to justify the constant fighting stance that quivered just under my skin.

This wasn't the worst.

I'd have guessed it would have hurt more. But instead, I was mortified, not devastated, to hear what she had to say. Hot tides of loathing pulled me back and forth while she yammered into my ear. But it was the wrong brand of reaction. I wanted *not* to know that my husband had been making ridiculous promises with his head buried in a stripper's cleavage more than I wanted for it not to have happened.

Angela kept me on the phone for forty-five minutes until I made myself burst into the tears she wasn't going to hang up without. She was furious with Patrick. I endured her biting, rambling rant and found, against a good percentage of my will, the tawdry little story tucked away in there between the lines.

He'd flirted when she served him lunch, outright hit on her when she brought the check, then called her up when she'd left her number on the receipt. He'd gone to see her at her other job—the less dressed and more lucrative one. He'd monopolized her time and teased extra attention out of her with big talk of bigger tips to be had in some vague, flush future. She'd stoked his bluff with nearly naked grind.

It must have been a spontaneous dare he'd made to himself. Patrick wasn't that brand of bold, and then he'd gone and underestimated a woman who was. She wasn't the sort of person you wind up, then brush aside. I couldn't imagine how he'd misevaluated Angela, because I could tell just by listening to her on the telephone that she was a semiprofessional pain in the ass.

If wallowing in drama is someone's favorite pastime, it's nearly impossible to disguise it. I didn't understand how he could not have seen that. But in a certain mood, these rocket-propelled people can be invigorating. When that frame of mind meets an unguarded opportunity, just the mere whiff of you-only-live-once whets a craving that's hard to resist.

Poor Patrick. He had certainly been towing a dark cloud over his head for a long while. He'd run right past the invigorating return of a good mood, straight past giddy, and headlong into insanity. Then, predictably, he'd come to his senses.

I wanted to stop her. More than that, I wanted to call her names. Not for being a stripper. A decent body and a bossy wiggle can be for sale and I'd have nothing to say about it. But she was low and stupid to bring me into this, to weigh me down with the details—as if she had the right to make a triangle out of the painful part of her job. I could feel my cheeks glowing, scalding with humiliation for having to hear Angela complaining to me of all people. Still, in the embarrassment I felt for Patrick, I burned with an extra dose of heat. Some strange shame brought me low for pitying Patrick in this moment.

He had called her after he stopped showing up as promised, wedging in some distance from the boasts he'd made, as she put it, "blowing smoke up my ass," but then he had switched off completely, soon afterward, pouring regret into her ear during a final good-bye on the telephone, saying he wouldn't be visiting the club again.

She'd spent money on his beery forecasting, too much money, and now found herself in the red. By her math, she'd sold him the inspiration for fantasies on credit. And the bill was due. Angela warned him against ignoring her over a barrage of unanswered calls and texts. Ferreting out my number and drawing me into the soap opera was her punishment for his disregard. But my sympathies didn't exactly nestle down where she'd expected them to.

"I just thought you should know, Mrs. Aldrich," she said, making *Mrs.* sound underlined and bold-typed.

That put the hard brakes on my conjured tears. I sniffed once and cleared my throat. "Really? Except that if he *had* come back like you told him to, then you wouldn't have called me because then I *shouldn't* know?"

"What?"

"I'm just trying to follow the conversation here. You're mad that he didn't do as you ordered him to do, so you called me and tried to blow up his life. What would you have done if he had obeyed you?"

"Excuse me?" Angela's scorn resparked brightly.

"It just seems like this whole call is a lot less about you thinking I should know what my husband is up to, than it is about you burning Patrick because you feel that he's crossed you."

"Don't you put this on me. Your sack-of-shit husband is the one you need to be talking to."

"Right."

"So what are you gonna do?" she demanded.

I sighed. "I don't know. Get tested for crabs?"

Inarticulate fury wrung a few strangled clucks down the line.

"Look, Angela, I don't know what you want me to say. Presumably you're not waiting for a 'Thank you.' If you want to know that I'm upset, I can at least offer you that. I'm upset, okay?"

"But what are you gonna *do*?" she shouted.

"I don't know!" I howled back, and stabbed the button, killing the call.

I hurled my phone into the sofa cushions and knelt on the floor. I rocked onto my heels. I'd been entirely frank with Angela. I had no idea what to do with this.

He'd been angry with me, and rightly so, but the ramp up from teasing and flirting with the young barista at the supermarket to pawing a pole dancer into a rage put Patrick too far from what I'd known of him. I didn't recognize the husband-shaped blur so far afield of our little life. It scared me hot and cold all over. My scalp tingled in waves of chills.

Part of my fear was in acknowledging my own hand in the distance between us. I had long since sworn only ever to lie out loud.

Within myself, in my mind, I was always honest to the point of discomfort. Patrick's wandering eye and kindled daring had a certain justice. I knew it and acknowledged it, even if he didn't know I did.

But he'd pulled back from this alley. He hadn't taken it all Angela's willing way. And every bit of the sincerity I could wrestle in my head wouldn't tally up an answer for that one. Why hadn't he gone all the way? Was it my worth or Angela's that had brought him back from the brink? Or was it something else entirely? Was this the end of his restlessness or the just the start?

Perhaps that was the price I would pay—ending up all alone with the facts and no sum to make of them.

12

Patrick found me cross-legged on the floor of the office, walled in by photo albums and boxes of books and papers. My mother's things. I'd spent all that afternoon avoiding him and busying myself away from the treadmill replay of Angela's phone call. She hadn't contacted me again, and every hour of distance from our chat was working that strange thing that is only the privilege of time to do—the rewriting of history. In this case, time managed its trick by sketching down the memory of my moderate reaction from what it had been into something abstract, a concept of a reaction instead of the reality of what I'd said to Angela.

With two days of real life for a buffer, what embarrassment there had been, and the odd wallow of sympathy I'd felt for Patrick, was faded more to watercolor than photograph. Now the surges of insult were so scalding I'd have to revisit the conversation, word for word, just to remember what I'd said to bring back even a shade of my measured calm.

But guilt had me thinking I had to make amends by being forgiving of a comparably weighted offense. The trouble is, betrayal is bigger on the inside than it is on the outside. However bad it looks, there are no scales to measure a pair of loyalties against each other. I couldn't tell which one of us was worse.

I wanted off the carousel, even for just a while. What I really wanted was to talk to my mother. Killing time rifling through the cartons of her things and remembering the stories behind the flotsam was a second-rate substitute for her electric presence and artful guidance, but it wasn't third rate, and it wasn't nothing. I took up the task of scanning her photos and letters into the computer for safekeeping.

The ongoing project had been meant as a layman's reach for permanence, a way to thumb my nose at fire and flood and tornadoes until electromagnetic pulse do us part. But in the drudge work of sorting all the snapshots, I'd swung into distraction at intervals and bent to the call of the laptop, and listless Internet searches for more information. I typed in variations of her maiden and married names with addresses or snippets of person, place, or thing that I recalled from my troll through her papers. Secret money, secret job. I knew the drill. I always had. But now more than ever, so much less stays secret. I looked for her in the immortal mountain of ones and zeros available to my every clickable whim.

"What are you doing?" Patrick asked, sitting down on the far side of my fortress of memorabilia.

"I don't know. Making some progress on our scanning project, I guess." Patrick and I had stacks piled up, intended for the electronic archive, but it had turned out to be somewhat of a one-mountain-forward, two-mountains-back endeavor. "With Paul coming around again and us getting the money in and just—you know, all the stuff that's going on. . . . Anyway, it made me think of her. I thought I only wanted to look at her pictures, then I thought I'd go ahead and get some of it scanned in. Next thing you know, I'm in here all day." I pulled out a postcard from the stack of pictures. "Hey, see this one?" The postcard was a once-glossy photo of a golden-rayed sunset on a beach, with a raw and wild jungle backdrop, nothing but green and shadow just past the umbrellas and lounge chairs of the resort. Safe and relaxing so close to wild and not safe at all, the picture was mesmerizing. The edges of the card had frayed to white fuzz, and the message space on the back had been left blank except for a smudged postmark from Thailand.

"This was the spider-catching card," I said. "My mother never crushed a spider. She always caught them with a glass and this postcard and then put them outside."

Patrick laughed. "You would think she could've just stared down even a tarantula and told it to scram and it would have gone straight for the door all by itself."

"You'd think."

"You okay?"

"Yeah," I said without conviction. The back of my throat tickled with tears. I hated crying and hated myself when I did it. I dared my eyes to water up, teeth hooked into the meat of my cheek, pinching what had been a vague sadness into a smoldering anger—at a show of weakness, at Patrick, at myself.

Patrick lifted a small stack of old-style, orangey, square photos off the pile and rotated through them without really looking. "It's not surprising, I don't think—the money, I mean. I wondered about that when the estate settled out. I always thought she would have had more."

"You always thought that, huh? Bold much?"

"What's that supposed to mean?"

"Nothing. It was just a weird way for you to put it is all. Like she owed us or something."

"I didn't mean anything by it, Dee. God." Patrick lurched up from the floor. "Nice little sucker punch, though."

"Pat, I'm sorry." A thrill of dread bloomed between my lungs and squeezed my heart to fluttering. If I picked a fight now, it would come out. I wasn't ready to talk about Angela, and in no small part because I hadn't decided how upset I might or might not be over it. The lay of our land was strewn with hidden traps, and not just mine.

"I should have known better," he said. "You're so touchy when-ever your mother comes up."

"I know I am. I'm sorry."

"Never mind. It's fine." Patrick kissed the top of my head with a loud, mocking smack and walked away.

My mother's games kept time in me like a second heart, the lessons thrumming away in the background, unnoticed, just like a pulse. I sensed the world the way she had taught me to without feeling the mechanism of it.

Something startled the galloping of blood and alertness through my veins. I felt eyes on me, but whoever owned the gaze had dropped it back into the crowded bustle of the mall's wide hallway before I was able to pin down the watcher.

My mother had grafted us, Simon and me, to a braided lifeline of intuition, tricks, and her stock of truisms. *There is nothing supernatu-ral,* she'd say. *There are only the things in this world that we understand, the things that we don't understand, and made-up crap.* The last part of that saying was always the best bit. *Pray at the altar of each of these things, my darlings.* She would be smirking by then. *They all work in their own way.*

Why, exactly, we should go through our days harnessed to a life-line at all, she never quite explained.

I scanned the bustling food court for the source of my ruined ap-petite. The trouble with top-of-the-line keenness (that my mother would never let us call paranoia) is that out of context, a pointed look could mean that I was being groomed as some sort of a target or merely that my sweater reminded the beholder that his wife's birthday was this weekend and that he'd best get a gift right quick before he forgot again.

I scanned the room and didn't see anything or anyone worth evaluating.

I sighed and forced down two more rounds of spicy tuna roll before tipping the rest of it into the garbage. The soft tingle of being watched tracked through my hair again, and I whirled to its call faster this time, half expecting to find a bristling woman with ANGELA tattooed across her forehead spotlighted somewhere in the crowd. But instead, my glance was tugged by the shoulder of a man turning away from me—tall with dark, wavy hair, and a jacket almost too nicely cut to be paired, as it was, over jeans. I looked back over the rest of the midday melee—munching, chatting, texting. None of them pulled crosshairs over my eyes the way Mr. Walking-Away did.

He didn't see me look again, but I double-checked to note whether his retreating stride still matched up with the humming compass in my brain. The doors to the parking levels turned him back in my direction, not full on, but even through two layers of insulated glass and nearly twenty years of time, I recognized his face.

I remember once drifting into my mother's office to find her studying the photograph of a man: blond, with nearly invisible eyebrows. He was clean-shaven and had a dent in his chin deep enough to look as if it might have had an ax buried in it at some point. The man's two-pronged jaw would have been interesting enough, but my mother's absorption was too intense, the whole scene unreal, as if maybe I were asleep in my bed and walking around only in my dreams.

She was motionless, staring at the picture, but with the image turned upside down.

"What are you doing?" I was little, maybe eight years old, and the only thing to make sense of it was to think of how I liked to watch my brother, just barely out of being a baby, talking upside down. We'd take turns dangling over the arm of the sofa, reciting rhymes to each other face-to-upside-down-face. It was good fun until the giggling made it all nonsense and somebody got spit in their eye. And even when it was fun, it was still a little creepy—the smile that was clearly a smile but all wrong with the big teeth bared below and the tongue tapping down instead of up. The fascinating deformity made the words look out of sync, as if they should sound wrong. But they didn't sound wrong. The singsong verses would play in Simon's clear little-boy ring. He always laughed first.

My mother looked up from her work, scanned me, and tallied up the sum of my discomfort with a speed and ease that, even then, I knew was disconcerting. But her smile put me one level closer to fine.

"It's a trick." My mother pulled me close and righted the photo. The room snapped back into plain old Saturday morning. "Your brain is amazing, Plucky. You can make it do fancy things that it doesn't normally do. Like if you study a person's face, like this guy's face for instance, upside down"—she inverted the photo again, much less disconcerting with her warm arm around me—"then it doesn't matter what he does to change the way he looks. I'll remember him if I ever see him again. He could change his hair color and it wouldn't matter. He could cover his eyes with glasses. He could wear a hat or grow a beard or get old and I would still be able to recognize him right away."

"Why would anyone change their face?"

"Now *that's* a conversation for an older and wiser day."

She often steered away from certain kinds of questions with that little word-rudder, sometimes to be revisited and sometimes not. If this one had ever come back around, I couldn't remember it, and I don't know if my mother ever crossed paths, or swords, with the blond man.

But, watching the glass door to the parking garage sweep closed, this particular day achieved instantly older and wiser status. I recognized Special Agent Brian Menary in the ridiculous food court of the equally ridiculous local shopping mall, and I'd only ever studied his face upside down once, almost two decades earlier on the night my mother left me twice—first by sending me into a lashing rain with my bawling little brother in tow, then later, in the foyer of our house on the worst night of my life.

The night my mother left us for so long, something in a storm had woken me. A sound had been running under the thunder as I slept, a sound I wasn't sure I had actually heard until I played back the end of my last dream. In it, my track coach had been talking to me about double-knotting my laces and the importance of pressing the balls of my feet against the starting blocks. He was sitting in a pile of autumn leaves raked up into a high hill in the corner of the gymnasium where we would run practice drills whenever the weather was too lousy to train outside. Then, to match the ambient noise of the house's waking reality, Coach Wells inexplicably slammed a door to nowhere that hadn't been there a second before.

Once my eyelids snapped open, the dark of my bedroom was immediately more solid than the bright nonsense reel I'd been playing in my sleep. I strained at the ears to hear the voices buried in the din of the rain on the roof. The runoff from the gutter spattered against the pane, and the wind hooting around the corner of the house snatched away the words, but the whispered whir of urgency slipped through the air. I picked out my mother's voice and also a man's, their conversation just a two-toned murmur under the sounds of the storm. At the top of the stairs, I heard her more clearly: "Nuh-unh. Not a chance. You're not taking them anywhere. I'll handle it."

Her usually light step was betrayed on the hardwood floor. I almost never heard her walking indoors. She was as silent as fog in the house, in her bare feet, missing every nail-rubbed spot in the boards without trying. She just seemed always to know where to step. Her strict policy was no shoes in the house, but that night she had her boots on. The clock read 1:12 a.m. It was just barely Friday.

My heartbeat thrashed at my eardrums before she slipped into my bedroom, trailing no light behind her. She and the man had been talking in the dark.

"I need you to do something for me, Plucky," she said. "I need you to take Simon out the back door. Take the path to the stock pond. Sit under the dock and count to one hundred." She laughed, a sound so disconnected from the scene it might as well have been another dream. But it was a real laugh, not a forced thing. Something in all of this was funny to her. "Then I want the both of you to sing 'American Pie'—the whole thing, all the verses—very quietly."

"What? Why are you sending us down there now? I was sleeping. I don't—Mama, it's raining."

"I know, baby. But it's not cold outside. You'll get dirty, but that's okay, and you'll be fine. But I need you to go, now, quickly. Now when you get back, if that truck"—she pulled back the bedroom curtain and tipped her head to send my glance out to where the streetlight cast the long shadow of a boxy, black Suburban over the lawn—"is still in the driveway, don't come in. If it's gone, then come around back and come on inside. If it *is* there, or if any car for that matter is in the driveway, go to Mrs. Anderson's house— the back door—and ring the bell." She tapped her teeth with her thumbnail, thinking. "And here's the second thing: if there aren't towels for you two on the back bench under the awning, same thing, even if the truck is gone—go through the yards to Mrs. Anderson's back door."

"You're scaring me! What's going on? Who is that out in the hall?"

"Don't worry, baby. He's fine. He's here to help. But it's almost surely a mistake. Probably nothing that has to do with me. And certainly nothing that has to do with you and your brother. I just need you to take him and do as I ask while I sort this out."

"Mama, I can't."

"You can't what? Walk? You can't count? You can't sing? Plucky, all of those things are easy. So is being scared—it's very easy. But being scared doesn't nail your feet to the floor any more than happiness makes you fly out the window. So go on, baby, scared or no. 'Can't' isn't very useful to us just now."

"Will you tell me later?"

"Not if you don't do what I say. Be a good girl, a brave girl, and who knows?" Incredibly, she winked. "I just might."

Her fingers trembled as she reached for the bedroom doorknob. Knowing that my mother was frightened flipped a switch in my middle. Suddenly, I didn't mind the thought of being far away from the house. Suddenly, it seemed like an excellent idea. I snatched Simon from a deep sleep and hustled him into his sneakers and raincoat, and we set out of the house as if the place were on fire.

I ran over the slick carpet of grass with Simon's hand in my grip, his sniffling sobs a high hum under the clamoring applause of the rain.

We did what she asked. We hunkered down in the squelchy mud by the last landlocked post of the pier. The fast, dull clatter of rain on the planks sang with the hard drumroll of my heartbeat. The two strains of staccato pounding raced each other, one over my head and one inside it. It might have been easier to tame the fear if it had been quiet, but in the quiet I would have been bending every nerve back toward home, toward my mother and the stranger and whatever they were waiting on inside our house. Maybe this was better. Tonight, no sound could hurdle the blanketing hiss of the rain. But at least there were our instructions.

The why of it was so far out of reach that we didn't even question it or wonder over the task list laid out to distract us from what was happening inside our house. Counting seemed right, seemed solid. One, two, three, four . . . In the farthest reach of the streetlight, I could see the fear-shine of Simon's eyes tamp down to just the glint of concentration as he tried not to lose track as we got into the higher numbers. Counting put the time of our return trip into focus. We were going home just on the far side of triple digits. Not far at all. Not long. We could do that. I could do it.

The singing was stupid enough that we eventually ended up sputtering rain as we laughed, which was exactly to my mother's plan. It put the heart back in us for the walk home. She knew we'd be scared.

We came up to an empty driveway with the secret-message towels stacked on the bench on the back porch. Inside, my mother's hair was curled with sweat and she was speaking low and fast into the telephone as we turned the corner of the living room. When she saw us, she tucked the phone against her shoulder and touched our faces with her hot hands. "I've got to go," she said to her caller, and without allowing time for a reply dropped the phone back into its cradle.

A very young Brian Menary huffed through the front door, red-faced and panting. He started stacking my mother's things in the foyer.

13

Patrick's phone burred in its holster. I didn't get the dinner plate that was in my hand set all the way into the dishwasher's rack before my cell also came to life, shimmying a little half turn on the countertop and pinging a text alert. We looked at each other, questioning the synchronicity with only a shared look while we both reached for our phones.

You deserve each other. 1 dog + 1 bitch. But when he turns you around next time, just know he's probably thinking about this.

Predictably, there was a photo attached. Angela's name wasn't tattooed on her forehead. It was, however, tattooed on her ass. The curly script underscored a delicate, impossibly beautiful, jewel-toned butterfly. I briefly wondered if the artist had regretted making a tacky name tag out of his nice work instead of letting the precision and color speak for itself.

Patrick and I locked eyes across the kitchen island. People sometimes say that the color drained from someone's face, but I'd never seen it in textbook presentation before. In this case, a distinct pale edge tumbled, forehead to chin, over the average shade of Tuesday on his face. The white drew down as his blood deserted his brain, where all the excuses and reasons lived. He opened his mouth but nothing came out.

"Pat—" I started.

"She's lying."

"Pat."

"I don't know who this person is. I think it's a wrong number. You know how they reassign numbers. This must be close to—I should call the telephone people. I—I've been getting these weird—these harassing messages—it's gotta be." The last three words made little sense, but he'd hit a sound stride and nodded his head as if it stood in for any kind of resolution.

"Pat!"

He froze. I mirrored his stance, chilled and stiff, bracing against the opening lines of this scene I'd hoped not to have to play out. There was no sloping into this one. A quick dive and a cold splash was all I had ahead of me.

I sighed. "Angela called me four days ago. She told me what happened."

"She what?" Patrick's pallor had curdled around flushed patches on his cheeks, as if he'd been slapped twice.

"I didn't know what to say to you."

"Four days? You didn't say anything about this for four days?"

"I just didn't—"

"You acted— We've been— Nothing. *Nothing* at all. Like everything was fine," he sputtered.

"It's not fine. I just didn't want to overreact. With everything that's happened . . ."

"With everything that's happened—what? What does that even mean?"

"Hang on. Wait. You're angry with *me*?" I asked.

"I don't know yet. Why haven't you said anything or even hinted that there was something wrong—something this big on your mind?"

"Why are you turning this around on me? I was trying to be understanding."

"You were trying? I dunno, you don't exactly look all worn-out from four days of *trying*. In fact, you look a lot more like you don't give a shit."

"This is ridiculous. I can't win."

"What are you trying to win, Dee?"

"So, you'd rather I throw dishes at your head? Is that what I'm supposed to get out of all of this?"

"Unbelievable." He got up from the table, the legs of his chair grinding across the tile. "You are truly unbelievable."

Patrick brushed by me, clearing the room in fast, angry strides before he'd have to offer one word in defense of being most literally bare-assed, blatantly caught.

"How am I in trouble with you over this? It doesn't make any sense. I was hoping that this was just a onetime thing, just a lapse, because you were mad at me. You know, getting back at me for the . . ." I left off, lost in the baffling indignation that billowed majestically around the statue of my husband as he loomed from the doorway.

Patrick was all offense now on an unfathomable high ground. He leaned in, somehow righteous in his fury, withering me under his glare. "Well, if I had known I had a hall pass, I might have spent it differently."

I shook my head. "I don't understand."

"I can see that." He stalked out of the room.

Just a few weeks later, after a run of tense days warming through discussion and tears, rolling over to tentative makeup sex and stunningly odd urges in me to apologize, Patrick forgot his cell phone and I interrupted him giving directions to a man in a blue sedan who didn't look lost at all.

Patrick was a man of preparation. Corporate presentations ended up looking effortless for all the effort he put into them, and he spent up to a quarter of an hour each workday morning in the driveway, admiring his shave in the rearview mirror and checking his voice mail and electronic messages for things to mull over on the way to work, psyching himself up with answers-at-the-ready for whatever he'd missed since he'd left the office on the previous afternoon.

So I was a little surprised on my way to the shower, one morning, to see his cell phone still in its charging cradle on the dresser. He'd only left just moments earlier, so I hustled into my robe and slippers to catch him before he could drive off without it. I yanked open the front door, still struggling with the robe's sash to stay decent. Patrick was bent at the hips, speaking into the open driver's-side window of a blue sedan idling at the curb opposite our house.

My flapping on the stoop drew the driver's attention. That was normal in and of itself, but something in the unmistakable *Oh, shit!* of the look on this stranger's face kicked my heart into double time. Patrick mirrored the man's startle, his eyebrows flying for his hairline before he could stop them. He composed himself, nodded at the man, who then pulled away from the curb without another look my way. Patrick met me on the sidewalk.

"Who was that?" I asked.

"What?"

I laughed for his benefit. Granting Patrick a sliver of time gave me one as well. Composure cuts both ways, and we'd been riding rough waters of late. Our peace was bruised and seasick. I'd made a second career of being careful not to upend a nice day without good cause.

I shielded the early sun out of my eyes with a sheltering hand across my brow. The blur of golden light receded under my shade so I could see his face clearly. "Do you know that guy?" I asked.

Patrick's color was high in bright circles over his cheekbones. "That guy? No, I don't know that guy." Parroting. A small giveaway that the statement is a lie.

"Well, what did he want?"

"Directions."

"To where?"

Patrick's eyes danced right and left. "The freeway."

"Oh. You forgot your phone."

Patrick took it and kissed my cheek. "Thanks. Gotta run. Love you." But his mouth turned down at the corners as he said it.

I went back into the house and pushed the whole scene from my mind and nearly convinced myself I hadn't memorized the license plate of the blue sedan.

14

My membership dues covered eight yoga classes per month, and my resolution to hit all ninety-six opportunities in a year was an achievement I had yet to celebrate. Still, some yoga was better than none, and I'd been a good girl, doing the diligent downward dog regularly of late. The studio was an addition to the instructor's home, a shoehorned-in upgrade stapled to the side of a funky, little house in a run-down quarter of town. The yard had been graveled over all the way to the chain-link fence for parking, but all the incongruence was forgotten over the threshold. The transition struck a mood of antiseptic reverence with spotless blond-wood floors, tall, gleaming mirrors, and gorgeous silk wall hangings in honor of the cascade of chakras we stretched and twisted our bodies to improve.

Offense was only my second reaction to the burglary at the studio. The first was mistrust. Of the four handbags that were upended from the nineteen full cubbies in the entryway, mine was the most thoroughly spread over the floor. Even the inside zipper compartments had been opened and emptied, and mine had been the only one with any cash in it at all, albeit only a few dollars. Beyond maybe enough money from my wallet to buy a Red Bull and a Slim

Jim at the bodega a block and a half away, no one at the yoga studio, a little too conveniently, was out anything.

A wad of pink aerosol string had blocked the studio's mostly-for-show security camera, and the police arrived at the reasonable and completely unsatisfying conclusion that a selection of local punk asses had been scared off their thievery before they could make off with anything valuable.

That might have been a good enough explanation, except for the niggling timing of it, wedged in as it was into my newly complicated life. I couldn't help but notice that, despite a rain shower's having stirred the dust into mud at the bottom of the steps leading into the studio, a hoodlum, or a gaggle of them even, had not tracked in any muck during a grab and dash.

The convenience mart down the street had a mounted camera as well, but that hadn't interested the police. It didn't point at the yoga instructor's house. My argument—that it covered the intersection closest to the scene—was met with the practical rebuttal that there would be no way to tie activity at the busy crossroads with the next-to-nothing that had happened down the street at the studio.

Undeterred, I resorted to forced tears to persuade the convenience-store owner to check the camera, only to find to his surprise, but eerily not mine, that it had suffered a fatal malfunction on the afternoon of the incident and that it hadn't worked ever since.

If my mother was ever followed while we were with her, I never knew about it. She wouldn't have made a game of it, anyway. There's no entertaining spin to put on a chase. I don't know that even she, with all her confidence and infinite stock of truisms, could have given me a mental talisman against the burn of being prey. Tag was always my least favorite school-yard game. Nothing stripped me of all cleverness, grace, and every coherent thought in my head like being hunted. Not even for fun. I heard the delighted squeals of the other children on the playground, but between my own ears was always loud white panic and little else. When the game was done, I kept my face turned from the group until I could tame my wild eyes and coax back my happy mask, showing that I knew, just like everyone else did, that it was only a game.

I checked the rearview mirror again. I was being dramatic. Angela's fire raid on our cell phones coming right on the heels of having seen Brian Menary at the mall and the dustup at the yoga studio had put me on buzzing alert for days. This was surely still part of that hangover. It had to be. The blue sedan I saw now looked very much like the one that had been outside my house that morning the week before. (Then I'd seen it again three rows over in the supermarket parking lot the very next day.) But it was a common enough model, and like getting a new one myself, as soon as any particular car imprinted on my attention, I saw it everywhere.

The other drivers in their not-blue-sedans rolled past me as I plied the brakes. The rest of the cars behaved just as they should have, their images sliding predictably into my mirrors when I ran down the gas pedal. But not this guy. I towed this single blue car as if it were on a peculiar hitch, fifty feet long and one lane crooked. I had just made up my mind to draw him out with a more decisive maneuver, zooming into the clear road ahead, when my nemesis (or probably just fellow commuter) ticked on his turn signal and banked innocently out of sight on the exit ramp.

The steering wheel showed the damp ghost of my grip, and the air wicked it away once I peeled my hands off their ten-and-two position to scan the radio channels for something better than the noise in my head.

The thing about the truth is that if it is any way complicated, it's slow. It gets weighed down with reasons and other people's agendas. I could smell Paul's brimstone wafting through my life. He wanted something from me, or maybe from Patrick. Poor Patrick. Paul would eat his lunch. It made sense. He had turned so nasty, so quickly. No wonder he was all wound up. If Paul knew what I knew about Patrick's finances and misbehavior, he'd have put Patrick on strings, pulled my husband any way Paul wanted him pulled.

The decision to use a lie as a shovel was easy enough. If Paul's people were nosing around my home in blue cars, buzzing my commute, and staging burglaries for a chance to paw through my purse when they weren't chatting up my husband right under my nose, Paul would never tell me anyway. No matter how hard I strained at the cleverness to drag a little information from him, I'd never get anywhere by asking him directly. Paul Rowland was more than a bit beyond me when I was armed with nothing but suspicion and a sliver of truth. I'd just have to go at it sideways.

Confronting Patrick would be unnecessarily stressful for the both of us, and if I was wrong about the whole thing, it would be pointlessly embarrassing, too. We certainly didn't need any setbacks in our timid dance over the floor of eggshells.

I followed the bouncing ball: Paul gave us some access to a reasonably large amount of money, and within two weeks I didn't recognize my own stream of consciousness. My hands tingled in the afterglow of paranoid blooms of adrenaline. And I knew everything had got away from me when I poured the sugar on the saucer and tossed its paper packet into my afternoon coffee out of pure distraction. The sight of the white paper twisting through the spoon-swirled wake in my cup pushed my resolve into the passing lane in my mind. Enough. No more cruising along behind this nonsense.

The money was probably the button to press that would summon either the blue sedan or the man who took my mother away from me on that night so long ago. What I'd do with either of those things once I'd got one of them on my hook was a guess best made on the spot.

So, to rattle loose a clue, I transferred $10,000 of the available balance of my mother's fund into Patrick's and my regular checking account at the bank, and after the form was signed and the keyboard was tapped, I made a detailed conversation with the manager, for the benefit of anyone possibly listening, out of what it would take, penalty-and-timeline-wise, to liquidate the entire account.

Then I had some lunch.

As the cherry on top of my performance, I treated myself to what every woman who is readying herself to bolt into the anonymous wild needs. I'd been wanting new luggage anyway, so there was no need for a lie, but the drive to the nearest department store later in the day didn't draw a blue sedan or any other obvious tail. I didn't note anyone overly interested in my show of struggling to load the new bags into the car either.

Back in my office, feeling somehow both foolish and disappointed, I thought I'd welcome the distraction of a phone call. That was until, of course, the phone rang.

"Dee, why did you move ten thousand dollars?"

"Oh, hey! Patrick, you're going to spoil my surprise." The revving lie leapt out of my mouth with a speed that startled me. I hadn't intended to leave the money out of the savings for longer than it took the withdrawal to play the dangling carrot to anyone who might be watching the account or my activity. And I certainly wasn't planning on leaving it out for long enough to have Patrick worry about it. I had thought I had plenty of time to decide how to explain it away as an accident or an oversight. The day-to-day finances were nearly a hobby of his, but I figured I should have had at least until the statement arrived.

"I just thought we could pay off a few bills," I said—no stammer, all dexterity. Two points for me. "And then treat ourselves—clear our heads, you know, to kind of blow out the blues and start fresh. We need it. We could relax and celebrate that we've finally got a little breathing room. Like a getaway. I was thinking a spa weekend? I mean, that's what I had in mind. But, if you'd like to do something else . . ."

"You know what I'd like?" I braced for the answer I could hear he had cocked and ready. "I'd like for you to let me know when you get the urge to play around with five-figure sums before I hear about it on the automated teller. That's what I'd like."

"Come on. Don't be like that. There's really no reason for you to get all pissed off about this."

"Why? Because it's your money and you can do with it whatever you damned well please?"

"Good God, Pat! That's not what I meant. Where did that come from?"

"You make decisions about our lives without me, Dee. You do it like I don't even get a vote. It's like I don't even exist. I hope you don't insult me by pretending you can't think of any reason I might feel this way."

I left it quiet, poised between a guilty angel at one ear and a devil tap dancing for attention on the other shoulder, squeezing a handful of hateful truths to justify a nasty argument.

Patrick's anger rolled through the gap in the conversation. "Don't you dare act like I'm coming out of nowhere with this."

"I didn't say anything, Pat."

"Well, you *need* to say something. Or would you like me to cite a recent example of why I might be just a little touchy on the topic of you doing stuff behind my back?"

"First of all, I didn't do anything behind your—"

"No? I don't remember talking about us dipping into that money to *pay off a few bills*. I dunno, maybe your head was under the bathroom sink when you mentioned it."

"Stop it. What are you doing? We've talked about this. And things have been good. I thought we'd made some progress after the whole Angel—"

"I swear to God, Dee, do not go there. No matter how hard you try to make it so, this is not a balance sheet where one mistake on my part—one mistake that I stopped on my own, I'd like to point out—makes up for a years-long scam you pulled on me until you got caught. You can't say you forgive me if you're going to keep trotting this out, because that doesn't feel like forgiveness. It feels like leverage, kinda like it did from the start."

"Keep trotting it out? First of all, I don't *keep trotting it out*, and second, that works both ways, Pat. And I've apologized a hundred times." I checked my tone, not that I wasn't furious, but because I wanted to be able to end the call with something other than his hanging up on me. "I thought we were getting past it."

"I thought we were getting past it, too, until you pulled this stunt."

"It wasn't a stunt." Not in the sense Patrick meant it, anyway. "I'll put the money back."

"No. Don't bother. Go ahead and pay off the bills. But I don't want to go anywhere this weekend."

"Okay."

A graceless exit would put us out of speaking terms for at least the rest of the day. I ransacked the script in my head for the best and the kindest parting line and hated myself for the bad habit. I didn't get there fast enough.

"Look, don't worry about it." Patrick sighed into the phone, a disgusted, exhausted sound that rolled into my ear with a hard thud that promised to leave me with a headache later. I shoved down the urge to hang up the call and skip the fizzling end of this pitiful conversation.

"Sorry I snapped," he said. "I'm just tired. I'm stressed-out. It'll be fine. It *is* fine. I'll see you at home."

"Pat, I'm—"

"I might be a little late, so go ahead and eat. See you later, okay?" And he was gone.

15

*O*nce *upon a time . . .*

I texted my brother in our shorthand. Our mother had started all of her adventure stories like that, but over the years *once upon a time* had come to mean a summons to the pub over on Carver Street. When the phrase was hers, she would toss it into a lull in the conversation at the dinner table by way of encouragement for us to tell her about what sort of day we'd had. For Simon and me, though, our tales had always been tamer than hers by a mile. He had kept the little intro alive more than I had, made it his own, and *once upon a time* between us was now just an invitation to buy each other an equal number of drinks instead of simply splitting the check down the middle as would make better sense.

I can be there by 6, he wrote back.

I'll save you a seat, I typed.

Simon tugged my hair twice, and I looked up from the newsfeed I'd been scrolling through on my phone, checking the headlines and looking at the pictures, but not reading the articles.

"Hey," he said as he took the barstool next to mine.

"Hey, yourself."

"Everything okay?"

"Yeah. I'm just on my own for dinner and I didn't feel like being all by myself."

"It doesn't look like you feel like having dinner, either. That's just french fries."

"And they're really good." I nudged the plate toward him.

The conversation slid through the slots and chutes of what was new in only the most surface of ways: what books we'd read, and what movies we'd seen, who was an asshole at work.

"Hey, now I'm going to get nosy," I said. "Are you thinking about quitting? I mean, doing something else, now that there's a little money in the bank?"

"Nah. For all the bitching I do, I actually like my job. I help people. Don't make that face. I do! I like it. Besides, it's really not that much money, is it?" Simon looked to the ceiling toward a heaven that our mother had never believed in. "Not that I don't appreciate it, Ma! It's great! And thanks. Amen."

"Mmmmm. I'd do it, I think. Quit my job, I mean. I could go for finding something else to do. Not that information logistics isn't riveting . . . I would do it, except that it would give Patrick a stroke."

"He'd stroke out if you spent your own money?" Simon had a special cranky tone reserved just for the topic of Patrick's shortcomings. I both courted it and resented it at turns.

"Don't say that! What are you, the devil? It's not only *my* money. Good Lord. I just had this conversation. It didn't go well. I'm treading very carefully these days."

"If you say so. I obviously know so much about being married. There. I said it before you could."

"Ha ha." I stuck my tongue out at him. "Seriously though, he's been really hypersensitive lately."

"My guess? He's still way pissed about the pill thing."

"Among other things, that would be a good guess."

"It was a pretty boneheaded thing to do, Dee."

"Whose side are you on?"

"Yours—always and obviously." Simon double-dipped into the ketchup. "And still it was a pretty boneheaded thing to do."

"I don't know how else to say I'm sorry about it. I've apologized to Patrick a hundred times. I've even apologized to you, just because you had to know about it. I've said it and said it. I just wasn't ready to have a baby. I know I went about it the wrong way, but then I can't do anything right. I've given him a hell of a wide margin of error, because I know he's upset. And he even gets mad about that. I tiptoe around all the time and make special dinners . . ."

"Do you ever think that maybe it's ruined?"

"Can't you just ever be that friend who thinks Patrick is great when I think he's great and calls him a rat bastard when I don't?"

"No."

Simon stared into my scowl until it unraveled and we both laughed.

"So what are you saying? My marriage is ruined?" I continued my new trend of not telling Simon everything. I couldn't yet face his reaction to the Angela episode.

"Yeah. Maybe." Simon shrugged.

"Really? You're just going to blurt it out? Just like that?"

"What's the point of not saying it? Things get ruined. It happens. You guys were always kind of a weird match. And I wasn't even all that surprised about the baby stuff. I remember how you played with dolls—giving them Mohawks and seeing if you could make parachutes out of garbage bags. Very maternal."

"You're horrible." I pulled the plate of my french fries out of his reach.

"Hey, I'm not the one throwing babies over railings." He reached across me and slid the plate back between us. "But seriously, if it is screwed up that bad, there's no point in taking forever to admit it. It's not the end of the world. It's not even the end of you, you know?"

"You just have it all worked out, don't you? A marriage is a process, Simon. Not a fixed thing that never changes. And it's not about 'matching.' People are too complicated to expect anyone else to be like them. It's more about . . . I think it's a decision, and then the handling and care of the life you want to have. Bottom line, it's not like I haven't forgiven him for things over the years."

"Yeah, I don't know if all that is actually 'forgiveness.' I think it might be part of the same problem: you not handling things head-on. Look, I'm not being hard on you. You're awesome. You know I think you're awesome. But I know you have this picture in your mind of what things are supposed to look like . . ." Simon let the conclusion drift in on its own. "I mean, what do you think Mom would say about all this?"

"I know what she would say. She knew."

My mother had known of the pill game from its first days. In the early weeks after she came to live with Patrick and me, there had been a scare, a missed cycle, and I'd run straight for the doctor. Except that my doctor was out of town and it wasn't the sort of worry I was willing to wait more than a week to unknot. I didn't trust the drugstore tests. I wanted blood drawn and an expert telling me to my face that I wasn't pregnant. I landed at the family planning clinic, waiting hours with a brain blanked by dread. When they called me back to speak with the doctor, my wool skirt was picked clean of fuzz and a small mountain of frayed lint was the only proof I had that I hadn't sat motionless the whole time. I would have sworn on a stack of holy books that I hadn't moved.

Once they'd reassured me I wasn't pregnant this time, they offered me birth control.

I actually soothed myself for quite some time with the deflection that it hadn't been my idea. They offered. I accepted. Simple. Unplanned and undevious.

That night, having not said a thing to Patrick about the worry or its solution, I imagined I could still feel the dry, little pill on the back of my throat. I checked in on my mother before I went to bed. She was, as she almost always was in those months, propped on a mountain of pillows, book in hand, nerd glasses somehow invisible under her eagle brows that arched over the frames. But she was smiling, too. I was stabbed straight through in that moment, washed in a preview of how much I would miss her looking up from her reading, distracted at my interruption, but warming up instantly to become all the way mine whenever I walked through the door. I often went through those days in a fog of sleepiness for how often our "good-night" turned into hours of talking. But I didn't mind.

I confessed the whole day to my mother—the bargaining with God, the frenzy, the pills, the secret. The whole time she was with us, my mother was sharpest at night. She was often foggy during the days, warm and sweet and subtly soft around the edges, but as she was dying, her glinting clarity rose with the moon. *Are you allergic to babies or just Patrick's babies?* We talked it through in hushed voices late into the night, behind the closed door, and only managed to clean and polish the obvious: my little, off-white lie wasn't a sturdy barge pole to push off with. It wasn't going to get me very far from my concerns.

"So did you give her a ration of shit like you're giving me?" Simon asked.

"To be fair, she was a lot smoother than you are." I stirred my drink.

"She always was."

Which, of course, steered us onto the rocks of our mother as a topic of conversation, her life and times, and what secrets she took to the grave.

"What's really bothering you, Dee?"

"What do you mean? I don't have an agenda. I just wonder, that's all."

"No. No, you don't. That's not all. You never wonder about her work, not out loud anyway, unless something else is bothering you.

What is it? What's going on? Whenever you itch, you scratch it with that. Why?"

"I don't know that I do that," I said, fluttering the sweetener packets in their white china holder.

"Do I have eyes? Do I have ears?"

"Do you have a big, obnoxious mouth?" I hit him on the shoulder and shut him down with a burst of horseplay until his beer got knocked over.

Our two identical checks came and went. I hugged my brother hard, then went home to a stiffly apologetic husband and an hour's stint at the computer with Google and my mother's name, and Paul Rowland's, and now Brian Menary's.

16

The corner of your eye is the watchdog of the brain. My mother was big on what we might or might not catch in the arc of our peripheral vision. She made games of the lessons that sharpened the farthest reaches of our sight. She'd write things, sometimes quite small, on a piece of paper, and if we could read it, off to one side or the other, without moving our heads or eyes, we scored points. But she was tricky. I got caught out on *to be or not to be* because she'd actually written *to be or not do he*. Of course, my brain had taken the shortcut and my overall score had taken the hit. *Never trust a shortcut,* she'd say. *Use one if you have to, but sacrifice a goat in thanks if it didn't land you on your ass.*

I remember seething with envy over Simon's points bonanza for translating *Your chores are (B), but you (Ar) to (Fe) your shirts anyway.* He'd been studying the periodic table of elements for an upcoming exam, so our mother took out two birds with *Your chores are boron (B), but you argon (Ar) to iron (Fe) your shirts anyway.*

The unreliability of the watchdog was also a way for our mother to teach us to take our own mental temperature. If a sharp pull from the corner of the eye resulted in anything useful, well, there you go. And if it didn't spotlight anything important or even anything interesting for more than a few times in a row, then it meant you had been working too hard and probably needed to power down and read a comic book or something.

My mother loved comic books. She memorized operas and devoured rich literature. She read novels, pored over poetry, and studied the newspapers. But none of that is love, and nothing lit her up like a stack of new comics. Simon caught the fever, but I never did. I was happy enough to avoid it because the medicine was expensive. I saved for a new bicycle while Simon's allowance evaporated weekly at the hobby store.

Now, in the food court, at my usual table, a male-shaped blur tugged in the margin of my right eye. Brian Menary took up a seat at a high table off to one side and midway to the exit from where I sat.

It could be that he lived nearby. People lived places. People, in fact, lived here. I lived here. My mother had lived here. Certainly, he had to live somewhere. So why not in this town? And if he lived here, he'd go out sometimes. Why wouldn't he eat here at this food court and take late lunches as I tended to do and . . . oh, hell. What if it wasn't even him?

And just like that, I derailed my first reaction, the crucial instinctive reflex, and accordingly, I also murdered its firstborn plan, which was to walk right over to his table, sit down, and look him in the eye with a fire that pinned him to his seat. We'd have a chat about the weather and the football scores and what he'd been up to for the past nineteen years—and just what exactly the hell did he mean by being aggressively in the same place as I was, at the same time that I was there, and on more than one occasion to boot.

Oh, boy. Not crazy-sounding at all.

Now gripped in doubt, I furiously pretended to read my phone, keeping my head cocked so that perhaps-Menary shifted, backlit and indistinct, at the farthest reach of my eye. I wouldn't let even his shoulder drift out of the frame. I couldn't bear the thought of his leaving the room, which would also have his leaving me with this ridiculous uncertainty to tote back home later.

My cheeks stung with the heat of my imagined audience's curiosity. Surely everyone was looking at me. I'd certainly be looking at me. They must have been able to feel the thrumming of my pulse and the pressure change it boomed into the room. Somehow it didn't help at all that not a single head had swiveled in my direction.

I bought a buffer of privacy in plain sight by mock-startling at the phone that had not rung or moved in my hand. I pretended to swipe the screen with a flourish, tucked the phone in under the curtain of my hair, and took a call that no one had made. Safe in the sanctuary of oh-she's-on-the-phone, I examined and discarded several options of how I could leave this food court knowing more than I had coming into it. It had to happen.

And why, exactly, should I be the only one in the room feeling branded and spotlighted? At least I knew I belonged here. Let him see me looking. Let's see what he does with that.

I raised my head, phone still at my ear, and let probably–Brian Menary see me find him in the crowd. A flicker of surprise zipped between our locked stares, and my bravery lasted only one tick of the second hand. I dropped my eyes to my knees and, for a heart-knocking moment, desperately wanted the previous minute back. A do-over. *No such thing, Plucky. You're in the soup now, little girl.* The memory of my mother's voice rang clear and smirking.

For the benefit of anyone who might be looking, I said my good-byes to the nobody on my silent phone and stood, snatching up my purse and jacket. On my feet, I found that I'd resolved myself to the only option that would guarantee any progress. I'd have to go ahead and walk over th—

Shit. He was gone.

In no more than a blink and a glance down to find the strap of my bag, Menary had slipped from his chair and faded into the thin crowd.

"Son of a bitch," I whispered, sorely disappointed and uncomfortably brimming with unexploded courage.

But God bless my mother and her games, I caught sight of him again, out of the direct line as was his trained habit. He was watching for me. There was still a chance to leave here wiser.

I walked past the shop window where he'd slouched low to browse some gadgety thing on the shelf in one of those electronic-wizardry gift shops. I stopped in the trickle of midday shoppers, made a small show of looking around, and turned on a purposed heel and headed back the way we'd both come.

I had to trust that he'd noticed the feint and would try to keep up with me. I would not risk looking around, even discreetly, to see if he was still there. If he wasn't, I'd feel foolish only to myself. And if he *was* there, I'd blow it. I slowed, knowing that he'd have to rein it in, too, then I took off at fresh pace, less than a dash but more than a stride.

The food court restrooms were set into the right side of the corridor: men's room first, then the ladies'. With more of a flail than a plan, I hit the ladies' room door hard enough so that it swung to the full range of its hinge and banged an echo down the short hallway. I blocked out the objections of my saner mind and doubled back instead and, quietly, slipped into the men's room.

Thankfully, the man at the urinal was done and just zipping up. I leaned my ear to the door, held up one finger against the startled outburst that might have launched from him, and mouthed, *I'm sorry!*

The din of the ladies' room door would have carried into the food court. If Menary hadn't seen me duck into the hallway, he would surely at least have noted the noise. I heard footsteps pass the men's room. The footfalls stopped in front of the ladies' room, but the door didn't open. I had him, or someone at least, in my trap, such as it was, with me between him and the exit.

Sorry, I mouthed again to the slack-jawed, red-faced man who stood holding his hands away from his sides, too stunned to make a break for the sinks. I pulled open the door and stepped into the buzz of the faltering fluorescents. Brian Menary turned easily, then with full flinch, to face me.

"Well, that was easy," I said.

17

ardon me?" he said. It was one of those passive-aggressive, trifly word-gnats that irked me in some indefinable way.

"Hang on." I raised a finger to put the scene on hold, in much the same way I had in the men's room. The door beside me opened. My lavatory hostage had at least rinsed his fingers, but whether he'd had time to properly soap up was in question. Maybe he was just really fast. He burst from the men's room shaking the water from his hands and scowling. Catching sight of me did nothing for the blood in his cheeks, and he bloomed even brighter and hustled away, muttering.

I let the man clear the entrance back into the food court, buying some time to pull in what I hoped weren't obvious deep breaths, before I turned back to Menary.

Nothing ventured, nothing nothing, much less gained. I led with bravado I felt only in my feet. Everything above the ankles was quaking. "So. Brian Menary. Long time, no see. But not quite as long as you'd intended, yeah?"

I watched him try not to react to the use of his name.

"Pardon me?" he said again.

"Please don't do that. It's annoying. I mean, unless you really are hard of hearing, and in that case I apologize. I'm ready to talk a whole lot louder if you'd like."

He relaxed just the slightest. Maybe we'd passed the part where I was supposed to pull a gun or something. "Have we met? I don't remember ever giving you my name."

"I read it on a name tag once."

He laughed. I didn't. "Come on," he said.

"Yeah. What was it? Nineteen years ago. We never did get formally introduced that night, but I never forget a face." It was only a little white lie of omission. I forgot faces all the time, but I never forgot a face that I had inadvertently studied upside down. It worked just as she had said it would. Three points for me.

"What are you doing here?" I said. "Please tell me you live right down the street."

"I was just checking in on you, of course."

"Of course." The trembling started all over again, with more rattle in it this time. I clamped down, at some expense to my ability to breathe, so that it wouldn't show.

He continued, "But I would have bet my next ten paychecks that there wasn't anything for me to actually find with you. Joke's on me, huh? Were you going for the Tag Site just now?"

"Tag Site?"

"You weren't going for the Tag Site?"

"I give up. What's a Tag Site?"

"Seriously?"

"I don't know what a Tag Site is. So what? And I don't know why you're here or what you want after nineteen goddamned years, but you can start filling in the blanks anytime you'd like." The daring zoomed through me. "Or I could just scream and see how badly I can mess up your day with security guards and any stray hero-types who happen to be sitting out there at the tables. I'm sure Paul Rowland would be thrilled to come pick you up and iron out all the shit that goes down when someone like you gets filmed from ten different angles by the security cameras. Or did you Silly String all of them on your way in?" My quaking had calmed to a heady buzz. I was beginning to enjoy this. "Not that Paul couldn't talk his and your way out of it, I'm sure. But still, there'd be anyone who took a video on their phone of the scene I'm about to cause. . . ."

Brian offered a palms-out surrender. "Okay, okay, hang on. Who do you work for?"

"Traynor and Associates."

"Well, I know that, but—really? That's it?"

"What is going on? I am just about out of patience and it's going to get very loud in here very fast."

"Okay, first off, that's a Tag Site." He pointed at the plain beige door across from the restrooms. A card swipe was next to the doorknob, but otherwise it was unmarked and, therefore, completely unremarkable.

"Yeah, that doesn't help as much as it could."

"A Tag Site is kind of like, I dunno, a covert-ops broom closet." He shrugged. "A few agencies use them. They're all over—in airports and hospitals. Sometimes shopping malls. You can get in by swiping your ID tag—hence *Tag* Site—or they can be unlocked for you remotely with a phone call. That's assuming you know who to call and how to ask."

"What are they for?"

"I guess it's not for anything if you weren't going in there in the first place."

"Yeah, that's not going to cut it. What's inside?"

"Secure communications. Supplies. Stuff."

"What stuff? Prove it," I said. "Show me."

"I can't do that!"

"No? Well, why are you telling me all about it then?"

Brian laughed, a warm, amazed chuckle. "Agh! Because you asked." He raked exasperated fingers through his hair.

"Other people don't ask?"

"What other people?"

"Nobody ever asks you to explain yourself when you're skulking around?"

"*Other people* don't ask me things because it doesn't occur to *other people* to corner me by the restrooms. I happen to be good at my job. Other people don't even know I'm there in the first place." The gap in the back-and-forth fell uncomfortable in seconds. "Speaking of, can we—" Brian's sentence was interrupted by a mother and a potty-dancing little boy hop-pulling past us to the ladies' room.

He waited until the heavy door had shut them out of our conversation. "Can we take this discussion out there?" He nodded to the bustle and blur of the open food court. "Maybe we could sit down and straighten out this misunderstanding?"

"You'll just ditch me."

"I'm not Houdini."

"Okay, so that's who you're not. How about who you *are*?"

I said it easily, with a confidence that felt tapped, and not necessarily by me. Brian Menary had a version of the same contagious boldness that my mother had owned. Confrontation in his hands, as it had been with her, wasn't the powder keg it could have been. They almost encouraged it, made it feel safer than it was, which made a certain type of sense. Information was their business. No gold stars were handed out for their shutting down the person across from them.

What scuttled through my head was of no use to him if it didn't tumble out of my mouth. Intimidation probably wasn't as useful as the spy movies made it look. Like hot-pepper flakes or eye shadow, it was best applied sparingly.

"Let's go sit down," he suggested again, mildly.

And so we did.

The situation was just as tricky out in the open, but at least sitting down felt less fidgety than standing up. That the air was fresher was a bonus, too. A big, bright window stripped our standoff of most of its clandestine mood, but the light made it more real, too. Brian Menary wasn't a figment of my paranoia, and that was both a triumph and a terror.

He was also better looking than I'd appreciated at thirteen years old or just now in the gloomy corridor. He would have seemed old to me that night if I'd even bothered to notice, but on closer and better-lit inspection now, he wasn't even two handfuls of years older than me.

In surprising candor, he explained to me that I was—and had been—under routine "follow-through" surveillance ever since my mother died. My Internet searches, not the money at all, had rung the bell.

"You're spying on my Internet?"

"No, not really. It's not even your computer, specifically. It's just an open alert, everywhere, an algorithm scanning the search engines and Web pages and whatnot. If enough key words get tripped in a certain way, in a certain span of time, then an analyst takes a look at a scramble of data. Sometimes they make a recommendation that we put eyeballs on the situation. Anything more than that and we'd need a warrant and an army of lawyers."

"Mmmmmm. I see. You guys are just playing by regular-people rules," I said. "Sure you are."

"We do. As much as we can. Seriously. We pick our headaches very carefully, I promise you. For things like this, we just put a very casual watch on the person's day-to-day for a short while to see if they're acting tuned up."

"And the yoga studio?"

Brian smiled quizzically.

"You owe me six bucks."

"Huh?"

"Yeah, right." I rolled my eyes.

"Look, almost every single time, it's nothing. It takes a lot to send us scrambling around for the invisible ink and self-destructing messages. It must feel very weird for you to hear this, I know, but, honestly, there's no one out there watching your every typo and Google search."

"Except the algorithm."

"Well, yeah. Look, your mother worked on some very sensitive cases in her time. They're all old news by now, but still, there are occasional developments in the field that call back to the work she did, even way back then. We'd just like to know before anyone else if her friends and family have any knowledge or even curiosities that could draw, you know, unwanted attention."

"So you're not recruiting me or Patrick?" I remembered Patrick's feeble covering for his conversation with the blue-sedan man. He'd make a terrible field operative. In the interest of national security, I hoped Paul Rowland had noticed that.

Brian looked genuinely surprised. "*I'm* not. And I don't think it's all that likely that anyone else is either. Nobody's looking at my reports for that sort of grooming intelligence. It's not that kind of thing. It's not what I do. I mean, I wouldn't definitely know for sure, but you're not—how do I say this without it sounding insulting? You're not high-desirability material."

Whatever telegraphed across my face set him backpedaling.

He took the bait and served up an apology, laughing. "Hang on. That's just jargon for 'not what we're looking for.' If you guys were seeking us out, or working in a field that bumped up against what we do, or, not to put too fine a point on it, if you were younger, then maybe. I mean, I know Rowland's big on pedigree and all that. . . ."

"So, like you said, you don't really know for sure. Paul's asked me before."

"Well, this is pretty much my job now. In all likelihood, I'd know. What I used to do had me a little more directly involved in operations. Now I mostly follow up on what, these days, crosses those same paths I walked way back when. It's semiretirement.

Now I only travel two hundred days a year instead of four hundred and fifty." He smiled and brackets of fine lines in the hollows of his cheeks made him look comfortable. Harmless even.

I wasn't that easy. "And you can just tell me all of this why?"

"Tell you what?" He smiled at me as if we were friends. Or as if we should be. A bright bubble of curiosity about what that would be like tickled up through my middle. "What have I told you?" he asked.

"That my Internet is being spied on, for one thing."

"It's really not, but again, what have I told you? Who would you tell? And they'd be able to do what with it? All's well, Mrs. Aldrich. I don't have to kill you just because I told you that stuff."

"Ugh. Let's just be Brian and Dee, if you don't mind. I mean, since we're such good friends and all."

"Yes, let's. This has been a very weird day. You scared the hell out of me back there by the bathrooms." Brian started laughing.

"I did?" The giggles got me then, too.

"Holy shit. Like I said, all of my errands these days—they're nothing. It's always nothing, and nothing is the only thing that ever happens. I get paid for a whole lot of nothing, and that's just fine by me. When I thought you were the one-in-a-million *something*, I didn't know what to do. It's been so long since I had to do any-thing."

"You keep saying that, but you're a lot younger than I thought you were. You guys retire awfully early."

"It's a high-mileage job."

Another lull didn't make the scene less ridiculous. Some sort of chivalry monster made Brian ask me if I wanted something to drink. I declined.

"So that's it, then?" I said. "I just put up with it—and with you—and that's that?"

"Come on. Put up with what? No harm done."

"You're not even going to give me the satisfaction of admitting that this is a huge invasion of privacy?"

"My idea of privacy is probably a little bit different from yours." He looked down at the tabletop. "Sorry."

"Yeah."

"It's really not a big deal. Amazon, Google, Microsoft, they're all keeping closer tabs on you than we are."

"This is a little bit different."

"Yes and no. The world's a big, tangly place and we're all just trying to make sense of it and keep it safe. At least we're not trying to get you to buy anything," he said.

"Except for the idea that you're completely harmless. And before you know it, I'm standing barefoot in line at the airport with a sandwich bag full of not enough mouthwash or hair gel, waiting for my dose of body-scan radiation—oh, wait."

"Hey! That's not me. You'll have to tackle that with your vote."

"Yeah, like you people don't control all the elections. Pfffft."

"You've got the wrong 'you people.'" As much as I'd enjoyed a flare of bravery, he was enjoying having his chains rattled. His smirk was catching. I felt it mirror in my own cheeks.

"Obviously, there's no winning this with you," he continued. "What, with me being me and all. I can only tell you that this is completely routine and you'll get an A-plus for business as usual on my report. Does that help?"

"Are you going to tell Paul about this little detour?"

"Interesting. Would you prefer that I didn't?"

"Why is it interesting? I guess I'm more wondering if you're allowed to."

"Allowed to what? Whatever else I may be, I'm still a grown man. Paul Rowland doesn't 'allow' me to type whatever I want into my reports. And it's only interesting because, in fact, Paul Rowland does take the time to bother with reports on team Vess."

"Yeah, I'm not surprised to hear that. He'd been looking into some money that my mother left to me and my brother. I don't know what he's up to. Paul's the original bad penny. Except that he's my mother's bad penny, so it's not fair. It seems like I should be able to shake him. Would you get into trouble if he found out that we had talked and you hadn't mentioned it?"

"Well, first of all, unless you're going to be telling him, I can't think of any way he'd know about it. As far as I'm concerned, it won't go any farther than this table if you don't bring it up and—"

"What if they're watching you, too?"

"Dee. I can call you Dee, right? It's not like that. There are certainly plots and conspiracies and all sorts of hinky business, just like everybody always hopes there is, but first off, not as much you might think, and secondly, what there is of it generates a hell of a lot of housekeeping. Very straightforward stuff. That's what I do. It's not glamorous, but it's important. And at the end of my report, nobody sends a SWAT team to find out why I wrote what I did or if I left anything out."

"They just send you back out to the next shopping mall."

"It's a job. Mostly very dull—"

"Sorry to have bored you."

"Not you. You win the Surprise of the Year award. I think my heart rate is right about back down to normal. It's just that what I do is a far cry from what people would think I do. Especially in the action and intrigue departments."

"Is this the part where you start complaining about paperwork?"

"I could."

"Well, let's don't and say we did." The tabletop became suddenly interesting, but mostly because looking down hid my unaccountable blushing.

He didn't leave me to glow into yet another stretch of awkward silence. "What were you looking for in those computer searches, if I could ask?" he said.

"You shouldn't ask, because it's nosy. And it's invasive. But since you did ask and since we've already established that Brian Menary will never mind his own business as long as the government pays him not to, the answer will only disappoint you."

"Oh, but do go on anyway."

I sighed. Brian looked interested. Friendly even. And I hadn't talked about her to anyone new in so long. "I don't know what I was looking for. See? Boring. I was looking for just anything, really. Nothing specific, anyway. Just something—anything—that I didn't already know about my mother. I miss her. For all the stuff I didn't know about what she did all day, I missed her even when she was here. So sometimes I just plug things into the computer to see what comes up. Should I not do that?"

"It's not a problem for you to look, but I can tell you, there's nothing readily available on the Internet that you're likely to find. And also, I'm sorry for your loss. She was a fascinating lady."

"Did you know her well?" There it was. I thought I'd wanted to know why he was hovering in my zip code, but even more than that, I'd wanted to know what he knew of my mother.

"No, not really. But I know enough about her to be sure that she would have laughed her ass off at you trapping me outside the latrines."

My phone buzzed on the table, pulling me from the edge of disappointment that Brian Menary hadn't known my mother well, then over to the edge of another disappointment—that our conversation had to be over. They'd be starting to wonder about me back at work.

"I need to be getting back to my office." I rose and extended my hand. "Brian Menary, it was something to have met you for real this time. I guess I don't have to point out that it might have been easier if you had just introduced yourself from the outset and said, 'Hey, just checking in. You know, making sure you're not headed to the Dark Side or anything.' That would have been a lot simpler. Or at least it would have kept that poor man safe from my barging in on him at the urinal."

Brian laughed and the ghost of the handshake tingled in my palm. "At least he's got a story to tell—the trials of the businessman's lunch. And, yeah, I could have come to you and said all that, but we were trying not to disturb you—trying to let you have your priv—"

"Don't even say it."

"Nice to meet you, Dee."

"See you around. I guess you're always just a Google search away."

18

didn't tell my brother about my confrontation with Brian Menary, much less the almost pleasant chat that it had turned into, even though the next-to-the-last secret I'd kept from Simon (as well as from my husband) had blown up in my face rather spectacularly. I hadn't revealed the adventure of hurricane Angela either, or my worries over Paul, and I felt alone and adrift without Simon's company in the drama. And still the list of things I didn't want to tell him grew.

There was no spiteful little spark in knowing something that Simon didn't. That wasn't what kept me from telling him about Special Agent Menary. I didn't want him to know we were being monitored. I didn't know how he'd take it, as dedicated as he was to the idea that our mother had been a mere translator. And I didn't want to wind him up about Paul.

As I'd walked away from the table in the food court, my mind was full of only the steady sound of my heels clacking on the hard rubber tiles and the small, radiant wonder as to whether Brian was watching me leave.

When there was room for more thought in my head, I lined up what I should have been feeling alongside what I actually did feel about the day. I resented the Internet auditing less than I would have expected. I think I'd felt more rattled the first time Amazon had gone sentient, when it had needled me by e-mail, flaunting that it had figured out by our purchases that we were doing a bit of remodeling. I started getting notifications of deals on garage door openers and lighting fixtures and all sundry necessary bits that fit eerily well with the next phase of our project.

On some level I had always expected it from Mother's circle. She had warned me in more than one way that they might someday come calling. *They* meaning Paul, but surely Paul's associates were an extension of the net. *There are no secrets with these people, but don't worry, there isn't any imagination left in them either. Paul knows stuff because he likes to know stuff, but that's all the prize he gets for it—the knowing. He's nosy as hell. Your secrets aren't safe but they aren't exactly in danger either, if you take my meaning.*

I didn't want to tell Simon because it would, inevitably, kick off the talk again, the nonconversation we'd had a thousand times about what my mother had or had not done for a living. I didn't need to have that conversation again. Ever. I was right about it. I'd always been right about it. But I felt no joy at all in possessing the trump. I could shut him down for good with the tale of my afternoon at the mall, but I couldn't imagine Simon's face when I did it, which was strange. I could always forecast his reactions to things in advance.

Simon lived in my head as much as he lived twenty minutes from my house. He was with me always and I loved him for it. But for all the times we had spoken of our mother's work, those were the only times I could remember Simon not seeming quite Simon-like to me. He had a wall around what he felt about her and how he regarded the off-center strangeness of our plain-picture upbringing. My brother's acting dismissive and disingenuous, when he was never either of those things on any other topic, did nothing for my warring feelings about our mother.

After the night she'd left, when I was thirteen and Simon was eight, it took an obstacle course over common sense to come to any conclusion other than that she was definitely into some sort of bigger game than translating memos. But Simon swung that course like an orangutan. He made it look effortless. And for all that he was reasonable about in life, he was also stubborn. He would not waver from his conclusions about her, would never entertain the obvious—that she had been a fully equipped and valuable field operative.

After leaving Brian at the table in the mall, and for the rest of the day, I felt hollowed out. Whatever I'd wedged into my nature to avoid confrontation—with my husband or with a cashier who couldn't count or with a driver whose time was obviously far more important than my safety—whatever blocked the font of daring in me, it had taken up more space in my everyday mood than I had ever realized. After having it out with Brian Menary, the void hadn't as yet been refilled. I was empty, and not unpleasantly so. I felt light and resonant, a bell waiting to be rung.

The shift wasn't lost on Patrick. "You look like you had a good day."

"I do?"

"Yeah. Did you have a three-martini lunch or something?"

"I had a regular lunch." Under no circumstances did I want to say anything more about lunch. "But I finally got all that big-project stuff put together and launched the whole mess of it off my desk. I dumped it right in the legal department's lap, where it belongs. So I guess I'm just relieved."

"Well, you wear it well, which is good. Thank God it's Friday," he crowed, very un-Patrick-like. "We're taking this good mood on the road, because I told Eric and Camilla that we'd be over to their place in a little while. They're having some people over for a housewarming party and I said we'd join them."

"What? We are? You can't stand Camilla."

"She's okay. She's all right. I can handle her. And Eric's been a huge help to me lately. He's asked me every day this week if we were

coming. They really want to show off their new place. Besides"—
Patrick watched himself in the mirror running the deodorant stick
up under his shirt. He smoothed the wrinkles out of the fabric,
eyes on his own in the glass, never once looking for a reaction from
me—"we need to get out. We need to see and be seen, before even
we forget we exist."

Eric and Camilla had just moved into a step-up-from-starter,
but-not-yet dream home. Their enthusiasm bubbled up for their
recent advance in the game of life. It frothed over right alongside the midpriced champagne that flowed from the moment we
crossed the welcome mat that still wafted a vague plastic-and-dye
smell. Popping corks punctuated the background chatter at intervals all night.

It felt good to be there with happy people. Good and unfamiliar, and a wide step away from what I was usually doing on
a Friday evening. All of which was in perfect congruence with
the second half of the day I'd already had, hours and hours full
of nothing usual. I took a third refill of champagne, skipping the
responsible math that usually came with the rare decision to have
just one more.

A hand silked across my back and around my waist, goosing
a startled gasp from me. I drew in some of the champagne along
with the air and doubled over, coughing. Patrick swooped down
and righted me before I was ready. He crushed me against him and
smiled down on me through the last of my fit. We'd drawn an audience. He dove in for a kiss, to everyone's delight, before I'd caught
my breath.

In the pause that our lips were pressed together, I felt heat coming off his body, fever warm, but his hands were cold through the
fabric of my waistband. I smelled his cologne and the champagne
he'd had. As much as I needed to take a breath, I didn't want to let
him go. What was it with this day? Again, unfamiliar equaled good
as my mildly affectionate husband heated up in my arms—in front

of a crowd, no less. I slid my hand over the back of his neck. Someone in the group hooted approval. I smiled against Patrick's mouth. Things could be better after tonight. I knew it. Finally. Something was still there, a solid safe place for us to get back to. We could make it past this. We could get back to norm—

Patrick's icy hand slipped around my waist, trailing the cold through my middle as he pulled away. I heaved in a breath, looking up at him, smiling into eyes that weren't smiling back.

His opaque gaze slid off mine. He pointedly didn't see me. He let me go and tapped his metal watchband against his glass. "Everyone! I have a little announcement to make," Patrick called.

A murmur of interest faded to expectant quiet. "Speech!" called a substantially drunk Eric.

Camilla squealed her guess. "You're pregnant!"

Patrick scowled down his front. "Uh-oh, does this shirt make me look pregnant?" He collected his due giggles. I could still feel the cold ring around my waist where Pat's hands had been. The chill worked inward. None of this show was anything I'd ever look for from Patrick. This unfamiliar turn dimmed the affection I'd been feeling for the strangeness of the day and reminded me why I was such a fan of the routine.

"Nah, we're not pregnant," he said. "No offense to all the parents here, all those poor souls who are, even as we speak, paying ten dollars an hour for a babysitter, but who wants babies? Isn't that right, honey?" He pulled me in, a nudge for a private joke. An unfunny, tremendously private joke. "Babies! Bah!"

I forced a smile.

Patrick kept going. "I have a present for my beautiful wife. Something she's always wanted. A dream come true to share with our best friends."

Beautiful wife? Best friends? We knew exactly four people in the room. I couldn't imagine where this was going. The guests shifted uneasily. Marital gift giving was hardly a spectator sport.

"Dee has been wanting to travel. She wants to get away. It's a wish she's had for a long time. So, I say, 'Let's travel!' " There was booze in his voice, and an edge that rang like good cheer painted over something much harder. "Today I booked the dream trip— a thirteen-day Rhine and Danube cruise. Baby, we're going to Budapest!"

There was a smattering of dutiful cheering and hesitant clapping. I patted his shoulder and planted a theatrical kiss on his cheek, but Patrick had effectively ended the party.

I tried to let it rest, but Patrick's newfound quirks and general moodiness scattered the sand from around my head faster than I could bury it over.

"Okay, what was *that* all about?" I said in the car twenty minutes later. "First off, that crack about babies was really obnoxious. And who announces their vacations at a party? What the hell? I thought you didn't want to go anywhere."

Patrick was unperturbed. "You know, I kind of thought there was going to be no winning you over, Dee. Even with this. And isn't that just like you? Just like us? I knew there was always going to be a problem if it was my idea. You want to spring a plan on me? Great. But if I want to take the initiative, if *I* skip putting an idea through committee, then, no, then it's all *What the hell, Patrick?* I figured as much, so, I thought I'd have a little bit of fun with it. The people at the party enjoyed it, even if you didn't."

"They didn't, Pat. No one enjoyed that."

"So you don't want to go? Say the word and I'll cancel the tickets."

The whir of the tires on the wet road played loudly into our silence.

"Why do you want to take this trip, Pat?"

"Probably for the same reason you wanted to book a spa weekend."

It was an impossibly loaded answer, but whether that was engineered or organic, I could hardly ask.

"Don't worry about it, Dee. I'll just cancel it."

"No, don't. That's not what I'm saying. It would be good for us, I think. It's an amazing present, Pat. It could be a wonderful trip, if we make it that way."

"Well, you just think about it and let me know if you change your mind."

The conversation looped in my head for days, stuck there like a snippet of song that has jammed its jingly way in without permission. It managed to erase every quiet moment.

I replayed our argument and couldn't find a hook to hang my preoccupation on. Patrick's trip was certainly more real than my little white lie of a spa-weekend getaway. But new money or no new money, Patrick wouldn't drop thousands of dollars to make a point that he'd caught me in a fib.

The folder from the travel agency was real enough—glossy and bulking with brochures for side excursions: history tours into Prague and castle-discovery rides through the Viennese countryside. There were travel advisories and pamphlets of packing tips, and our names and details bold-printed in every blank on the pages and pages of endless fine print. At the end of it all was Patrick's bold, left-slanting signature beneath an impressive dollar amount cheerfully stamped PAID IN FULL.

The awkwardness of the announcement, the expense of the whole thing, then the naturally following concern that we were throwing money at a problem that didn't have a solution for sale, it would set anyone on edge. That must be it. Any reasonable person would rehash the discussion and turn the scenario this way and that, in hopes that a new facet would catch the light and make some sense. I wasn't being weird. It was normal, all this obsessing.

And as "normal" usually did, this time it didn't fix the worry even a little bit.

But like all ear-burrs, the nearly continuous playback of the argument rubbed off eventually. I stopped rewinding and replaying the conversation. I was able to blank daydream at stoplights again. The song faded away, but I would always know the lyrics by heart.

19

Friday

I'm trying to imagine the ride back down this road. Or more likely, I'm only stalling, still sitting here with the car idling the gas away. I twist the key and kill the engine and the silence rolls over me like syrup, rising into every space. My ears fill with quiet. It slides down my throat. I can't breathe. I'm drowning. It's so heavy. The conch shell roar of the blood in my veins takes over, a tidal sound. I'm not deaf. I'm not drowning. I'm treading water. I can do that. I'm an expert.

I'll wait for my hands to feel more under my own direction and my heartbeat to steady out to a canter. I just need a little while longer. I'm a mess. But, I do wonder how I'll be on the way out of this. Will it be in twenty minutes, empty-handed and none the wiser? Maybe an hour. Two? Or will all of this take so long that I'll be wheeling these turns in the dark, head full of answers, heart full of . . . what? And will I be alone, barreling back to what I know, home and husband, on this road that will look just as alien going the other way as it does now?

I always watch my route carefully wherever I go. I never sleep on planes or in the passenger seat of car trips. For me, the travel isn't a throwaway or a given. It's the way back again if I ever wish to return, or it's the route to avoid if I'll never go back.

Patrick wasn't wrong about my wanderlust. Of course, my mother's journeys never came with photos to chronicle her stops, but the specific destinations didn't matter. Because of her, I craved a headful of private travelogue, too—a whole world within, my own version of the world without.

Patrick and I had done some limited domestic touring, but vacations are expensive and there never seemed to be a good time. When I thought about where I wanted to go and what I wanted to see, I never admitted out loud that I most often imagined myself alone on Tower Bridge in London or peering through a screen of forest primeval from solitude in a deep green somewhere.

It's not that I didn't want to go places with Patrick. He was, or had been at some point, good company. It's just that when I sketched out the daydreams, accidentally he wasn't there, with no malice intended. The dream space to my left and right was open air, and my imaginary stride kept pace with no other legs.

Huh. Funny that. Thinking about not thinking of having someone with me has just twisted around on itself. I just imagined Buda Castle from Patrick's travel brochures, the ones that should have thrilled me into planning mode, but had failed to do anything but worry me. The palace, flung long and looming along the Danube, is something I've always wanted to see from the Pest side of the river. I can summon the image at will. But this time there's a ghostly outline next to me in my mind, a sketch of man, taller than my husband, wavy-haired. . . .

When I couldn't make sense of Patrick, with his plans and his moods, my mind skipped tracks to the next man-puzzle within my reach. I typed in a string of Al Qaeda names culled from recent news articles and added in my mother's name at the end. Then I put *Brian Menary* into the word soup for good measure. I hit Send to launch the search and got ready for work. At lunchtime, I took a book to the food court at the mall and waited.

"Don't do that."

I'd drifted deep into the plot of the novel in my hand, and Brian simply scared the hell out of me.

He took the chair across from mine, his starchy collar drawing a sharp, white line under his grimly set jaw. "It's not funny."

"I'm not laughing at that. I'm laughing at me. You scared me to death."

"Do you know how much trouble that could have caused if your little summons had vaulted over my head?"

"Oh my God," I said, trying for light mocking, hoping that it was somehow appropriate even though his face and his posture suggested otherwise. "Was my mother involved with Al Qaeda? Are you?"

"No. But linking all that up in an Internet search makes you sound crazy. It's not just an algorithm, remember? It's analysts, too. If they think you're maybe just a little too curious about something, they send me. Curious is watchable. But crazy makes us have to do something, and if you'll recall, I don't *do* things anymore. A little weirder and you could have drawn down a different kind of surveillance altogether."

"Oh, no. I didn't think of it like that. I'm so sorry. I really—it won't happen again."

"It certainly won't." Brian slid a business card across the table.

"'Hoyle's Compounding Pharmacy and Alternative Medicine Center'?" I read from the card. "Huh?"

"Yeah, I'm an herb guru in my other life," he deadpanned. "Either that or it's a private voice mail that will route a message to my regular phone if, for some reason, you feel you need to reach me." He shook his head at me. "Jesus, what happened that made you pull a stunt like that?"

"Nothing happened." My cleverness had crumpled to mortification. "Shit, I'm so sorry. I didn't mean to cause a problem."

"You didn't. You could have, but you didn't. It's okay. They sent the memo to me, thank God, since I was still out this way. Maybe I was too flippant when we talked before. I was just trying to put you at ease. My job's not usually a big deal anymore, but it's not exactly a joke either."

"Brian, I'm really sorry."

"It's okay." He sat back in his chair. "So, nothing happened, but you waved a red flag at the cyberbull to get my attention. Is this officially our first date, then?"

"What?"

"So that's a no."

"I'm married."

"Well, sure, but you know . . . ," he teased, and earned only blinking from me in response. "Okay, so that's *no*, underlined. Right. Got it. What are we here for then?"

"Now I feel like an idiot. Let's never mind the whole thing. I'm so sorry."

"After all that? 'Never mind'? You can't be serious."

I sighed. "Now it seems so wrong to ask you. It's just that I've been kicking myself since the other day after we talked. I chickened out."

"You chickened out?" His smirk had returned, full simmer. "What did you want to ask me that you didn't have the courage to? Now I'm intrigued for sure. But I'm glad I already checked that this wasn't a date."

"No. It's still not a date," I said, unable to pry my eyes up off the tabletop. "I didn't ask you more about my mother. That's all. I just didn't know what to ask."

"Ah. Probably because I said that I didn't know her very well. I've got nothing, really. I imagine you could tell me a lot more than I could tell you."

"I know, but you'd been very open about why you were here and how the whole system works and the Tag Site thing and whatnot.

You were talking. I should have asked for more—you for more in-formation." I was stammering. I bit down on the tip of my clumsy tongue and drew in a breath. "I just wanted to ask you about that night at least, about what she did for all those months when you came to get her."

"I wasn't with her on the trip."

"That's not the same as you not knowing anything."

"I was only a messenger and her driver that night. Like I said, it was my first real assignment. I drove and I messenged and then I drove again."

"That's it?"

"Of course not. But now I'm a little concerned about setting you off on another Googling frenzy."

"I won't."

"You don't need to, Dee. There's nothing to find. But it would be a little too pointed right now, after all this."

"I understand."

"Hmmmm." He stared into me unself-consciously. "You probably do. Okay. Let's see. It goes back a ways. Anyway, once upon a time—"

"You start your stories like that? My mother always did, too. So does my brother."

Brian smiled. "It's a spook thing, I think. Occupational hazard of sounding like a goof. But it's like breathing to me now. I can't seem to help it. Anyway, once upon a time, there was a very young, very green man-boy who dropped out of college because he was bored and heartbroken. A very cruel coed had dumped him for an upper-classman, and it left him not interested in studying anymore. In fact, it left him uninterested in doing much of anything except sleeping until noon, eating his way through his tiny little bank account, drinking way too much beer, and watching whatever was next on TV. None of that stuff pays the rent very well.

"So, the young man joined the army because he had seen too many movies. The young man had really not taken into account exactly how much he hated being yelled at. Very foolish, all the *not* thinking that boy did. He wasn't bright. But he did have a talent. This boy was almost completely immune to jet lag. And he could stay awake for several days with very little adverse effect on his coordination and concentration."

"Really? That's your superpower?"

"Hey, don't knock it. Staying awake never paid so good." Brian laughed. "But it's a trick. Like all magic, it's just sleight of hand. I really do sleep. It's just that, for some reason, I can doze very deeply for a minute or two—sometimes only just a few seconds, even while standing up. I can nod off practically on command and most people can't. It can be helpful. In school it meant I could stay up all night playing video games. And in the army, their sleep-deprivation tactics didn't really zonk me out like it did the other guys. Then *they* heard about it and came to see the Amazing Wide-Awake Man-Boy. They asked me if I wanted out of the army. To which I replied, 'Yes, sir. Yes, sir. Three bags full of *yes, sir.*' And before you know it, I was sent places and taught things.

"Then one day, in a galaxy far, far away, someone in charge came up to me and told me that they'd gotten some information and that there was an important *asset*, which by that time I knew was super-secret-agent codespeak for 'person,' who was going to be needing some on-scene assistance, and that I had to get there faster than some other people who were already on their way.

"And the rest, you know." He laid both hands on the table as if there had been some sort of conclusion.

"You're kidding, right? I don't know anything. You just told me about you, not about her."

"I was hoping you wouldn't notice."

I sucked in my cheeks to keep the corners of my mouth out of a smile, but there was no winning with my left eyebrow. It arced right over at Brian's grinning command. "And why would you be hoping that?"

"Even if this isn't a date, you can't blame a guy for trying to see if he can still impress. It's such a drag. I never get to tell my story."

"So." I straightened down my eyebrow and set my face to unreadable. "Am I impressed?"

"Shit. Finally get a chance to try my game and I pick Annette Vess's daughter to run it on."

"That'll teach you. So you can't tell me anything about that night? Or you won't?"

"Well, there's not much to tell, really. I mean, I came to the house. I got there just ahead of who they were worried about, so that was good. And for a short, crazy while I helped out in any way I could. Which mostly meant cleaning up after she kicked a solid bit of ass. Then I put her bags in the car. She wouldn't let me anywhere near you and your brother. I hardly did anything. And still I was thrilled. She was a legend."

"That's it?"

"Well, that was my part of it. I can tell you that she was absolutely furious with Paul Rowland and miserable to be leaving her children."

"The fight in the house. It was bad, wasn't it?" Having her send us out into the rain was terrifying. But coming home to a house full of charged air and broken things was the first mile marker in the distance between my mother and me. "It was like I could feel it still echoing off the walls. Did she kill somebody that night?"

Brian hesitated. "She wasn't an assassin."

"That isn't what I asked."

"The simple answer is yes. The full answer is not as harsh as all that, but it's more than I can go into."

"I knew it. I swear to God, I always knew it."

"She had to do it."

"What about you? Where were you? Why didn't you stop it? Or why didn't you help her?"

"Dee, it was all over, start to finish, in less than three minutes. But it was a hell of a long three minutes. A lot happened and *I'm* not an assassin either. I can only tell you that she didn't have a choice. Let's just say that sometimes people hire someone to do something, but there's no way to guarantee that the type of person who'll do one thing for money might not be prone to do other things as well."

"Someone hired out to kill her?"

"Not at all. That was the 'other things' I was talking about. It's just kind of hard to trust people who will do stuff for money that other people won't. They aren't what you'd call 'stable.'"

"Where did she go? What was the—I don't even know what you people call it. Mission?"

"I don't know where she was headed or what she ended up doing for all that time. But it's always been that way. I'm more useful the less I know. I got over being offended by it a long time ago and made a career out of being a clueless errand boy. I'm about as in-the-know as a Swiss Army knife. What I can tell you is that her trip was fallout from a project from years before. A lot of that stuff is declassified now. You could probably read up on it yourself if you wanted to sift through a ton of bureaucracy first and then two tons of old paperwork after that.

"But I know it was some sort of loose end from her big show. It's the one that made her famous. It was called Operation Little Miss Muffet."

It stung. Of all that I knew of her and all that I suspected of her throughout the years, there was no doubt that my mother was a force. The reckoning kind, wickedly smart and endlessly capable. I welled up with a pride for her and a belated protectiveness, and a disgust for the rampant sexism that allowed them to tack a cute, dismissive tag on her best work.

"Unreal," I said. "Were they really that small? Were they that threatened by her? It's so petty. It's disgusting is what it is."

"Huh?"

"With as good as she was—and you know that she was—the

code name they gave her was Little Miss Muffet? Really? You actually think that's okay?"

"What? I don't— Wait." Then, Brian burst out laughing. "Oh, God. She wasn't— Oh, no. That's not what they called her. As if! No, no, no. Her handle was always Spider."

Along came a spider who sat down beside her . . .

My chin dropped, and the perpetually thirteen-year-old girl inside me, the one stubbornly bereft for the mother who had tried so hard to prove that she was there all along, that girl swooned away.

My mother had always been particular about spiders. She'd sift a fly's guts through the mesh of a swatter or squeeze a millipede into a crumpled Kleenex without fanfare. I even once saw her whip a wasp clean in two with the flick of a dish towel. The antennaed head and foresegment fell at her feet, and its striped, barbed back end, still throbbing, hit the linoleum a full two yards away at my feet as the whip snap echoed off the kitchen walls. She and I split a root beer in celebration of the coolness of that one.

But spiders were left alone in high corners or caught under drinking glasses to be turned loose in the front yard if they ever dangled inconveniently in our way or insisted on menacing my brother or me.

"Freer than me," she always said while sliding away the postcard she had clapped over the rim of the glass. The postcard was actually the Postcard; the one I had shown Patrick so recently from the stack of keepsakes in the spare room.

She kept it in between the cookbooks on the kitchen counter specifically for spider-wrangling. When called for, one of us would fetch a glass and the Postcard, a race that was always worth a point to the winner. Whichever of us hadn't got the postcard ended up serving as doorman for the spider, hoping for a chance at a bonus point.

My mother would often say "freer than me" in one of the many languages she had learned the phrase. The point on offer was earned for correctly naming the language.

The summer Simon was ten, he packed cheerfully enough for two weeks away at Adventure Indian Camp. Five days in, a glossy postcard arrived in our mailbox. The picture was of the log-and-chinking camp store, authentically inauthentic with a split-rail perimeter, a carved wooden Indian chief, and a row of fiberglass canoes leaning against the sunlit wall. My brother's widely spaced handwriting decorated the back—*Freer Than Me* was all he'd written.

My mother was not a crier, and by the time I found her howling and clutching Simon's card, it was difficult to tell how much of the noise and the tears were from laughing and what percentage was just in sympathy and love for Simon. She was ruined and wrung-out at the end of the fit. She rescued him from camp the next day.

It became one of our little family codes then, another in-joke to bind us close. Wherever and whenever we traveled apart, all throughout our lives, we'd send home a *freer than me* postcard, regardless of whether the truth of the trip was that we were having a great time or slogging through a fraught disaster. Each postcard was slotted into place with the others, between the cookbooks, ready for the next rescue mission.

My mother was Spider. Spider was her. Whether the name came before the reverence for the creature or because of it, I couldn't know.

"Are you okay?" Brian asked.

"I'm fine. My mother just had a thing about spiders. I didn't know that it meant anything. I guess I still don't know what it means. But it's at least something to know that there was anything more to it at all."

"I didn't mean to upset you."

"You didn't. Anyway, I asked. Thank you."

"I did get to work with her again after that. But just little stuff. I ran some documents for a couple of different projects; facilitated a few interviews for her over the years. That sort of thing."

"Why does that sound like you nabbed guys into white vans and dumped them on a warehouse floor at my mother's feet?"

"Because I'm sexy and dangerous and I belong in the movies?"

"That must be it."

"Then it was years and years before I saw her again. I was the last one who got to work with her, though, right before she died."

"When did you see her last?"

"Just a few days before—" He hesitated. "Before she passed away."

"Huh? You saw her then? Where? Did my mother meet you somewhere?" My mother, as far as I knew, had almost never left the house at all in the months she'd lived with us. She dug in, curled up in bed, or on the sofa, or on the porch swing, all day every day. She set to battle with an intimidating stack of books, and a catalog of films and television shows. She said she'd seen enough of the real world and wanted to wallow in fiction at the end. I bought comic books to add to the pile and brought her coffee in the morning, tea in the afternoon, and a nip of nightcap in the evening that she shouldn't have mixed with her medicine, but did anyway.

"No, I came out to the house to talk with her a couple of times."

"The house? You mean *my* house?"

"To be fair, it was her house, too, at the time. I mean, that's where she lived."

This was another of their shared traits. Both Brian Menary and my mother had the uncanny ability to deliver uncomfortable, even offensive, lines without squirming. My brother could do it, too. It was as if nothing, no matter how awkward, ever made any of them uncomfortable. The freedom was so breathtaking it leapt right over being obnoxious.

"You've been in my house? When I wasn't there?"

"I promise I didn't look in the medicine cabinets."

"Okay, that's more than a little unnerving."

"You have no idea. They wanted transcripted interviews to close out her files. Actually, what they wanted—what *Paul Rowland*

wanted—was for her to move into an agency-approved hospice facility. It would have been first-class care for sure. I mean, not that
she didn't get that with you. That's not what I meant. It's just that
her comfort was more of a secondary concern for him.

"He sent me in to wheedle her about it at first, to try to convince
her to go to one of these places when she first found out she was
terminal. But she wanted to live with you. She was adamant. He
was really annoyed with her. Those places are like the Ritz Carlton,
only with doctors. And everybody from the janitor to the chef to
the accounting manager has top-secret or better security clearance.
They spare no luxurious expense in exchange for getting the drop
on any deathbed confessions. But your mother refused.

"So instead of the Ritz, she got me nagging at her for the interviews. It was all so cold. I felt terrible about it, taping her when
she was so weak. But she was utterly gracious. So patient with all
the boring questions and the pointless prying. I would never have
forgotten her anyway, but the grace she showed in those last interviews . . ."

"Paul punished her for not doing his bidding. Even at the very
end?"

"Hey, I don't know that I was her punishment exactly. I'm not
that bad."

"No, of course not. That's not what I meant."

"She was a great storyteller."

"She really was."

An empty space opened in the conversation. Empty of words,
anyway, but more than full enough of unspoken questions.

"Is it always like this, do you think?" I asked.

"Like what?" He was already smiling.

"Like the more you know, all you really know is that you don't
know anything."

Brian gasped. "Are you trying to steal my job?"

Brian had a plane to catch and I had my life, such as the state of
it was, to catch. I dragged my attention out of the past, through the

present and pleasant company across from me, and into the start of the rest of the day still ahead, anchored in an evening with Patrick. There was melancholy in the equation. My husband was less friendly by the hour, it seemed.

Brian double-checked that I had his card. I did. I double-checked that he wouldn't have to lurk after me to get information about my curiosities anymore. He didn't.

20

Patrick started leaving the lights on and having nightmares. In that order. He had always kept track of the utility bills in one brand of spreadsheet or another, and we had negotiated over the finer details of household maintenance. Mild debate on things like the merits of turning up the temperature on the hot-water heater versus its effect on the bottom line were what we used to have for nuts-and-bolts conversations instead of the thorny small talk we'd had to cultivate to fill up the echoing silences.

Growing up, the Aldrich family, with one income and six kids, had kept steadily (if only just barely) in the black with a tight hold over the little leaks in the budget. It was in Patrick's blood to keep score on such things as gas mileage and credit-card points. I didn't mind cutting coupons or stalking the sale racks for bargains. They were such easy brownie points to win with my husband. Such simple things to do to put him at ease. He appreciated it. It was responsible, and mature, an easy way for me to be like them. And it was my favorite: it was normal.

The first time I asked him about the lights, Patrick flinched and said that he'd run to get the phone and must have forgotten to switch off the lamp after the call. That didn't quite work unless he'd run a zigzag through the house to do it. Lights were left on in three different rooms.

Even with the hallelujah of wattage lighting up every corner of the place, day and night, Patrick wasn't seeing all that much. He regularly escaped our overbright rooms to the length of his thousand-yard stare. He went missing, more and more often, into the unfocused middle distance, overshooting his barely touched dinner plate, the television, or my face as I tried to stitch together a chat about anything.

"I'm just tired," he said, and conjured up a self-fulfilling prophecy. His gritting teeth and midnight mumblings left the both of us groggy and dull in the mornings.

But he wasn't too tired to drag us to baseball games and barbecues and any number of things offered up by the office and neighborhood cultures that, until recently, we'd never bothered with. He would say that it would be fun, but he'd say it without smiling. He would scrub at the dark circles under his eyes with the heels of his hands, then sigh and say that we needed to get out more. I couldn't help but think that what he felt we actually needed was a stage.

He was courting approval. He always had in his own way, but over the years he had, just like me, lapsed into our hermited, comfortable routine, endorsed enough by his day-to-day successes to get from sunup to lights out without expecting a trophy for managing it. But now he was back, head up and keeping track of who was watching, and making up for lost time by all accounts. An anticipation was crackling in him, a nearly electric hum that buzzed under his forced chatter and big, un-Patrick-like laugh. He seemed to be pulling out of his usual patterns in a showy stride so as to be found far ahead of where everyone was used to seeing him if they ever bothered to stop and note his progress.

Was it a problem with midlife on the near horizon? Or was it more commentary on *our* life, right now and all around us? The math seemed simple enough: Patrick wanted to look like a good guy to these people. But I couldn't quite make it all add up to his wanting to *be* a good guy, not to me at least. At home he was prickly when he wasn't distant.

"What's going on, Pat?" I slid my shoes off and faced him from the closet doorway. He looked as wrecked as I felt, with all the flint out of his spine, sitting there on the corner of the bed hunched over, scrubbing his brows with his fingertips as if he could work enough energy in through his skull to get over the last hurdle of brushing his teeth.

I was simply too tired to take the long way around the block to start the conversation I'd been dreading. He had gnashed and thrashed all through the night before, even more than had become his usual, and yet we'd still gone bowling with his boss and her husband, exhausted as we were.

"What?" he answered.

"I'm trying to see all of this—the bowling tonight, all the dinners and these get-togethers—I'm trying to see it in a good light, but I'm just not feeling it."

"Seeing what? Feeling what? It's late. I don't want to play twenty questions, Dee. What's the problem?"

I stepped up to the suspicion that had been tethered to the center of my thoughts for days, then I let it off the leash. "Are you getting ready to leave me?"

"What?" He launched from the bed and went from zero to shouting in two seconds. "Are you kidding me?"

"I'm not trying to make you angry."

"This is *not trying to make me angry*? What would trying look like, huh? I'd love to know what crazy shit you would say if you were actually trying to make me angry."

"Stop yelling. I just want to understand what's going on. You're not eating. You're not sleeping. We're going out four times a week, at least, so that we can what? It's like a circus around here. Something's obviously on your mind."

Patrick ground his teeth and took in a deep breath through flared nostrils. Whether he'd blow out the candles on his temper or breathe fire, I could only wait and see.

He came through his showy sigh in the hard, brittle mode of forced patience. "Are you actually concerned, Dee, or are you just looking for the exits? Let's just go ahead and get it out there in the open, because I'm being accused—"

"Pat, I'm just asking, not accusing. You're not yourself lately—"

"And what do you think 'myself' should act like for you to be able to recognize me? I'll be honest, Dee, you might not have seen this me before, but that's because it would have been kind of hard to predict what I would turn out to be when I got left holding the bag on our marriage."

"This is nuts. I'm trying, you know. I don't know what to say to you anymore. You're so goddamned touchy—"

"I'm touchy?" He laughed without a shred of humor in his voice. "Come on, you're setting me up. You have to be. Poor, mistreated Dee. Is that going to be the angle? Is that what you're telling your friends? That I'm touchy and mean? That you think I'm going to leave you, even though you're a perfect angel? You've got some big balls, lady, after what you pul—"

"Enough!" I rarely raised my voice and it slammed a full stop between us. "Enough! I'm not listening to one more roll call of your disappointments. I'm not sitting here while you tell me—again— how lousy it was for me to take birth control pills without telling you. You don't get to run me over with that anymore, not without it coming back on you, you don't." I paced, sock-footed on our bedroom carpet, rolling up the cage on the storefront of my knowledge about our marriage. *Careful, Plucky,* I heard my mother in my mind. And I ignored her. "You fucking hypocrite! *I* have big balls? You're amazing.

"Tell me, Pat, have you got anything you'd like to 'get out in the open' with everyone? Maybe tap your glass and make a big reveal about why you're so psychotically cheerful in public and a growling son of a bitch at home? Anything *you*'d like to get off your chest instead of playing charades with your coworkers? Pat, the good guy. Pat, the devoted husband. Pat, the *family* man . . ."

"What are you talking about, Dee?"

"You must think I'm really stupid."

Patrick scowled and took one slow word at a time "What—are—you—talking—about?"

In which our hero takes a stick to a hornet's nest, my mother would say when Simon or I were about to go too far in an argument. I pulled the punch on my mother's oft-given warning. I looked at Pat's face. The anger there didn't surprise me, but the electric aura of fear around him snagged me off the trigger. My shoulders sank. "We need to see somebody; talk to a professional or something. We're falling apart."

"I think you said it all at 'enough.'" Patrick snatched the pillow from his side of the bed and pounded down the hall to the living-room sofa.

I didn't read anything into our not speaking. I wouldn't have known what to say to him anyway. But the silence left a clinging weight to the quiet days as they dragged on. The dread of the silent house jousted with the dread of picking up the fight where we'd left off it. It hurt.

But if time heals all wounds, then distraction heals the insult of time's sluggish pace. And nothing is quite so distracting as finding your belongings rifled through. Again.

When Simon was seven years old, his best friend told him that Santa Claus wasn't real and that it was only our mother hiding all the presents, every year, somewhere in the house, until she, not Saint Nick, put them under the tree on Christmas Eve. Simon checked with me and I didn't deny it.

He accepted the challenge and deployed his second-grade sleuth. He soon dragged me to his prize find and we squealed out our discoveries as we nudged each package aside for the next one. When the stack ended at the back corner of our mother's closet, we retraced our burrowing, tidying everything as we went, all the way to the screen of boxed books and folded blankets that she had set up to hide it all.

In the days that followed up to Christmas, the galloping anticipation we normally rode dragged its hooves a bit. The fever of counting down the days only simmered on low with no danger, for the first time ever, of boiling over. Even Simon realized our mistake, and we agreed without having to speak of it that we'd never spoil a surprise again. Lesson learned, we welled in maturity and contrition—safe and undiscovered. And on the bright side, after all, there were still presents to look forward to, even if the big reveal would be a bit of a song and dance on our parts.

Only on Christmas morning, the scant flat packages arranged around the tree didn't match up with the bulging mountain that would have held all the goodies we'd found in the closet. Simon fought tears as he unwrapped puzzle books and Val-U packs of underwear. My cheeks bloomed red as Burl Ives sang "Holly Jolly" and my mother watched me, over the rim of her coffee cup, open a box of assorted teas.

"Would you guys like a tip for all future snooping missions?" she asked.

We nodded at the carpet, unable to meet her eyes.

"There are two things you can't leave disturbed when you go through people's stuff: the stuff and your face. So, if you ever again get the urge to poke around in closets and whatnots that are not yours, I would suggest a big deep breath and a good, hard think beforehand. If you look, you're going to find, and once you find, you can't unfind, so you'd better have your face well in order."

We did get our presents later in the day, but Mother drove home the point by moving things in our rooms, just an inch or two out of place, so that we could see how clumsy our attempt at slyness had been. Spot-the-difference became a new favorite game for points, and my brother and I got wicked good at it.

Whoever had been in my house was more careful than Patrick would have needed to be. That everything was so close to the order I'd left it in spoke to stealth, and the air still fluttered in the fading wake of someone else's path through the halls. *Forgive us our trespasses.* Right. Will do. As soon as I figured out who needed forgiveness for what, I'd get right on it. The light sting of chills surged over me as I walked the rooms, playing the game for no points this time. Or maybe for all the points if the person turned out to be still lurking somewhere inside. I grabbed one of Patrick's golf clubs from the front closet.

I held my breath and cocked an ear for any sounds that didn't fit. The attic fan whirred its sigh through the vents. An airplane grumbled overhead. It didn't *feel* as if I had company. Whatever that meant. I made my rounds, rolling my feet to tread as quietly as I knew how, my palms sweating into the little divots in the rubber grip on the putter, ears ringing, straining for any indication that I wasn't alone, and having no idea what I would do if I found out that I wasn't.

The stack of bills on my desk was only a shade to the left of where it should have been, and my prescription eyedrops were in the back part of the front bin in the drawer, instead of in the front part of the next bin where *my* hand would automatically have set it. Amid a few more scattered incongruities, nothing appeared to be missing.

I even looked in the pantry and pushed every door that stood angled open in its jamb, dreading that each would stop against a firm someone behind it. But no one was there.

The three obvious possibilities were that my husband had lost his cool to an attack of rather pointless sneak, or a burglar had come in and not found anything worth taking, or Brian Menary was still poking around. If it was Patrick, the basicness of the search confused me. If it was a burglar, my untouched jewelry and the intact $300 in cash in the desk drawer confused me. If it was Brian, it wasn't all that confusing. Only infuriating.

Since I'd left a message at Hoyle's Pharmacy, I was fairly certain who would be on the line when the display showed *unknown caller.*

There was a smile in Brian's voice. It irritated me that I felt a tug of willingness to be cajoled as he said, "I'll tell you, Dee, I don't know whether to be concerned or flattered. Now that you've met me, you can't seem to stay away from me for very long."

I smirked in spite of myself. "What were you looking for in my house?"

"We weren't looking for anything. I promise, there was never any video surveillance in your home. I never sent any guys rifling through your stuff either. I respected your mother way too much to take my orders past their minimum, whatever the trouble was between her and Paul. I thought he was being kind of ridiculous about the whole thing anyway.

"I meant it when I said I hadn't looked in the medicine chest. We just needed to know what she said, just in case. That's all. Pain and the narcotics they prescribe for it can be a real problem. It makes the higher-ups paranoid. That's why Paul wanted to have her in an approved facility—to avoid all that. But he also wanted her there to get the nice-guy points for sparing everyone the hassle of the recordings."

"Huh?"

"That's what I meant about the agency hospitals," he said, as if my disorientation meant something to him that it didn't mean to me. "It doesn't matter what anyone says in those places. The staff is cleared for just about everything. She wouldn't go, as you well know, so they sent me in, but I kept the taps to the bare minimum. And it was only at the very end, anyway. Even so, I'm sorry. But there was never any video. We weren't watching you."

"Wait, what?" My outrage caught up with my train of thought and his disparate one. He thought I was asking about when he had been here with my mother three years earlier. "No *video* surveillance. No video? You kept the taps to a minimum? You had audio. You left microphones. You were listening in while my mother was dying."

"She knew, Dee. What are we even talking about?"

"*I* didn't know! It's my house! And you told her that you were leaving microphones in my house and she was fine with that?"

"We didn't talk about it. We wouldn't have had to. It didn't seem to be a problem at all until that last day. . . . There was nothing to wonder about until she turned up the music."

"Oh my God. I am so stupid." I was stunned and then not. She had asked to have the music turned up loud in the last minutes of her life. She asked me twice to dial it up until violins rang off the walls and tore the last of the air she breathed to gilded shreds. I had thought she'd wanted to drown out something—pain, fear, memories. And all that may have been true, but only as a secondary goal. She had been shutting the door on Paul, to die without his supervision, to leave him first of all before she left the rest of us. The last control she had wrested from him had been the volume knob on the stereo, and she'd used my hand to do it. Did she know they would wonder? Did she offer up my privacy to their curiosity on purpose?

"You checking in on me isn't routine at all, is it? You don't keep tabs on every former employee's kids and cousins and goddamned dog walkers. That would be ridiculous. You son of a bitch. You guys have been worried for three years about what she said to me in that last hour as she died."

"We haven't been worried. The follow-up is exactly like I said it was. It's casual and we just check in from time to time."

"Well, have you figured it out yet, you asshole?"

"Okay, hang on a minute. Calm down. Figured out what?"

"Do not tell me to calm down. Have you figured out what she said to me? If you wanted to know, you could have probably just guessed. She said what she always said—she said nothing. That last hour was for us. About us. And she hardly said a word at all. She never betrayed her position. As if she ever would. Are you satisfied? Paul had her muzzled perfectly. Even in pain and even loaded to the gills on morphine. Congratulations, Paul! If you're still listening in on my phone calls . . ."

"Dee, it's not like that. We're not—"

"Well, now you know. Although I guess you figured out how harmless and dense I am after meeting me in person the other day. God, I'm so embarrassing. Is that it, then? Since everyone's convinced I'm safe and clueless, you just snuck in and packed up today?"

"What? Today? What are you talking about? I told you the truth. You haven't been under any detailed surveillance since—"

"Do not mention truth. Please. I'll tell you the truth: if you ever bug my house again—"

Apparently, I'd reached the end of his patience. "If we ever bug your house again, you'll never know it. So just live your life, Dee. I made a mistake in talking to you, but you've always known how important your mother was. You've known that and you've known what Paul is. None of this should be that big of a surprise. Most particularly because it's not that important in the grand scheme of things. I was telling you the truth." Then his tone softened. "Look, I'm sorry I've upset you like this. I really am. I wish she had told you that we were there. It would have been better coming from her. But in the end, none of it matters. Everything is fine."

"You have no right to tell me what matters."

"Okay."

Silence weighed down the line.

"So, you're not going to even do me the courtesy of admitting that you were in my house today?"

"I don't think you'll believe me no matter what I say, but I wasn't there. I think I've made you jumpy, and I'm very sorry for that. We weren't there and we're *not* there, if you take my meaning."

Maddeningly, that he had regained his composure only spotlighted my own impotence. I could rail at him, or I could tear into Paul through him, or at the whole stupid system by hurling insults at the both of them, and that was about it.

Resignation was the new black, whereas avoidance had been the new black before that. Was there ever just black?

Not at my mother's big show. And it was always and forevermore my mother's show. But what choice did she have? For her to die in any kind of peace, she had needed my help. And I had, as unwitting accomplice or unsuspecting red herring, been there for her.

21

As it turned out, it wasn't something that Patrick mumbled in his sleep that gave him away. When he said it, he said it out loud, conversationally, although he wasn't speaking to me and didn't realize I had heard him.

The only exchange he and I had was well before that, earlier in the day as we were both ready to leave for work. It was Monday morning and I had scurried faster than usual to get out of the airless cabinet that our house had become over the way-too-long weekend. Staying out of each other's way had become a game of dodging each other's shadow and trying to look comfortable while veering around nothing to keep from being in the same room at the same time.

There is a point, pre-olive-branch, when orbiting the same space becomes simply too awkward to go on without communication. You can either start leaving notes for one another, which is more thought than you'd like to give to every little detail of the day, or you start talking. Someone has to say something eventually. It seemed to annoy Patrick that this time, the task fell to him.

His voice broke the glassy silence, startling me, as he spit out his announcement suddenly in a postargument monotone into the quiet of the kitchen. "I'll take your car today."

"Why?"

"The inspection is due. It expires today. You didn't take it in."

"I never saw the notice."

Patrick only shrugged.

"It's okay, Pat." I bumped my tone into the peacemaking range. "I can do it. You don't have to drive it all the way out there for me. That's a hassle. I'll take it in."

"I said I'd do it," he snapped. "I'll take it in now. I've got to be over that way later this morning anyway. We can switch back at lunchtime if it bothers you so much to drive mine."

"It doesn't bother me. I just didn't want to send you out of your way."

"Whatever. It needs to be done today and I'm going that way anyway." He knocked back the last of his coffee. "I need your keys." His own keys hit the counter in an irritable jangle, and he answered my question when it still was only a look on my face. "I don't know where the spares are."

I pulled the keys from my purse and set them into his aggressively outstretched hand as gently as I could, aiming for kind without scraping as low as timid. "Okay, thanks," I said, mostly to an empty room. He was already halfway out the door.

I was in Patrick's car and two turns away from my office when I realized he had my work ID. It was on its lanyard in the cup holder where I left it most days.

I could have got into the building without my ID, but it would have meant that I'd have to talk to Victor at the security desk. And I never talked to Victor if I could help it. I took the stairs at the side entrance every morning and every evening, and both to and from lunch, all the way to the seventh floor to swipe the bar code on my card to get into our office suite. I told everyone it was for the exercise. While it was certainly good for my heart rate and calf muscles, it was even better for my productivity. Any run-in with Victor meant a goodly amount of time spent shaking off the chill of his boldly roaming stare. If I had to go in without my ID, he'd take a sloth's pace in coding my temporary pass card and ask me where I'd been hiding, saying it *hiiiidin'* with a sidelong leer.

"You keep smilin', pretty lady," he'd say. *Smiiiiiiiiilin'*. And on his greasy command, I, like an idiot, would paste a smile on my face that didn't fit and walk stiffly to the elevators, willing away the sway that I was sure his nasty stare was trying to collect.

On its own, my not wanting to bask in Victor's slimy aura would probably not have been enough to tempt me into being late on purpose. But as it was, Jordy was out of the office for two weeks. While he wasn't a tyrant, he was on the obsessive side when it came to counting heads. If he noticed any of us chickens missing as the clock ticked over to 8:30, he was sure we had died in a fiery commuting disaster instead of maybe oversleeping or running low on gas. Our trespasses on his fussiness sometimes went noted on our performance appraisals, so it wasn't worth it. But Jordy was in Puerto Rico, hopefully taking the edge off, and no one else in the place would care if I took the stairs half an hour later than usual.

The idea of going back to Patrick was also a gift to my dissatisfaction with the way the morning had played out. With the entire weekend if I was honest. I'd had an opportunity to cut the stalemate short before he left with my keys and my car, and I'd let it slip away. Patrick was doing me a favor. That had to be a good sign. Given even another two minutes with him in the kitchen, I felt sure I could have got him to smile or at least look me in the eye.

So I swung through the drive-through for two overpriced dessert-for-breakfast coffees and sped off to fetch my ID and salvage a step forward in our long road back to peace.

The queue of cars showed that I was hardly the only person to have left off having my state inspection until the last minutes of the month. It wasn't like me to lose track of those things, and I would have sworn I never saw the notice. I did, in fact, swear to it later. My car sat third in line for the service bay, and Patrick was out of the driver's seat, turned away from me, leaning against the wall of the shop while smoking and talking on the phone. *Smoking?* We'd quit together over four years earlier. Both of my parents had been smokers, and they'd both died of cancer. Once I was finally able to quit, with nicotine patches and lots of yoga, I had been appalled that I ever took up the habit in the first place.

It was so jarring to see Patrick with a cigarette in his hand that time wavered and I could feel, just for an instant, my slightly younger self, cigarette in my own hand, watching my husband, warm and there, right where he should be, and me with him, contented, and completely clueless as to what he was thinking. Why had I never wondered? You should always wonder.

With the arrival of all the curiosity I'd never had about Patrick's internal gears, and every bit of the sidecar unease it ignited, I stopped at the edge of being able to hear his side of the conversation.

"One fourteen Reeves Road."

. . .

"No, Reeves."

. . .

"Reeves. With a *v* as in *Victor.*"

. . .

Victor. I shuddered. *Where you been hiiiiiiidin'?* And what was that about 114 Reeves Road? I went there twice a month, to a little hole-in-the-wall spa for a facial and a massage. My next one was—

"Saturday. Yeah, this Saturday. She goes in early. Like eight o'clock. The entrance is in the back. Off the street."

. . .

"No, I understand. Not that there are any guarantees in life anyway. I know. Whatever."

. . .

"I understand. And, yes, I'm sure."

. . .

"I know."

. . .

"It *is* sad, but just one fucking thing needs to be easy with her. I'm done. I'm not putting myself through all that. This needs to be over. Now. I'm sorry, but this is how it has to be."

. . .

"I understand."

. . .

"I've got it for a few hours. I'll take care of it."

. . .

"Yeah, I know what to do. I won't go all the way through it. And then I'll get you a copy of the keys you need."

. . .

"If you say so. Plan Bs are your thing, not mine."

. . .

"No, no. I understand. I appreciate your, you know, flexibility."

. . .

"Then I'll just wait to hear from you until after, then. Okay?"

. . .

"Oh right, or from them. Hmmm. Yeah, hadn't really thought of that. Okay."

. . .

"I understand."

. . .

"Keep me posted."

. . .

"G'bye."

On autopilot, I stepped back under the screening wing of the brick wall, then ducked through the door of the service station before Patrick could turn and see me. I left the full coffee cups on the counter in front of the bewildered cashier and clipped right through the service bay and out the back door.

There was no helping it. I noted that it was Monday. *File that little episode under Monday. Whatever the hell it was.*

Back in Patrick's car and pointed, more or less, in the direction of my office, I barely saw the road as it spooled out around the turns and over the hills.

I'm going to be served divorce papers on Saturday morning. I'll be in yoga pants with no makeup on and I'll have to stand there and have some stranger tell me that it's not going to work out for me and Patrick and I'll have to nod my head and sign my name and then what? I'd snagged this conclusion out of the roar in my head and kept twisting it this way and that to fill in the blank spot, like a puzzle piece that has almost all the right notches.

But my own voice wasn't the only one I heard in my mind. *Plucky, it doesn't fit.*

"Nothing fits," I said out loud.

It will.

I had to see my old shadow in the blue sedan twice that day before I called my brother. If it had been only the once on my lunch break, spying the round-headed silhouette behind the wheel of the car tucked in like a dull sapphire between a pair of minivans, it might have been written off as a coincidence. It's not that big of a town. It could maybe even have been a different car with only a similar guy behind the wheel. Except I knew that it wasn't. Five points for me.

It wasn't Brian Menary, either, and it never had been. Private detective? Perhaps. That could make sense. If he had permission from Patrick, and soon a set of keys, his being in our house whenever he wanted wouldn't be breaking and entering. If blue-sedan man was a private investigator, I had a strong candidate for who had been through my stuff and who might be back for another look.

The second time I saw the car in under four hours, it put a pain low in my side, while a choking anger bloomed hot in my throat. Simon answered his phone before I'd had a chance to clear my voice.

"This is Vess," he said in his professional monotone.

"Simon, do you have a minute?"

"Dee? Are you all right?"

"Yeah. Can I ask you to do something with no strings attached? I mean no strings on my end and no further poking around on yours."

"What's going on?"

"Probably nothing. And definitely nothing if I don't get a promise out of you," I said.

"What do you need?"

"A tag number run. I want to know who owns a car. But I don't want to know anything more than that. And then I need you to leave it alone. If you can't guarantee that, I'll understand."

I had a long wait. I could hear his office humming in drawer-banging, phone-ringing industry in the background while he checked his conscience.

"What is it? Is Patrick messing around for real?"

"Probably." It was a convenient likelihood. I guessed that he'd started up a new game of flirtation with someone, as far as I could tell by his behavior, in the weeks after the Angela fiasco. In the intervals between his spells of cranky preoccupation, he had that moody flush, the waxing and waning cheerfulness that signposted guilty excitement. Once I realized that it might not have been the thought of me that had steered him clear of the stripper, I only pried listlessly into looking for a possible real girlfriend. I didn't have the heart for the hunt. Before today, I specifically didn't want to find out anything more about Patrick. In fact, I would have drunk a potion or maybe agreed to a targeted head injury to know less about him, but I wasn't acquainted with any witch doctors or surgically precise thugs.

After the birth-control saga and the electrocuted embarrassment of the tandem-texted butterfly photo, I had no appetite for dealing with whatever I might find, so instead, I let myself get distracted over Brian Menary and remembered that Pat's ego had taken a hammering. I had given it a pass, albeit perhaps one with an expiration date.

But now I was being followed, and Patrick had inserted unknown plans into my itinerary for the coming weekend. I had my own wrung-out concerns to wrangle. For my purposes, his track record of wandering-eye syndrome would smooth the way to news I *did* want at the moment, news that my brother could get for me.

"You think this is her car?" Simon's voice yanked me back to my quest.

"Um, yeah. Maybe."

"Your pauses are the worst, Dee. Might as well hold up a sign— THE NEXT THING I SAY WILL BE DODGY."

"No, I don't know whose car it is."

"Are you worried?"

"Not particularly." Lie, but no pause for me this time. I wouldn't be caught out twice. Not in the same conversation. He took a turn at dead air.

"Simon, I really need you to respect my privacy on this. I'm embarrassed as hell at how my life is turning out. And you pointing out the other night that it's probably all ruined anyway no matter what I do—it just didn't help. You made me feel like an idiot. This is hard enough without you judging me. Just let me handle this mess my own way, okay?"

It was a bit of a low blow, but it was the truth, if not the entire truth.

"Wow. You know I didn't mean to hurt you with that," he said.

"Didn't you?"

"No! Of course not. He's the one who should get hurt."

"And your sister's self-respect just got caught in your cross fire?"

"I'm sorry."

"It's okay."

"All right, I'll do it." He was now squarely trapped into making amends. They should all be so easy. "I'll do it if you promise me that you'll ask for my help just before you're one hundred percent sure that you need it."

I smiled into the phone and felt our mother smiling with me. To her, swaggering past rational fear was the greatest folly of all. It was a betrayal of the instinct she'd constantly groomed in us. She'd say, *Don't be stupid. Under the guillotine, you're only one hundred percent sure the blade has dropped when your severed head is staring back at its stump.*

"Why do you pretend she didn't train us up like good little soldiers?" My voice caught on the sentiment.

"What's the license number, Plucky?" His voice was as thick as mine.

22

I knew the very moment I laid eyes on Patrick when he came through the door that I didn't want him back. I didn't want to salvage the life we'd had, and I'd already done the last double-back to make up with him that I would ever do.

I did want more information, though. I wanted to know what he was up to for Saturday, and I wanted to understand why. But I knew that I was no longer interested in fixing things between us.

Then I realized I had known it an hour earlier when I'd changed clothes.

I'd put up with Victor to get into my office, blessedly too swamped with a gaggle of new interns to give me much of a hassle, but I didn't make it through the day there. I claimed a migraine and left early. I didn't suffer from migraines, but no one seemed to mark my inaugural complaint with anything more than distracted tut-tutting and standard government-issue sympathy.

I tried running errands. I bought a roll of stamps we didn't need. I gassed up the car and took advantage of the pennies-per-gallon discount for adding in a wash with my fill-up. It was only practical. So, the car was clean and I'd shaved another four minutes off my spinning. The grocery store was stocked with not a single appetizing thing, and I had looked over each aisle with care, so I left with only two bottles of the pricey pinot noir that Patrick bought whenever he was in a particularly good mood.

At home, an inadvertent glimpse of myself in the bathroom mirror pulled me off the track I'd been wearing into the hallway floor, zipping back and forth—with a haul of collected garbage, with a two-course trip for all the recycling, with a pass of the dust broom, and now with a load of laundry.

I'd run out of frantic busywork at the office. Hence the phantom migraine and, ultimately, the shiftless drifting from room to room back at home. Onward and upward, the house would be tidied all the way to the baseboards at the pace I'd stirred up. By God and by elbow grease, I'd get control of myself. I would have order, but the mirror showed that it would come at some great cost to any chance of being taken seriously. Patrick would come home to a madwoman looking every bit the part.

A tuft of my ponytail had tried for a jailbreak but hadn't made it past a hairy hiccup on the top of my head. Blurred mascara ringed my startled eyes. My face was a waxy mask the color of bad news. And for the finale, a splotchy flush blazed up from the neckline of my shirt. I'd be lucky to fetch even a sympathy point.

The clock showed that a hurry would make me presentable by the time Patrick got home, but as I reached for one fragrant bottle after another in the shower, the choir of butterflies in my middle hunkered down, quiet and wary, almost of their own accord. The calm soaked into me with the creams and lotions, settling my stampeding pulse with a false pharmacy of lanolin and lavender. I was changing the script as I went, with strange clockworks shifting to the foreground in my mind, recommending new lines for me to speak, and new responses to expect.

I stole peeks at the transformation in the mirror. It was safer to give all the credit to the drugstore potions. Otherwise, there was no way to deny a hatching was going on, an unfurling that would not fold back into its box anytime soon. With every swipe of the brushes and with each stroke of powdered color, everything that had been rattling inside me stilled and cooled.

I went into the closet with a mind to put on the jade blouse that always earned compliments from Patrick. It was my go-to power shirt, the one I didn't merely wear, but rocked. I loved the green blouse. Or I had.

I stared at my reflection again and tried to remember a time that the green blouse had worked any magic. I turned to the side, shook out my shoulders, and relaxed the edge off my rigid, green-blouse-makes-me-fierce posture. But it was practically pulsing its greenness into the room. I wasn't Dee wearing a green blouse, I was a green blouse with an agenda to keep Dee from being naked. I hated it.

I wadded it into the wastebasket and took up a black, long-sleeved T-shirt and jeans. Now the mirror didn't shout green. It didn't shout anything at all, which was a relief. I straightened up to find I owned a fierce-is-in-my-back-pocket-if-I-need-it posture that was, while not exactly familiar, very suitable. No sympathy point would be needed. And no automatic two-tenths deduction for trying too hard.

"Fuck it," I said to the mirror, and went to open Patrick's wine.

I was deep into the second glass and also deep into the big armchair in the living room, legs tucked under me, when Patrick finally came through the door.

"Hey," I said neutrally. I took a deep breath, committed to not raising my voice.

"Whoa! Crap. You scared me."

With no inflection of pleading, I said, "Come give me a kiss."

"What? Why are you sitting in the dark?" He flipped up the switch for the overhead lights.

"I didn't need a light. I was just sitting here thinking. Thinking about you. And waiting for you to come home." I nodded at the low table in front of me and at the bottle with its empty, expectant glass beside it. "I bought that wine you like. Have some. One good turn deserving another and all that. You did me a favor today with the car, and we're speaking actual words for the first time in a few days. So let's end this. Right now. Let's just take the shortcut. To hell with it. Kiss me and I'll pour you a glass of wine and we can get on with our lives."

I knew he wouldn't do it. There wasn't a kiss to be had, for love nor money, anywhere in our emotional zip code. But no matter . . .

"Just like that, huh?" he said.

"Yeah. Why not?"

"Because I'm tired, that's why not. And you're being weird. Give me some space, Dee."

"Have you been smoking?"

"What? No!"

"I can smell it."

"No, you can't. You know that Darren smokes around me during the day. You're just needling me."

In my best impression of my mother's measured tones, I asked, "Do I do that? Do you feel needled and hassled, or are you just assigning me random faults so that you can stay mad at me for, what, ever?"

"Well, I'm certainly feeling hassled right now. I don't kiss you on command and suddenly I'm getting analyzed before I can even take my jacket off?"

"By all means, take your jacket off."

He did. He set down his computer case, where it slumped against the table's leg. His jacket went over the back of a chair. When he didn't make a move toward the wine, I did it for him and offered up the filled glass. He let me sit there, arm extended for a few beats longer than it took indecision to crest over into outright rudeness.

"No, thanks," he said finally.

"You might as well." I set the glass on the table in front of the chair. "We need to talk."

"I don't feel like talking, Dee. It's been a long day and I just want to relax for a little while and then go to bed. That will go a lot farther in getting us back to normal than you dolling up and staging an intervention."

Dolling up? I wondered what the green blouse would have bought or cost me.

"We're not going to drag this out," I said.

"Right. Because you say so."

"No, because I've put a lawyer on retainer," I lied.

In the span of Patrick's tardiness, while I'd sipped the wine that I was at first sure I'd bought for him, I decided to give him a dose of what he didn't even know he'd served up that morning. If he had orchestrated a private investigator and a legal ambush for my spa day, it might help me get a little of my own back if I caught him out of play here at home this evening.

Whatever else, I needed him to react. I needed to take the temperature of his surprise, or to shake loose a bread crumb to track back from. He was going to be, at the very least, furious. And I'd known now for five minutes that I couldn't care less.

Recklessness reaped what recklessness generally sows. Patrick simply freaked out.

"You did *what?*" He took what should have been the two full strides between us in a single leap. He had me by the shoulders and pulled halfway out of my chair before I could put down my wine. "You did *what?*" he bellowed again as my glass arced through the air and splash-thumped into the carpet. "What did you do, Dee? Why did you talk to a lawyer?"

I was unprepared for the bright, sparking outrage that surged through me. In more than thirteen years together my husband had touched me in affection (even of the manufactured variety) or not at all. We didn't snuggle without its signaling sex. We didn't casually hold hands. We didn't roughhouse, wrestle, or push each other into the pool. And the thing was, I didn't know which of us wasn't the cuddly one. His fingers crushing bruises into my arms put us instantly into unmapped territory. Into unimagined territory.

This was only one of several scattered thoughts and revelations cast off as the lava swell of fury carried me the rest of the way to my feet, clutched and struggling in Patrick's clawed hands. Also noted was that Patrick wasn't just angry, he was terrified. And PS, the carpet's ruined. Monday got a subtab for Monday Night.

"Are you out of your mind? Let me go!" I shouted.

"What have you done?" He shook me with each word and then flung me out of his grip. He raked his hands through his hair.

Either he was terribly, explosively even, distressed at the prospect of losing me, or—as I'd tried to avoid knowing all day—I was very wide of the bull's-eye on what was happening in my life. I stepped back from him and put myself close enough to the chair to jump behind it should I be unable to wiggle off this powder keg before another eruption from Patrick.

"Jesus, Pat. I didn't do anything yet."

"Tell me exactly what you said to him. And how much you paid him." Patrick was pale and panting. He was wilting before my eyes.

I split the lie in half. In truth, I hadn't even thought to pick up the sharp stick I'd just poked him with. There was no lawyer. I'd never made the call. I'd only invented the scenario at the top of the second glass of wine. Not that I'd backpedal that far now.

"It was a *her* not a *him*." I made it up as I went. "And I didn't actually make the call or give her any money. I didn't even actually talk to her. I only looked into it."

"Have you told everybody that you're leaving me? Is that it? Am I the last asshole to know?"

"Patrick, I'm just trying to get you to talk to me. I exaggerated about the lawyer just now because you won't get into what's going on with us. You are out of my reach. You're either angry or spacing out—all the time—and I can't take it anymore. I haven't packed my bags or anything. But neither have you, right? *Right?* And when have I ever, since you've known me, *ever* aired my personal business to anyone. It's not exactly in my blood, now is it?"

"What about Simon?"

"What about him?"

"Does he hate me?"

"No." It wasn't a lie and it wasn't the full truth. Simon would put up with whatever I would from Patrick. As such, his attachment was all but over, but that little detail didn't feel useful for Patrick to have at this point in the conversation.

The spent adrenaline burned in my legs. I sat down and retrieved my wineglass from the floor. I picked a bit of fuzz from the rim and refilled it from the bottle.

"I should go get some club soda for that." Patrick pointed to the stippled trail and ragged rose of wine in the carpet. It looked like blood.

"It doesn't matter. It's ruined. Leave it."

"I'll get a new one."

I sniffed. "Maybe we'll even get a new one together."

Patrick took up his own full glass and sagged into the chair opposite me. Nearly half the generous pour went down in a single, open-throated swallow. "I'm sorry I wouldn't kiss you."

I floundered in the pause. The lying pause. "I'm sorry you didn't want to."

Fibber. Both of you.

I tried to imagine us in the morning, awkward and grimly shy in our sunny kitchen. I reached further out to cast us into next week, next month, our retirement to old age spent treading all the inevitable uncomfortable silences, enough of them to fill a library. A dozen libraries. *Shhhhhhhh.* I couldn't do it. I couldn't see us in any future.

But wasn't it supposed to be one day at a time? Wasn't it folly at best to invent futures for ourselves? Wasn't it almost a sin to do the math and live in any time but the Almighty Now? That was what they told you to do. Don't project beyond the moment. Live in the now. That was what you did when you were successfully normal and inspirational-poster healthy. It didn't matter that I didn't love him or that he didn't love me. According to the experts, we had an endless parade of nows in which to deal with those details.

But in this now I was too tired. In this now, I wanted only to buy some peace.

So I launched the bid for a happy intermission (never to be confused with a happy ending). I laughed to get Patrick's attention, a little shaky, a little sad, and very much a lying white flag to keep his hands off me. It was just a short-range goal anyway, not for the now, but something to take care of the hours, and maybe even days, just on the other side of now. It was the best I could do so that I could go to bed and get the hell out of Monday. "Well, we'd better figure out a way to get along before our trip or that's going to be the tensest the Danube's been since 1944."

"I'm not worried about the trip," Patrick said. And then he cried.

23

We slept in the same bed with no negotiation. With no discussion at all. After a blowup like none we'd ever had before, it surprised me. He'd slept in the living room over much less. I thought there would have to be a summit. A treaty adopted. Something formal and announced. Something.

But all the aggression drained from the silence while Patrick cried quietly—three tight sobs and maybe half a minute of refuge behind his hands. He wiped his eyes, took a deep, shuddery breath, and drained his glass.

He fetched a towel for the spilled wine and spent a pointless few minutes blotting the stain, folding the towel over to a clean spot, dabbing at it again and again to soak up a little more. In the end, and much like our argument, the juice was out of it but the flaw remained. The rug was wrecked and it would be carted out and replaced, sooner over later most likely. Nothing useful would come of fretting over it. I tried not to measure that against the state of my life, but the stain and its verdict plagued my peripheral vision as I moved through the house.

Our evening routine came back on autopilot, only minus any chitchat. We were armored, each hunkered down in our own shad-

owy little shell, but both breathing easier with no more steam to
weigh down the air from our collective boiling. For the first time in
days, my mind wandered as I got ready for bed. There was no more
urge to disappear from Patrick's radar; no need to walk carefully,
cringing at every knee pop. I didn't miss the obligation to try to appear both invisible and put-upon every time I found myself in the
same room with him.

In the past few mornings, I'd been self-conscious of the coffee gurgling into the carafe and the knife scraping the butter over
the toast, as if breakfasting was a sign of weakness, an embarrassing
admission of need. The hours of setting things down quietly and of
scanning the background noise to keep track of where Patrick was
in the house had put my teeth on edge even more than I'd realized.

With the tension of the past days blown to vapor, my jaw unclenched and I was left with my thoughts and the smooth, solid,
automatic gestures of home. Just for the span of the rest of that evening, I didn't even worry myself with imagining what Patrick was
thinking.

As for what I was thinking, I pointedly ignored the throbbing
finger marks in my arms and planned my search.

I checked my e-mail before turning in, as I always did. The
only message of any consequence was from my brother. The blue
car was part of a fleet belonging to a company, Carlisle Inc., that
built metal-skinned self-storage and warehouse facilities. The name
meant nothing to me.

I woke before the alarm, snapping alert with a blaring *Where is he?*
clanging in my head. Patrick wasn't beside me. I listened for his
breathing and reached out for a sense of him in the room, primed for
any echo of ill intent from the dark corners. Then the toilet flushed
and I tried to laugh at myself, but succeeded in only laughing at myself for wanting to laugh at it. *Don't be a fool. You know damned well
you should worry.*

Patrick shuffled into our room and rolled back into place on his side of the bed.

"My turn," I mumbled, and scooched out of the blankets, calculatedly graceless, as if I, too, were barely awake.

As soon as the door clicked shut behind me, I lifted the toilet lid and let it thunk purposefully against the porcelain tank. I braced the vanity drawer for stealth and slid it open to pick carefully through Patrick's toothpaste, razor-head refills, and floss picks for just a bit longer than it would have taken me to pee. The bottom two drawers took their rifling under the screening rush of water as it ran into my sink. I rattled the towel ring while I pried open the few boxed sundries under his vanity cabinet. Nothing but the usual stuff, in the usual amounts.

I went back to bed and waited for the alarm.

Sleep recharged us—and in the most electric sense. As the dawn dialed up the light seeping in through the curtains, I could feel Patrick awake in the gloom, but pretending not to be. The energized air tickled like spiders' feet. He eased up from the pillow, bracing his arm in an effort to turn out of the bed without creaking the springs. I murmured and snuffled and turned toward him, freezing him halfway through a stealthy sit-up. He held it for an uncomfortable stretch while I made a production of snuggling down into a new position.

He eased back down and waited for the radio to kick on.

"Morning," Patrick said in the kitchen. It was a greeting neither of us had ever used.

"Howdy, Sheriff."

Patrick rolled his eyes.

"You okay?" I said.

"Yep." He put his cup in the sink. "You all done in the bathroom?"

"Um, I guess. Are you going to lock me out or something?"

"I just wanted to know if you were done." His bristles were fully extended now.

"Okay, okay." I put up my hands. "I was only teasing."

I tossed over his car while he showered. There wasn't so much as a credit-card receipt or a gum wrapper.

I dallied over breakfast with a third cup of coffee and a book.

Patrick's unease rose like mercury in a hot thermometer. "You're not going in?"

"Of course I am. Everybody's just kind of enjoying Jordy being out, though. All last week it was a mini-vacation of tardiness, long lunches, and ducking out early."

"Must be nice."

I put down my book. "You know, it really has been. He'll be back next week, and for the first time in a long time I can't say I'm looking all that forward to the weekend. For a change, when Saturday comes, this time it means the fun's all over for me."

I shrugged and held his gaze steady in mine while I watched him flinch at every reference to Saturday I could work into the conversation. "At least I've got my spa day to perk me up. That'll be nice, right?"

It would have looked to Patrick as if I'd dropped my glance back into my book, but from the corner of my eye I watched him go gray, then flush back to life, then crest over to full sunburn red.

His voice chirped out past a knotted throat, sounding not like his voice at all. He stopped and coughed and tried again. "Well, the traffic isn't getting any better, so you're only making that part of the day worse for yourself."

"It's okay. I'll find a radio show to keep me company. I've got that new audiobook, too. It'll be fine. I don't have any early meetings, so I'm not in a hurry."

He fidgeted another minute off the clock. "I can't be late."

"Okay. Have a good day."

He started out the door, then doubled back to my side. He kissed my temple, a dutiful hammer tap that rocked my head sideways, and then he stiff-legged it into the garage.

I stared for ten minutes, unseeing, at the blur of words on the unturned page. Then, of course, I took the house apart.

Every scrap of workaday debris was gone from his wake. There was nothing that indicated he'd even ducked into a grocery store or hit an ATM in the past several weeks. It didn't fit. He hadn't left any glitter on his collar from Angela or any blatant signposts to his more recent distraction, but he was only as careful as I ever appeared suspicious, which was hardly at all. There had been plenty to find, if you knew where to look. Being my mother's daughter a good deal more than Patrick ever realized, knowing where to look had never been much of a hurdle. But now there was nothing, and somehow that worried me much more than even the Carlisle man in the blue car did.

The itch wasn't scratched and I couldn't even write it off to the fact I hadn't found anything. The absence of any writing to analyze or receipts to puzzle over or any empty, dust-bordered spots on the bookshelves to reverse engineer, all of that was only part of the problem. There was careful and then there was too careful. And still it wasn't the Thing. Whatever it was, I'd overlooked it somehow.

Easter-egg hunts, hide-and-seek, and scavenger quests were some of my mother's favorite games. Simon loved them, too. I generally approved of the results of the contest, but I was more impatient, more easily frustrated than both of them. In some fit of grace, they were both perfectly comfortable to stand in admiration of other people's cleverness. Both of them could somehow be delighted to find themselves stumped. I, on the other hand, learned to curse.

"Shit!" I yelled to the foyer ceiling.

My phone rang in response.

I found it and looked at the display before it could drop into voice mail. Of course, it was Patrick. I studied the background photo I'd set for his number, an ancient picture of us in college, one that had made it through the stacks of the scanning project. I tried to remember the last time Patrick had called me on a weekday morning. I couldn't remember one.

I hit the red button and declined the call. "Yes, I'm still here, you squirrelly bastard," I said to the screen.

The wine stain on the living-room floor was even more garish in the daylight.

I wandered back into the den. With the possible exception of the kitchen, this room had the most variable contents. Even so, it was still mostly all the same—all the time. The bills and the letters on the desk changed in amount, creditor, and subject matter, but the stack rotated through the same general acreage on the polished wood. We'd swapped out a desktop for a laptop a couple of years earlier, but the computer had been in the same spot since the day we moved in. Current catalogs were where there had been older ones, and all of them had fluttered out exactly nothing when I'd shaken each by its spine. The pens changed color and size as they broke their springs or ran out of ink, but they always bristled from the same cup. Even then, I'd not overlooked the thought to take them out and scan the bottom for any miniature clue.

I had already played spot-the-difference in here.

There was an advantage to not knowing what you were looking for, though. In my mother's version of the game, when it wasn't Easter eggs, she'd wind us up with a gasp. *Ah! I'm thinking there's something hiding in this house,* she'd say. *And I'm thinking there's fun riding on it if one of you finds it before supper.*

Sometimes it was movie tickets, or a new board game, or a coupon for a two-for-one dessert special down at the diner. Once it was a brochure for Disneyland, and another time it was fishbowls for each of us, Mother included, a coppery, chiffon-finned fish turning laps in each of the three. Sometimes she'd even pick one of us to do the hiding so that she could play along in the search for a change.

But before the find, before my inevitable irritability set in, there was the little thrill of possibility—it could be anything, and it could be anywhere.

The wide-focus perspective forced a keener vision. You played the game to secure a goal, but in the meantime you saw, *really* saw, your surroundings. By imagining what each thing could conceal (and how it could manage it) you knew it better.

Everything is more yours for wondering at all that it could disguise.

Patrick and I had lived in our house for more than eight years. All the furniture and belongings were more or less in the same place where they (or their equivalent predecessors) had been set when we unpacked them. Certainly there were places to hide things, big and small, but as frustrated as I would get with the game when I was young, I had learned that the best way to avoid the crawling annoyance of being baffled was to win.

I was very good at looking for things. Yet, here I stood, empty-handed.

Perhaps, I thought, this wasn't a matter of spot-the-difference in this room, or any other room. Maybe the clue was tucked into something more subtle. Maybe today's game was a matter of spot-the-difference in this life, not necessarily this house.

I turned a circle in the middle of the den and remembered the floor strewn with boxes. I remembered having been concerned that we didn't have enough stuff to fill up the upgraded space. We were just kids, barely able to afford a real house. I remembered complaining that it echoed. We talked about throwing parties, not having babies. I remembered the alienness of not knowing how far down along the wall to reach for the light switch, and not knowing for the longest time which one controlled each fixture. I remembered the blissful little realizations that I felt at home as the weeks turned to months turned to years. We had been content here for a long stretch.

My mother and I had solidly reconnected in this house, finally. She'd come here to read her last books and tick off the lists of the films she'd missed. She'd been allowed to end it all when she chose to because she'd been here and not in a hospital. She had been grateful to me here, and I'd been so, so grateful for her gratitude.

Then life had slid down, slowly, and in so many ways, to something less satisfactory, and eventually into a lousy mess. But at least in some areas we'd pulled up, hadn't we?

That was the difference.

Up until recently, we'd been grinding away since my mother died, more contentious, less at ease in our niches. Then we'd been rewarded with the distraction of a windfall: my mother's legacy fund. We were doing better on paper, anyway. Anyone who had seen us on brash display in these last few weeks would have seen fit, smiling, smooching fools. He'd made such a show of us lately. And I, to try to avoid looking abnormal, would go ahead and dance when he would metaphorically sing so that our audience wouldn't feel uncomfortable—or would at least feel less uncomfortable. We were about to take the trip of a lifetime. . . .

I'm not worried about the trip.

My eyes stopped on the rich navy portfolio with its slick, gold-foiled logo: Best of All Worlds—Travel Agents and Timeshare Brokers. I sat in the swiveling chair and took the file into my lap. I'd already read through it days ago, which was the excuse I'd used to skip over it today, the very day I was actually looking for something important. I went through it again, page by page.

The tickle got a solid clawing at the back of the contract. When I'd first looked through the file, I hadn't read every bit of the endless fine print that Patrick had signed for. I had read the itinerary. I had admired the brochures for the ports of call and imagined the day-trips and excursions. I had tried to feel happy that I'd soon see

the views in those artfully snapped photos, but with my own eyes—
and with my dour husband, hopefully getting happier, beside me.
But I had glazed over at the beginning of the fat ream of addenda
and agreements and disclaimers that padded the back quarter of the
stack.

Historically, my husband had declined every extended warranty
he'd ever been offered. He shunned the salesmen's enhanced-protection
provisos and any additional rust, fire, loss, leakage, insect, hail, and
act-of-God plans for whatever might get ruined by such sundry. Those
crafty deals, according to Patrick, were nothing but scams for suckers
who couldn't say no. He'd said it a hundred times. He didn't second-
guess his well-thought-out purchases, and he wouldn't part with an
extra dime against the possibility of vague what-if scenarios.

But Patrick had bought travel insurance for this trip. The top-
shelf policy, too, that covered luggage loss or theft, weather troubles,
travel delays, medical emergencies, and provided a full refund or
transfer of tickets for passengers unable to complete the itinerary due
to serious illness or death.

24

It seemed there wasn't much my mother hated more than denial. It was lying, laziness, and wasting time all rolled into one tidy sin. And it had only one remedy: stop it. If she ever wrangled the offense, I didn't know what it looked like on her face. I never felt farther from her than when I was, in her words, *leaving poor, old reality standing on the side of the road with its thumb out.*

Once I had read the travel-insurance addendum all the way through, I tucked it back into the obscenely luxurious folder and left for work. I ran the radio up loud and babbled a running commentary on the relative merits of my fellow commuters, wishing terrible things on every driver who distinguished himself in any way from the pack of whirring metal boxes around me—from whatever brand of moron would buy such a fucking ugly snot-green Martian box, to the ridiculous hipster singing his heart out, blessedly behind safety glass, to the undoubtedly nice old lady who should have had her license cryogenically frozen to be reunited with her once they'd figured out how to do courage transplants on the terminally flinchy.

By the time I got to my office I thoroughly hated myself.

I had my ID this time, but I went through the lobby anyway, unsure of what I wanted out of a confrontation with Victor.

"There she is! Hey, lady, where you been hiiiiidin'?"

"What's my name?" I clapped my hand over the photo badge dangling around my neck.

"Huh?"

"What's my name? I mean, you miss me so terribly all the time. Surely you know my name by now?"

Victor rolled his ogle-y eyes and smirked. "What did that guy say? That *Romeo and Juliet* guy? He said, 'What's in a name?' That's my philosophy, too—what's in a name? It's all the same. See? Poetry."

"Hmmm. Shakespeare. Okay, I didn't see that coming."

He pursed his lips and nodded. "Mmmm. Hmmm. Well, you're lookin' fiiiine, Miz—" He leaned in well closer than he needed to read my tag, which I'd let go. "Miz Aldrich."

"Oh, I doubt that I'm looking anywhere close to fine." I swiped my card and the turnstile allowed me through.

"Aw, no. It's all good. Miiiiiiighty fine, just like I said, 'cept I'm thinkin' you could do with just a little bit of a smiiiile on your face."

I leaned into his space and thumped my palm on the counter. Victor's eyebrows did a twitchy little dance to the top of their reach. "You know what I think? I think you practice all the long *i*-sound words you can think of. I think you practice them in the mirror, actually. And I think you probably do this a lot because there's nobody around at home to tell you to cut it out. But it's creepy and I think you know it's creepy. And for you, it's funny to be a creeper because you're bored. And I can see where you'd get bored sitting down in this cave all day. But you know what, Victor?" I leaned in a little farther. "You don't bother me anymore. So let's make a deal, you and me. I'll come through this lobby every weekday morning, and every weekday evening, and twice on the lunch hour, and you can long-*i* and eyyyyyyyeball me all you want and I won't file a complaint with"—I leaned in well closer than I needed to read the embroidered logo on his uniform shirt—"Gateway Security. In exchange, you leave everyone else alone."

His eyebrows found an extra millimeter of distance from his eyes.

"I don't want to hear of one more woman all skeeved out by her walk through the lobby. You got that? You keep your eyes and *iiiiiiiis* to yourself. Of course, I'll be missing out on my daily exercise up and down those stairs, but I don't need to worry that I'll gain any weight. I don't mind being your little thrill if you don't mind being my appetite suppressant."

I left him gawping and turned for the elevators.

"Stop watching my ass, Victor," I called without turning around. A bump and a rattle of keys, then an officious rustle of paper, came in answer from the security desk behind me.

I don't know that I felt better exactly, but I'd at least cut the blue wire for a while.

Then, all of a sudden, back-to-back meetings had never been so interesting. I made concentration an Olympic event for the rest of the morning, and in a burst of not letting my mind wander during the second roundtable discussion, I discovered a pretty tidy solution to the problem of a nagging data conflict that had been plaguing our development team for half a year. I earned gold-star nods from everyone at the table.

But I kept talking. I ate up every pause so that no one could gather up their things without looking rude. I had an epiphany for a third meeting just as the chair races were under way, mere inches from setting everyone free. The squeaking wheels and groaning vinyl muffled their sighs as they all scooched back into position at the table, and we planned the agenda for my latest (and last) bright idea.

The clock eased forward to noon. Lunch was calling them. It was screaming at me.

On the way back to my office, I insinuated myself into a con-versation about an upcoming 5K charity race even though I wasn't a runner anymore. Then I stopped by Marco's office to see if he had pictures of his new baby. He had loads, thank the gods.

"There you are," said Jill. I could have kissed her. Marco had been trying to get rid of me for five minutes and I was running out of small-talk ammo.

"Hi! What's up?" I sounded like a lunatic.

"Security has been calling. They're looking for you. There's some guy downstairs, waiting to see you? Brian Men—Menefee, Mena—something."

Oh.

"I'm not sure I can adequately express how much I do *not* want to talk to you right now," I said from the turnstile.

From behind the safety of his desk, Victor offered Brian a sym-pathetic look.

"Can we talk?" Brian asked.

"What about?"

"I don't like the way we left things."

"What, they didn't give you an A on your report?"

"This isn't a professional visit," said Brian. "Can we get out of here? Have you had lunch? Let me at least buy you lunch."

I had to kill the next hour somehow anyway.

I ordered soup.

"That's all you're having?" Brian asked.

"I'm probably not even having that. I'm not very hungry."

Water was sipped. Napkins were flourished into place. Windows were stared through. It was nerve-racking enough to completely blank my brain, which made it my new favorite thing ever.

Brian broke my reverie. "Okay, look, I had a lot of respect for your mother. And I respect you, too."

"You don't know me well enough to respect me."

"Right. But I generally start out thinking well of people and chainsaw down the pedestal from there as things go along."

"It shouldn't take you long to bury me, then."

"Don't say that," he said.

"Okay."

"But it was more than just standard respect. You have to understand. I admired Annette. And I liked her. It's a funny thing, even in the years between working with her, if her name ever came up in passing, she just came right back to me—vivid, you know. Even now. She gets stuck in your head, like a song."

I sighed. "Yes. She was something, my mother."

"She really was. And if she were alive, she'd be ten kinds of pissed off that I've upset you like this."

"You think so?"

"I know so."

I laughed in spite of myself. "Knew her that well, did you? Are we getting to the part where you make a confession I don't want to hear? Were you almost my stepfather or something?"

"No. Good God. Nothing like that. I know because she told me." Brian slid a jump drive across the table. "Like I said, whenever she comes up in conversation, I remember her so clearly. So all of this, it made me think back to part of the last interview she and I had, right before we were done. I went through the audio and snipped it out for you. Hopefully it'll clear up any lingering questions about my attachment to this case, about why I'm here. Maybe it could even serve as an apology of sorts."

I looked at the gray plastic bar on the table, but didn't reach for it. "How much trouble are we going to get in for that?"

Brian chuckled, a little perforated exhale. "You've got us all wrong. You know it's not like that. It's a bureaucracy made up of a million little, low-tech cogs. And a few big, toothy important and fancy ones. Nothing rests on a snippet of old conversation on a jump drive I bought yesterday at Office Depot. It has to be that way or the whole machine falls apart. You have to see that. It can only work as a hive of bit players. They have to let people be able to live a life while they do the job. They'd get no takers otherwise. There aren't many who are cut out for nonstop cloak-and-dagger. I mean, your mom was Annette Vess, for God's sake, and there weren't any exploding pens in the drawers or villains lurking behind every door."

"Only on the night you were there."

"Touché."

"So let me rephrase. How much would this annoy Paul Rowland?" I tipped my head at the jump drive.

Brian shrugged. "He wouldn't like it, but not because it's sensitive or anything. There's something about Annette that was hanging over Rowland's head. Everyone kind of knows it and he's extra-cranky about anything that has to do with her. Your mother had him by the short hairs somehow. But the interviews were pretty standard.

"Admittedly, his insistence on leaving the taps until the end was a little less typical. But after all of it was filed away in the end, there was nothing of special interest, except that last seventy-two minutes of music. So if he knew that you had heard this, it wouldn't really be a big thing. He'd just . . . Well, you'll see."

My soup arrived. I surprised myself and finished it all.

"You sure you've had enough to eat?" he asked, forking in the last bite of his omelet. "You should take advantage. I'm a stingy bastard. I almost never buy."

"I'm fine. Thank you." I finally took the memory stick from where it had been burning a hole in my concentration. "And thank you for this."

"You're welcome. I hope you—*enjoy* isn't the right word, is it? I hope it's a good thing. I hope it does something positive for you."

"I should get back." I stood up and offered my hand.

His palm slid over mine, a solid, earnest clasping. "I guess I'll see you around," he said.

"Do you think that's going to be necessary?"

A brief, wounded look rippled through his expression. "No, probably not."

My throat clenched, locking out the next breath. "Well then, take care." I meant it more than the generic crumb of etiquette that it was. But it rang flat from a voice that wouldn't cooperate, that didn't admit to being hurt over hurting him.

"You, too," he said.

The jump drive was warm in my hand, or more likely in my imagination.

Brian called out to me after a few steps, "And, Dee, maybe think a little kindlier of me after you listen to that?"

But I was still angry, and Brian Menary, in everything from his curly-topped height to his globe-trotting loafers, put a name and face to the all that seeded my acre of discontent. I came back to within whispering distance. "After listening to a conversation with my dying mother that you snuck into my house and taped without my knowledge?" I squinted at him. "Yeah, I'll try."

The trick of breathing while not giving over to crying was a painful struggle with the knot in my throat. I shut my office door and plugged the drive into my computer. The player launched and my mother leapt from the little speakers. She'd said plenty of words in her lifetime that I'd never heard, told a thousand stories I didn't know, but none at all for more than three years. I thought I'd never again hear her say something new.

This time machine took me back to the weeks when my heart was broken in a series, a run of healing over and then recracking each time I entered her room. Every day, she was weaker than the last, wavering, flickering. She wasn't going pale as much as she was lightening. She glowed with a terrible cold radiance in those last weeks, before the very end, as if her spirit would outpace the cancer and burn right through her. But at least she was still there.

Patrick was still there, too. I suppose that had been the best of us, such as it was when we were still holding out hope for our life together. It was the end of the middle, the last of the time we fed and watered the expectation that the other person would eventually become what we'd paid for with our youth and with our stubborn oaths.

And there she was—

. . . and those maniacs on two beat-up scooters, racing down the road, wrestling over that duffel with nothing in it but Pritchett's laundry. My mother laughed here, a rougher version of the harp-string sweep she'd had in health. Her laugh was possibly the most beautiful thing about her. On the surface it honored whatever was funny, but it was layered with wisdom, secret knowledge, and unknown connotations that made you want to pin her down and force her to tell you every-thing, to hold her captive until you understood the entire trill of it. As if you ever could. *Honestly, that no one died was almost a shame. A stunt that stupid should end in flames and flag-draped coffins.*

Brian laughed here. It was a jolt to hear and recognize it. It's not like our last conversations had been bubbling over with comedy.

Is Paul going to listen to these? she asked.

I don't know. I kind of doubt it. They're only going to run transcripts and just put them in at the end of the file.

"End of the file." I like that for a euphemism.

Oh, God! That sounded terrible! I—

My mother burst out laughing again. *It's fine. It's fine. I was trying to be funny. I'm so sorry. Please don't worry about it. Here's something for them to translate, just for Paul, from me to him, here at the end of the file.*

Presumably she shot the bird or made some other rude gesture, because Brian belted out another laugh.

But seriously, Brian, I want you to steer them away from Dee. I startled, a reflex at hearing my name in her voice again. *Make them leave her alone. She hates this stuff. She always has. She's trying so hard to have a normal life. Trying even too hard, maybe. But she'll figure that out. I don't know that she ever quite got over me leaving for so long when she was a teenager. I don't know that I ever got over it either. It was terrible timing on top of just being a terrible thing in general. Hey! That was the first time we met, you and I.*

Indeed it was, said Brian. *Not sure I ever got over that night myself. Talk about trial by fire, man.*

You were just a baby. Oh, God, the look on your face. You seemed barely older than Dee that night.

A different caliber of laughter from them both. Grimmer, and complicated with images they shared that I couldn't imagine.

My mother took up the thread again. *And I guess this will be the last time we meet, eh?*

I guess so. Is it corny if I say it's been a privilege?

Very corny, but don't let that stop you.

Well, it's been a privilege.

Thank you. And as such, you owe me, right?

Uh-oh. Let me get my wallet.

I just want this one favor. Remember me. And when you do, ease him away from my daughter. Distract him if and when it comes up again. I know it amuses Paul no end to imagine a stable full of Vesses at his command. He wants to know what I've put into their heads. He thinks he needs to control everything. He worries too much, but there's no telling him that. I'm used to it. I just can't stand the thought of him bending her, convincing her. She's so capable. She's so beautiful. She should be freer than me.

Some muffled rustling.

Brian said, *I'll be handling all the follow-up anyway. I'll see to it. No big deal. There's not that much more to cover. Or should I say not too long to cover it? He's got to retire soon, right?*

Please tell me you're not pointing out that I should have outlived Paul Rowland?

They both laughed on the recording and I seethed with a jolt of envy. My house. My mother. My benediction.

My mother sounded suddenly very tired. *It's funny, it seems you're supposed to have these aspirations for your children. You're almost an absentee parent if you don't try to put down a rail for them to ride, but from the moment she took her very first step, all I ever wanted to see was what she wanted to do. It fascinated me. It didn't matter what it was, only that it was what she chose next.*

I like that, Brian said.

Me, too. So get between them, if and when you can, Brian.

I will. You know I will.

Rustling . . .

Brian speaks again. *Okay, just one more set of questions on Cordriss and—*

The recording cuts out.

At home, Patrick asked me if I was feeling okay. I said I was. It was true if only in the sense that I had a pulse and my cholesterol was within the recommended guidelines. He suggested we go out for dinner. That was fine with me.

"You're just having soup?" he asked.

"I'm probably not even having that. I'm not really very hungry."

But I ended up eating all of it.

My mother lost her ring finger for love. She'd always said it was a gardening accident, but on the day she died, she told me the rest of the story. I had just been in to give her a dose of morphine.

"Leave the bottle, Plucky."

"What?"

She reached for me with her damaged hand, looking for all the world as if it were covered in gray paper. Her luminescence had receded in what felt like just a few hours. "It's time."

"No." I shook my head. "You haven't even complained once.

You're just having a bad day. Come on. Hang in there. Give this dose a chance to work and get some rest. It can't be that far yet."

She was still her, if only in her flashing eyes. The whites of them had gone yellow days earlier, but their beam was just as spearing as it ever had been. "And since when am I defined by what I choose *not* to say?"

"Since forever." I slumped next to her on the bed and finally took her proffered hand. I ran my index finger over the vacant knuckle ridges.

She flattened my hand next to hers on the bedspread. "I'm so used to it, it doesn't even look strange to me anymore."

"Me neither."

She told a version of the jailhouse brawl, and as it always did, it turned me eleven years old again, close to her and stoked proud to be sanctioned ready for a story, ready for a trust, even if the names had been changed to protect the innocent and the not so innocent. Or maybe they hadn't been. I'd never know. But now I knew that those parts didn't matter. They never had.

She touched the next knuckle. "And then my wedding band got caught up in the tiller blade."

"No, Mom, you lost that finger before I was born."

"I was married once before you were born."

"Huh? When was this? You said it was gardening."

"It was. Sort of. And like I said, this was all before you were born." She waved away the details. "It wasn't even in this country."

I propped up on my elbow. "What? Well, where was it? Who was this guy?"

She sighed. "Oh, Plucky, it's a long story and I don't have the energy. It was another life. Not a very good one, really, except for Ramon. I quit my work for a little while and we bought a farm."

"You on a farm?"

"Me in suburbia? Me in heaven? I'm me wherever I go, aren't I?"

I couldn't disagree. "Go on."

"There was an accident. One of the hired men started up this rattletrap old tiller we had, but he didn't look first to make sure that my husband was clear of it. He wasn't. He'd stumbled. I was coming across the field when it happened. When I got there, they were cursing and screaming at each other, but not getting very far by way of stopping the tiller from chewing right through his leg. He was bleeding all over everything. They finally stopped the blades, but by then, my man and the machine were more or less all one thing. We realized we were going to have to reverse the blades before we could pull him out."

She stopped, winded. The rest of the story slipped out on a whisper, fast and pained. It was the first time she'd let me see how much it had worn through her reserves.

"So the hired man set the switch and eased the power back on, and I reached in to pull Ramon free. One of the blades nicked my finger and almost glanced off, but it snagged on the edge of the wedding band. It happened so fast. The next blade came behind it and took the finger clean off."

"What happened to Ramon? What happened to the farm?"

"Ramon never even made it to the hospital. We got him into the truck, but he bled to death before we got to the main road. I cried for almost a year, then sold the farm, and came back to work for Paul again."

"That's awful."

"Yes. It was. But that's life sometimes, Dee. There's so much of everything if you last long enough. Some of it's lousy." She stroked my face. "But so much of it is amazing." She'd thrown a stone into my well, too. She studied my face to get a fix on my depth, but whatever echoed back only caused her to sigh and pat my hand. "You're going to want to have some stories to tell." She smiled and closed her eyes.

So my mother had run for normal once, too. An off-the-main-road kind of normal even, with trucks and farmhands and tools, and

Andrew Wyeth–style fields. Yet in the end, she went back to Paul and his coded directives. I would never have existed if she hadn't. She made a way for us, Simon and me, even without the usual brand of normal.

She'd had both kinds of life in multiple measures. More life, but never more than she could handle.

We were quiet for so long, I thought she'd fallen asleep. I was glad of it, stupidly hoping that a nap would let her feel better for a little while, that morphine dreams would distract her from her pain and delay the inevitable. Just for another day. Maybe two.

"Why don't you go out for a while? It'll be fine. Go get some air . . . maybe run some errands," she said with her eyes still closed.

"I want to stay."

She thought about it for a moment. "I'd like that. Put on some music for us, Plucky. Turn it up loud."

25

*O*nce *upon a time, there was a sandwich. . . .* Simon's text came in while I waited on Wednesday morning in the sticky-floored lounge of the auto-service center. His message interrupted me from sipping again from a cup of brown water purported to be coffee. It tasted awful, but I was restless and stubborn to pin down what was wrong with it. Ultimately, I was skeptical that they had used the right kind of beans. I tried to suss it out with tiny little tastes. Pinto beans maybe. Or limas. With food coloring dripped in to cover the mistake.

Can't, I typed. *The car died. I'm at the repair shop now.*

How about after work? Need to talk. His reply came so fast, I hadn't even set down my phone.

Ok. Quick one.

Earliest?

4?

Cool. See u there.

"Mrs. Aldrich?"

"That's me." *Sort of,* I thought.

"It's good news, bad news. Or maybe bad news, good news?"

"Isn't it always? I mean, I'm here, aren't I?"

"Yep. Because your serpentine belt gave it up. That's the bad news. But it won't take long to fix. That's the good-news part. If you can hang on for just a little bit, we'll have you under way shortly."

"The car was in here just a few days ago for inspection. Wouldn't you guys have seen that the serpentine thing was about to go?"

"Nah, those state requirements are mostly checking for lights and gauges and emissions and stuff."

"Okay."

"So we're good? You want me to fix it?"

"Yes. Thank you."

He turned back toward the service bays.

"Hang on," I called to him. A faint Klaxon wailed in my head, hitched to nothing specific. A random jolt of acid spiked my blood.

"Yeah?"

"How did it break? What happened to the belt?"

He shrugged. "They all go at some point. Most times it's just regular wear and tear. They get ragged after about seventy-five thousand miles or so. Lemme see." He checked the paper on his clipboard. "Yeah, it's a little early maybe, but not by too much. It happens. It was probably just a little defective from the factory. One little nick and it'll wear through sooner than later."

"Could it have been dangerous?"

"What, losing the belt?"

"Yeah. I was just pulling into the parking deck at work, but what if it had snapped while I was going fast on the highway or in a curve or something?"

"I doubt it would have been a huge deal. I mean, like you saw, you'd lose power steering and then it's like driving a whale through fudge. You might have caused a little traffic jam trying to get over, and of course you'd be stranded, but you wouldn't burst into flames or anything."

"Okay."

"So we're good to go?"

"Yeah. Thanks."

What in the ever-loving hell was that about?

But I knew very well what it was—and what it was, was a far cry from common sense. Just no. I scolded my overtaxed brain for torturing a manufactured if-then scenario to the point that I'd just pictured my husband, odd as he'd been lately, sawing through the guts of my car. I was exhausted. And I was ridiculous. There were ways to sabotage a car into real trouble. What good would it do for him to force an arbitrary breakdown?

You don't have to know the end of a story to know it's a sad one. Thanks, Mother. I'll take it from here, if you don't mind.

I watched the clock and my own wandering thoughts.

"Okay, don't be mad, Sissy."

I was a little early to Carver Street and Simon was a little bit late, but I could tell he wasn't apologizing for tardiness.

"Tell me you didn't just say that. What have you done now?"

He hadn't pried into Carlisle Inc. He'd followed the letter of my request, but not the spirit of it. Instead, he had followed Patrick.

"That crack you made about me blowing up your self-respect really got to me. I don't want to be able to hurt you like that. I'm your brother and I should be able to tell you things. If I can't say what's on my mind and if everything's gotten out of hand to the point where me just telling the truth as I see it is so painful for you to hear, then something is fundamentally flawed.

"I'm not telling you what to do. And I love you and stand by you and promise to let you handle it any way you want to handle it—just like you asked me to. But let's all be talking about the same 'it' that needs handling, okay?"

"What is it? Say it, for God's sake." My heart was pounding, every thought and nerve poised to recoil from what I thought he would tell me, to what the longest reach of my imagination had suggested to me earlier in the day when I'd learned of the damage to the belt in my car's engine. "Simon, what? What did you find?"

"He's fooling around again. For real this time."

I deflated and rolled my eyes. "Okay."

"You are the weirdest woman I ever met. Why doesn't that make you angry?"

"I'm angry."

"But you're not, though. It's like Patrick is just fucking around with your abacus, or your pots and pans or something. It's like he messed up your Rubik's Cube, not your heart."

"Can I ask you what you know about it, Simon? I mean, here we go again. I'm not trying to be hateful here, but what do you know about it? Have you ever even had a girlfriend for more than six months?"

"That's not the point—"

"No, except that it *is* kind of part of the point. Even though you don't want it to be. You keep judging me and you've never even been in a long-term relationship. Ever. Are you too cool for school, Simon? What's your deal?"

"This isn't about me."

"Right. Because that would be uncomfortable."

"You're twisting this around."

"I know I am. It's not an accident. It's because this is too easy for you. And it's pissing me off. You're looking down from some sort of ivory tower, but it doesn't make any sense. Why are you so far above it all? Why won't *you* let anybody in, huh? Maybe afraid you won't get it right either? At least I tried, pitiful as it may have turned out."

"My job makes it difficult."

"You're a cop, Simon, not a priest."

"So, because I don't have a girlfriend, I'm not allowed to have an opinion?"

"Way to miss the point."

"I didn't miss it, though," Simon countered. "I got it. I know you're upset. And I know it has to hurt. I just want to help."

"Do you think that maybe I might be able to stay upright in my seat because you didn't tell me anything I didn't already know? *I told you*, remember? You only went looking because I said that he was probably messing around. So I'm sorry I didn't fall apart like you were looking forward to."

"Okay, now that's just stupid."

"Look, I don't mind you following Patrick. I really don't. I know you were just looking out for me. And I don't mind you telling me about it either. I know it's awkward, and I know it isn't fun. Okay, maybe it's a little bit fun for you, because you never liked him in the first place, but I don't resent you for that either. Not for any of it. Just don't script out how I'm supposed to react, all right?"

"Fair enough. But let me just ask—do you love him? Do you really love him? Because I can shut up and deal with it if you do. I don't have to understand it. Maybe you're right. Maybe I'd be different if there was true love in my history. Maybe—"

"You're not allowed to ask me that question."

"What?"

I had hurt him with that one. No matter everything I'd said on the subject and no matter how well I'd swiveled the gotcha-gun around in his hand tonight, I hadn't shut the door on him like that before. Not that he'd known anyway. I put my hand on his arm. "And what can you tell about the situation if I answer you with that?"

He read my face until he understood. "Hot damn. You're all done."

"I still don't know what I'm going to do yet. You have to give me some space on this."

"I'll let it alone. I promise. But will you look at the video I shot? Maybe it will help you decide how to play it."

"Oh, God. I don't think I can."

"No, it's not like that." Simon took out his phone.

She was a real estate agent, Simon had discovered. I remembered seeing her once, from across the room, at a Chamber of Commerce function I'd attended with Patrick. Simon told me she worked mostly in furnished rentals, which, I could well imagine, had afforded them plenty of rendezvous points in these last few weeks that were somehow slightly less seedy than the rank motels at the edge of town, and a convenient way around generating any receipts as well.

Tracking them wasn't difficult for Simon. The video images were more or less tame, except in their warmth and natural grace. I wasn't jealous of the usual thing. She wasn't taking my toys. He wasn't out playing the stud. I just didn't know that Patrick and I had ever looked like that.

Despite my mangled opinion of Patrick, I had to clamp down on a frantic place in my mind, an unwieldy switch that needed to be thrown to keep me in my seat when I saw the tiny, but clear, image of their heads bent together over the center armrest, nuzzling at the stoplights.

This was my replacement, or more like the new and improved model, if I was honest. What he'd always wanted. Hell, what I always wanted, too. I imagined her as every good thing that I was not, and it wasn't difficult at all to picture him there beside her, biding his time until it was legal. What I couldn't see was what route he'd take to get to happily ever after: the rocky, open road or the shortcut through the darker, more treacherous woods.

I was amazed that Patrick could sleep with the riot blaring in my head. That none of the clanging rang out of my skull into the dead quiet of our bedroom was hard to believe. I'd managed all through the next day, getting Thursday morning done on two cups of coffee and the last vitamin C tablet in the bottle and took the evening on two vodka tonics and an aspirin, somehow speaking when spoken to and not drilling holes straight through him as I stared at his face, searching his expression for some hint as to how he pictured the end of us. I needed a sign that what he had planned for me on Saturday morning would or would not make any plans for Sunday completely moot.

When had I lost faith in the simplest conclusion, the comforting resignation to the most normal outcome? It was still likely only divorce papers. Hell, maybe the bald guy in the blue sedan had snapped pictures of my meetings with Brian. Maybe from a certain angle, with me constantly blushing at the tabletop the way I had, it looked less innocent than it was. Could be that I was about to find myself tipped over with adultery allegations. That would be rich, to be sure, but it would make nonviolent, noncriminal, nonpermanent sense. If Patrick had pictures and he thought I didn't, maybe he had a plan to beat me to the jump, which should include half my mother's inheritance. Or would it?

Round and round I chased my tail, at turns veering off to thoughts of my mother's taped interview and how I wasn't living up to her opinion of me. She had thought I was capable. She had thought I was freer than her. But I couldn't even manage to conclude whether my own husband might be plotting to have me killed. I was vaguely wary of my car, and I'd all but burgled my own house, but I had only got as far as finalizing my mistrust of Patrick's extraspecial tidiness and his newfound respect for insurance.

After back-to-back sleepless nights, following weeks of iffy rest to begin with, my edge was bound to be dull. My worship of clean, simple reasoning wasn't the only toppling god. I felt unreliably paranoid, and terribly rusty in the instinct. I wasn't going to be getting any smarter, that was for sure.

As Thursday night rolled into Friday's dawn, I had to concede the inevitability of the next step. If I was going to do anything to spoil the surprise, today was all that stood between us and Saturday morning, whatever that would bring.

There was still one thing he couldn't sanitize, and that was his mistress's face.

26

After all that had happened, I knew now that the hook that lashes the mind to the heart is flimsier than I would have guessed back at the beginning when I was plotting and planning my life to the fine details. My decision to stay with Patrick had not been nearly the same as an imperative to do so. The attachment I'd felt to this illusion of obligation was voluntary. It could be unhitched in an instant, with only the will to make it happen.

Just having faith that it's so easy; simply believing that all it takes is a small adjustment of mind-set, nothing but a quick trick of resolution to let it all go—that's the only thing that keeps the majority of us on the far side of this freedom.

Once faith becomes knowledge, all it takes is a little practice. I'd had plenty.

I'd only ever seen Christine Ames from a distance. She was much prettier up close. Beautiful even. Wide-eyed terror only made her more so.

I stood in her office doorway, dressed in my best suit and matching poker face. "Hello, Ms. Ames. May I speak with you?"

In less than two minutes she was shuddering her shame into her cupped hands, streams of mascara raking black tracks down her flushed face. Annoyingly, she was still lovely. She would have told me everything, in lurid detail, if I hadn't stopped her from pelting through a heartfelt confession. Once I realized she was desperately and genuinely in love with Patrick, I wasn't sure I could sit through the broken play-by-play of her remorse. She wasn't a terrible person. If there was any sort of plot against me, she was completely ignorant of it. In fact, it seemed Patrick had represented me quite kindly to her.

A tickling fear of having been wrong about everything (or right about everything in the times I'd felt stupid for it) crept up my spine again. My head ached with the noise of frantically retallying my "facts" to the point I nearly missed out on the only key she had to my mystery.

"I'm sorry, what did you just say?"

She was hiccuping now, and her nose had finally puffed up. "When?"

"You just said that you only call him now on his *other* cell phone since he told you to. He has two phones?"

She nodded her guilt-heavy head, unable to meet my eyes.

"How long has this been going on? When did he ask you to use the other number?"

"Maybe almost two months ago. Something like that. I'm so-o-o so-or-ry." Fresh, bouncing sobs gave the last words too many syllables. I forced my eyes not to roll. I held my tongue between my teeth to keep from telling her that I didn't care nearly as much as she thought I should.

Instead, I was the Goddess of Patience, the Pardon Fairy, somehow someone who was comfortable patting her husband's mistress on her pitiful, shaking shoulders.

"Christine, please. I know this is horrible for you, but believe me when I tell you—I don't hate you. These things happen. I know you didn't do this to hurt me."

She looked up; the hope for absolution, and maybe even the fear of it, pulled a trembly smile on her lips.

"I only need two things from you. I have to sort out a few is-
sues, a couple of important things with Patrick. If you can do these
two favors for me, and once I've talked to him, I won't stand in
your way. I promise. I'm okay. Or I will be. Really. It's going to
be all right. It's plain you love him. If he feels the same way about
you . . ." I finished with a sympathetic shrug.

Her nose ran and her chin quivered. "What do you want me
to do?"

She would have agreed to whatever I asked, but the ghost of any
vengeful feelings of mine had faded away in the face of her sorrow.
I almost regretted that I was likely only to make it worse in the days
to come if what I suspected proved true. Of course he would have
said nice things about me. Her eyes dazzled pure sunshine on blue
water when Patrick was the hero. He'd never risk her sweetness. In
her company, he wouldn't say shit if he had mouthful of it.

In the end, she gave me Patrick's alternate cell phone number
and promised to play ill, avoiding him and not taking his calls until
I contacted her again.

I caught my reflection in a gilt-framed mirror on my way out
of the building. I hadn't felt the look of purpose rearrange my fea-
tures, and I'd missed the moment when my eyebrow had cocked a
gleam into my eye. The calm I felt now fit the new look too well.
The sting of surprise was what seemed out of place. I should have
known this creature in the mirror. I should have felt her coming
all along.

By my own invitation, perpetual déjà vu had slowed time and
sharpened my senses. This clarity and detachment made me feel like
someone else, but sure as lies in church, it was someone jarringly
familiar.

I turned away from my mother's daughter in the mirror. But I
took her with me.

•   •   •

It was hardly a surprise that a quick Internet query showed that Patrick's second phone number traced back to Carlisle Inc. The listing
saved me further typing by providing the address and a handy map
link as well.

27

My mother had a prescribed method for doing almost anything. There was a right way to research a science project and a right way to make a bed. She schooled us in the order of operations to best compose a photograph, and she showed us the proper technique to prune a rosebush. She was less dedicated to securing our undying loyalty to her way of doing things than she was interested in our mastery of her techniques—for just at least one go-around. She taught us her model of everything.

Just once, do it her way, and she'd rarely mention it again.

Except for the problem of mull, which included its cousins: sulk and fret. If we had got into trouble or fell broody over anything—be it unrequited love, or how much we wanted a car, or how worried we were over an upcoming exam, or how annoyed a brother might be at a sister (or vice versa)—there was always only one way to handle it. Even when we were little, the process was ever the same, except it would be with her alongside, hand in hand, for the routine.

"To the dock with you," she'd say, rain or shine.

Our neighborhood bordered a small, muddy-banked lake that was too cold for swimming and too tight for growing fish big enough for people to eat. The dock was more for show than anything else, a long, silvery arm into the water that made a nice focal point against the backdrop of fall foliage or winter freezes. In spring and summer it was a pleasant halfway point for a stroll. Sometimes herons decorated the end posts, motionless until a bird-size dinner swam by.

The command would actually be "To the dock with you. 'Feliz Navidad.'"

"Mama, it's August."

"Sing it anyway."

The remedy consisted of a walk to the dock, thinking only of the problem at hand. We had been trained to take this walk in a strict meditation on whatever troubled us. No woolgathering allowed. Eyes on the path, mind on the worry. Nothing else, all the way to the end of the dock. Then the song, which was almost always something ridiculous and never had anything, by design, to do with the problem. It was to be sung to the lake. I tended to only hum the songs, as if I were somehow getting one over on my mother if I didn't belt it out with jazz hands. I never skipped the step, though. I lived in superstition of ruining the spell. I didn't step on cracks or walk under ladders either, even though my mother-stoked store of *You know better* told me it was all nonsense.

The cure wrapped up with a riddle for the walk home. My mother wrote down riddles on strips of paper and rolled them into an old film canister. The little plastic cylinder snugged in just right at the joint of the dock's skirting and last pylon. I always stirred the hole first with a length of reed grass to rout out the daddy longlegs that liked to hunker down next to our stash of brain teasers.

At journey's end, back in the kitchen or tucked up in the den or on the cool concrete of the front step with the firefly channel winking into the gloom, we talked out the riddle first, then the problem with its resolution or its next step, or sometimes its uncanny dissolution under scrutiny.

Psychology courses in college had made for easy dissection of my mother's dock exercise, but even knowing why it worked couldn't wring the mystery from her greatest construct. When you did it as she had taught us to do it, it felt like voodoo.

I left Christine Ames and drove back home. Not to my house, but home to where I'd learned to unpack a problem properly.

The house was painted a creamy off-white now. It had been a light gray-blue when we'd lived there. The current owners had added heavy-hinged, stained-wood shutters to the façade. It looked good, and I was somehow glad to see how much it didn't look like my house anymore, or her house either. She was, we were, free of it all. Being there now was devotion, not obligation.

I parked in the empty cul-de-sac and went for the anti-loiter, purposeful-looking stride, straight for the lake. At ten in the misty morning wearing a business suit, it was already a strange thing to do, to be walking the squelchy trail in Dry Clean Only. It wouldn't do to look unsure of myself. I assigned myself the song—"Bus Stop," by the Hollies.

In the meantime, though, there was the walk and the think.

I chewed the details of the past few weeks, mindful of finding bones. Hopeful of it even. There weren't any, so my conclusions remained mushy. But either way, at the end of the dock, it was time to let it go. I felt as absurd as I ever had, with my antique pop song and my stage of weathered wood and the audience of trees and tiny fish. I hummed.

I pulled up a thin reed and stirred away a crumpled leaf from the hidey-hole only out of respect for the entirety of the ritual. We'd taken away the trove of riddles when Simon went off to school. Surprise flashed up my arm when the reed bent straightaway against something solid. My hands shook as I jimmied out the little black cylinder, an old 35 mm film canister. Inside, a strip of curled, crispy paper:

What belongs to you but others use it more than you do?

It wasn't my mother's handwriting. On the other side of the paper was a smiley face and *Hi, Sissy.*

"Damnit, Simon." I'd had to use the voice command to dial him because the shaking in my hands made the numbers on the keypad too small by half.

"Hey! Double damnit to you, Dee." Simon laughed.

"The answer is your name."

"The answer is Simon Vess?"

"No."

"The answer is Simon Garrett Vess? I thought the answer was always forty-two."

"No! It's what belongs to you that others use more than you do."

The line went quiet to the point I suspected I'd lost the signal. I was just pulling the phone away to look to see that we were still connected when I heard him again.

"You're at the dock?"

"Yeah, real funny, you little asshole. You scared me to death with that. I thought I was going crazy."

"Dee, why are you out there? You acted fine the other night, but you're really upset about that woman, aren't you? I didn't mean to make it worse."

"I'm okay."

"Oh, yeah? Sounds like it."

"Bite me."

"Okay. So anyway, once upon a time, a brother and a sister had some lunch if she wasn't sick of him. . . . Come on. Last time sucked. Let's do it better. You've got to eat, right? My treat, to make up for the riddle. And for the other night."

I sighed. "You're not working?"

"Nope. Got the day off."

"Me, too."

"So, half hour? Be there or be square?"

"I guess."

• • •

A vodka cranberry sat waiting for me on the bar in front of my seat. Simon was into rum and Coke these days and this day, too.

"I see lunch is poured," I said.

"It sounds like it's been that kind of day again."

"As you well know, it's been that kind of week. That kind of month, really."

"You look spiffy for a day off." Simon flicked the cuff of my jacket's sleeve.

"Thank you. I had an appointment."

"Want to talk about it?"

"Not at the moment."

"I'm sorry about the riddle. I didn't think it would freak you out so bad."

"How would finding a riddle there, just like my dead mother used to do, not freak me out?"

"I put it there ages ago. I just wanted to know if you ever went out there."

"Do you go out there?" I asked.

"I have. Obviously."

"Well, were you disappointed I hadn't thought to leave you any riddles?"

He laughed. "Kinda."

I didn't laugh. "Do you have any idea how dismal it is to have everybody wishing I was her?"

"Now, that's not what I meant. Come on, Dee. That's not fair."

"Oh, it's not just you. You're in some fine company. My husband wishes I was her. And Br—"—I pulled a hand-brake turn on my tongue. I didn't want to talk about Brian with Simon. Not yet, anyway—"that brainwashing bastard Paul Rowland."

Simon startled at my babbling. "Why do you think Paul wants you to be like Mom?"

"Oh, he's always making the comparison. You know how he is. She said he'd probably try to get me to come work with him at some point. With *them*, whoever *they* are. Does he try to get to you, too?"

"No. Has he been around recently?"

"No," I glowered into my drink. "Not since the money thing. I'm just pissed off in general. Don't worry about it. I didn't mean to bring him up. Sorry. No use the both of us being in a bad mood."

Our chatter drifted, but Simon kept steering back to Christine Ames and to what he presumed was bothering me. I bumpered the truth and told him stories of Patrick's and my recent squabbles, including an edited version of Angela's wrath. Simon was dutifully, brotherly indignant on my behalf.

"So, what was with the car, then? The plate I ran. Carlisle Inc.?"

"It's nothing." Shit. I'd said it too quickly. I could practically watch the antennae extend from Simon. The idea of seeing Carlisle Inc. for myself had been throbbing in my mind, ramping up its boom all morning. It was the gift of the dock walk, the answer it gave. I knew where to go next.

"Dee?"

"Simon."

"Does she have some connection to Carlisle?"

"Who?"

"Who? Seriously? The fucking tooth fairy. Or maybe this Angela or Christine? Are you being dense on purpose?"

"No. It's nothing," I said.

"I don't like this. You always talk to me. We talk. That's what we do. Now there's this wall that I can only knock holes in by sneaking around behind your back. What is going on?"

"Nothing. You promised you'd leave it alone and you've already played Twister all over that one."

"And you promised you'd bring me in if you needed help."

"I have not broken that promise."

"Dee."

"I haven't."

He got up from his barstool. "I'm gonna hit the head. But we're going to have this out when I get back." He winked at the bartender and said, "Don't let her leave," and headed to the back of the restaurant.

I had minutes, at best. And I knew what I wanted now. The want bordered on a need. Before I made a fool of myself and took this any further with Simon, I had one more errand to run. I wasn't going in half cocked on this. Whatever shred of pride I had left, whatever could loosely have been dubbed *capable* in me was already hanging by a thread.

The first part of the last part of my quest involved neutralizing my brother so that I could take the leap I needed in peace. Then I would know what was going on and what to do with it and when to involve SuperSimon.

I pulled a $50 bill from my wallet and waved the bartender over. I slid the bill across the wood.

"I need a favor."

She took a step back, hands raised. "Oh, boy."

"No, it's nothing bad. Nothing you'll regret. I promise."

She had a skeptic's eyebrow. Or maybe just an experienced bartender's.

"No really. See that bottle of Grey Goose? It's almost empty. I'd like you to fill it halfway, right now—and very quickly—with plain tap water. When that guy comes back, we're going to start drinking for real. He's on rum and Cokes, but I want you to make all of my drinks from that bottle of mostly water."

I got only a hard squint in answer and took a chance. She was wearing both a crucifix and a medal of St. Amandus, the patron saint of bartenders. A showy Catholic with at least some sense of humor, hopefully from a big, devout, pain-in-the-ass family.

"He's my brother and I need to get something done today without his brotherly interference. You got brothers?"

She sneered but not without affection. "Yeah. Three."

"Okay, so you know what I'm talking about. You don't even have to worry. I'll get him home in a taxi, safe and sound. I love him, but he's a pain. And right now I need him to go home and go to sleep."

"Okay." She shrugged. "It's your fifty."

"What's your name?"

"Yolanda."

"Yolanda, you're my hero."

Simon returned with his serious face on.

"You've got the whole day off?" I said before he could start in on me.

"Yep."

"Then I want to get shit-faced. I'll tell you all my sorrows if you'll drown them with me. I've been trying to do the stiff-upper-lip thing. But I feel like hell."

So we drank, and I played it. I could feel the bartender watching my performance and hoped that Simon didn't notice her attention. I cried a little. I waited until the fourth drink so he'd believe it, confessing that I thought Patrick was going to serve papers on me soon. I made much of my humiliation over Simon's discovery until he swore and slurred that he was sorry and that I wasn't a wimp, that I was "the srongesss woman since Ma." Which was, of course, ridiculous even by drunk measure.

By his foggy seventh drink he was the one shushing me down from singing at the bar. The concerned glower from Yolanda, our drink-pouring new best friend, was as good as an Oscar award to me. I'd almost convinced her that I was drunk on watered-down cranberry juice, and she had been in on the whole thing from the beginning. I bit down on the corner of the sober smile that tried to curl my lip out of character.

We had one for the road (of course we did), and I primly righted myself and, giggling, asked Yolanda to call us a taxi.

"You okay for the ride?" I said to Simon. "You're not gonna puke in my lap, are ya?"

I heard the driver's neck bones pop as he craned his head back to take stock of us. Pitiful midday lushes, his sad eyes summed it up.

"Nah. I got iss," said Simon.

We rolled along, the both of us swaying and overcorrecting through the turns. It was like a dance. Simon led, I followed.

"I'll kick his ass. I really will." Simon's liver was extremely unhappy with my husband.

"What are you gonna do, bury him in parking tickets?"

"Parking tickets? Pfffft. Oh, no—s'not cop trouble I'm talkin' about." Simon's head rocked in a loose nod that was trying for wise, but only looked likely to send him to the chiropractor after his hangover let him get out of bed. "He'll be begging for cop trouble if I ever set my real sights on him. You don' know, Sissy, how good I've been. I do what I'm supposed to, but oooohh, man. Oh, man. If I could do what I *can* do . . ."

"Okay, baby badass. I mean baby brother."

His beautiful sincerity shrugged out of the sopping booze blanket for just long enough to make the simple point he'd wanted to convey all afternoon. Or even before that, ages ago, way back when he left the riddle for me at the dock, and even when he'd pried into my business by following Patrick. "I don't want him to hurt you. I want you to be happy. You should be happy. Ma wanted you to be happy."

"I know, Simon. And I promise you, again, I know where to go for help. I know you're there for me. I always have." I patted his hand and the haze refilled his eyes.

I watched him spill out of the taxi and stagger up the steps to his plain, low rancher.

"Where to now, miss?" said the driver, watching me carefully for tears or nausea.

I blew out a deep breath, shook off the stage show I'd been playing, and found the driver's eyes in the rearview mirror. His confusion set in before I'd even spoken.

"Hello." I smiled. "Sorry about all that. Everything's fine. I need to get something from my house first, and then take me back to my car at the pub, if you don't mind."

28

Friday

Time to go. I twist the key and the car rumbles awake. The last bend before Carlisle is just ahead. Foot to the pedal. Please let me not come back this way bewildered.

Carlisle Inc. is a sloppy compound made up of dusty assembly yards under mammoth scaffolds dripping with hoists and pulleys, the whole complex worked around clusters of the cheap aluminum dome sheds that the company makes for its customers. As Friday's business hours wind down, a mild commotion of people, cars, and work trucks buzz over the worn tracks that lay out a winding maze through the site. A pleasantly warm sun is westering over the end of this workweek, and the promise of a weekend that's made out of all the same loveliness looks as if it's motivating everyone to keep one eye on the clock and the other on what needs doing in order to punch that clock on time.

The few glances that could mark my approach have slid right off my car as if it isn't there. I feel invisible in a very pointed lack of curiosity. Either slippery ignorance is a job requirement here at Carlisle, or no one wants to acknowledge my presence for fear that it might pull them off the fast track to Friday's happy hour.

Cars are haphazardly parked in the grassless spaces between the buildings, but the blue sedan I was hoping to see is fortunately easy to find. It's all alone and deep in the shaded alley alongside what looks to be the main office.

I slide the gearshift to Park. Then eyes closed, deep breath. I don't get even a full minute before the door of the office opens up and two men step out onto the concrete apron. They're talking, nodding over a clipboard in the bright, lowering sun, and they wrap up their business with a handshake.

The bald one on the left looks very much as if he could be my guy, but I've only ever seen him at a distance and, even then, only sitting in the car. But once they separate, Baldy veers off toward the left side of the shed in the direction of the blue car. With that, I have as close to an answer as I'm going to get.

My available options make their arguments. I could follow him, although getting out of the compound discreetly behind his car now would be something of a trick. He would almost certainly know I was there. Getting it wrong and setting him on high alert would surely undo any progress I've made.

I could play a ruse—hunker down and let him go on about his business, then bluff my way into a conversation with his buddies and hope that Friday's secondhand information will be enough to tilt Saturday out of the crosshairs. Weak.

He's slid in behind the steering wheel of the blue car and I'm here at the decision. Move or don't. You have two seconds to make up your mind. Heaven help me, *Mother help me,* I get out from behind the wheel of my own car before he can leave.

I don't have a plan, which is probably a good thing. She always said that plans were for professionals and that people who didn't know what they were doing only fouled them up. So I scrub my mind a determined blank and leave the engine running, and the driver's door wide-open. I pace off the distance to the other car in long, steady, Annette-Vess-style strides.

I wait to draw the gun from my bag until the shade of the building unsquints my eyes.

Baldy is just reaching for his seat belt when I draw even with his rolled-down window. He turns his unconcerned face up to me, no doubt expecting his colleague for a follow-up last word. What he gets instead is the barrel of my gun pressed into his forehead.

"Don't move."

He moves, but to his credit, only to raise his hands, palms out, above his shoulders.

"Do you know me?"

The answer dawns across his face before I even finish the question. He swallows hard and gives a redundant nod.

"What's your name?"

"Jim."

I push the gun a fraction closer to Jim's skull, whitening the skin in a halo around the muzzle. "Well, Jim, I have never yet killed a man who told me what I needed to know."

He searches my eyes and finds no lie there. "Are you wearing a wire?" His color is coming back.

"I'm holding a gun to your head. How likely is that? Now, how do you know me?"

I get the sense that his line of work has given Jim a certain fatalistic resignation in the face of disaster. He sighs. "Obviously, you already know."

I press the gun harder into his head and Jim winces.

"Okay, okay. Your husband has hired us—more specifically me—to have you killed."

My lungs shut down, the bellows simply refusing to fan full or fold up. There's enough air in me for another question, maybe two. Beyond that, I'm not sure how I'm going to reboot the next breath.

"Tomorrow morning?"

"That was the plan." It's derailing how much sympathy and matter-of-fact detachment Jim can telegraph at the same time from deep down in his sad brown eyes.

My own eyes tear up. But it's from lack of blinking, not sadness. I'm not devastated yet. I'm barely anything at all, only stiff, brittle, and so cold. A great reservoir of reaction is frozen beyond my reach. I can feel it like sap in a tree waiting for its time.

"Why did I see you at my house a few weeks ago?" My voice falls quiet, but I haven't turned the volume down consciously. The idea itself isn't loud. It whispers. I just remember being in my drive-way, unconcerned on a beautiful morning, shielding my eyes against the same sun that warmed my body through the comfy cotton robe that I know is hanging right now on its hook in my closet. No, the idea that I almost didn't have this day isn't loud. It's low and cold. "Were you there to—to do it?"

"No."

"Then why were you?"

"We'd given him a phone when we'd started the deal. He was waffling. I'd come to see why he wasn't communicating reliably and collect it, if necessary. He decided to keep it. Obviously."

"And my car? The belt? Did you do that?"

"It was just one of several possible alternatives. Plan Bs and all."

It's what I had expected to hear, but the blow knocks my heart out of rhythm and horror finally flits like icy-winged moths, bumping and thumping their heavy way through my middle. My hands and feet buzz with a charge that fizzes up my legs and down through both arms. My knees are thinking about letting go. My throat burns. My head, however, is still on the job. Sort of.

"Okay." I'm still stunned, but warming up. Life has returned with the first order to flee. I let the pistol drop against my thigh and turn for my own car.

People never do what you expect them to do. This was true for me and true, apparently, for Jim. My simply walking away was not in his playbook. "What?" His bewilderment borders on indignant. "That's it?"

I stop, zapped sane, and turn around again to face him. "You know what?" I stride back. "You're probably right." I raise the gun and shoot him, point-blank, behind the ear.

29

A paintball to the skull from an air pistol is rarely fatal. Well placed, it's good for a stun. I had been hoping for lights out, but no such luck. Jim never got a good look at the convincing replica before the sting. It had been one of Patrick's favorite sporty toys, and I had snagged it while my relieved and well-tipped cabdriver waited in my driveway a lifetime ago, or less than ninety minutes ago, maybe. It's all the same thing now.

Jim falls across the steering wheel, his hand wobbling for the back of his head, but losing its will or its way repeatedly as his senses waver.

Maybe I should wait to see if he'll fade out entirely, but the moaning is going to be a problem. I wince a quick look over each shoulder, turn the gun butt out so that I'm gripping the barrel, then sidle up to give my batting arm some room to swing.

My first stroke is less than committed. I couldn't look, so I'm not exactly sure where I clipped him. It has woken him up more than put him out. He yelps and that sets a match to my resolve. A confident thump delivered over the knot I'd already raised and Jim has the decency to go quiet. And limp.

In short order, he's gagged with his own socks and bound at the wrists by his belt. I trot back to my running car, kill the engine, and lock it up. I fetch some bungee tethers from the trunk and fortify my handiwork, securing Jim's ankles to finish the job. The shoving struggle to drag him over to the passenger side of his car leaves me trembling and sweaty, but he's still not come all the way around by the time we pull to the back end of the deserted wasteland behind the Carlisle Inc. compound.

I slam the gearshift back into place, pry the gag from Jim's mouth, and brace my back against the driver's door, foot poised to kick a hole into my new friend if he wakes up cross or noisy. As it is, he wakes up slowly and sweetly groggy. When his focus comes back online, I prod him with the toe of my shoe and level the paintball pistol at his face.

"Hiya. How much was I worth?"

"Excuse me?"

I toe-poke him again. "Don't do that. I'm not in the mood. How much was I worth?"

"Fifteen thousand."

"Well, now you work for me. I'll pay you fifteen thousand and twenty-five dollars."

"What?" He actually laughed.

"I'm sorry. Did you think I'd offer double? I'm not the one who knows what my socks taste like, now am I? How about this: I'll pay you fifteen thousand twenty-five dollars and *not* shoot you in the throat." I press the maw of the barrel into his neck. "Now who do you work for?"

"What do you want me to do?"

"I want you to call Patrick and get him over here. And then"—I shrugged—"do what you do."

"I can't kill him here."

"No?" I crane around to look out every window. Early on a Friday evening, the back margin of Carlisle Inc. might as well be the dark side of the moon. "It looks like a nice private place for someone to meet their end, don't you think?" I put the gun back in his face. "I think it's perfect, if you have the right incentive to improvise." His eyes cross and water as they skitter over the gun. I've no doubt that he has a crushing headache.

I hold the phone for Jim while he talks Patrick into a detour to Carlisle Inc. on his way home from work. I encourage Jim's cooperation with the muzzle of the paintball gun jammed firmly into his crotch.

I listen to the one-sided conversation, imagining my husband in his steel-and-glass office building on its carpet of crayon-bright sod, talking to his hired thug on the phone while he admires the fountained lake outside his office window, all blue and sparkling with reflected sky. How does he feel inside that jewel right now? Safe? Impatient? Did a cloud just pass over the sun where he was, canceling out some of the warmth from the air against his cheek? Did the room go suddenly dim in some cool warning that my hand rests right on the other side of the voice in his ear? Can he feel me as a cold spot in the place where he keeps his plan—am I already a ghost in the attic of his mind?

And how does he look to them today, the people who think they know him? Did he seem out of sorts on the day before he bought himself a $15,000 avalanche of sympathy and a wide-open vista of no-strings freedom?

When the call ends, I strangle the steering wheel to squeeze the shakes out of my hands. There is a terrible power in me, jousting with a gut-melting fear. I'm running out of time. The workday is winding down and Patrick will soon be out of his office and on his way to me. Jim is almost irrelevant, especially bound and gagged. But it wouldn't do for him to know just yet that I will never pay him, and also that I have no intention of letting him kill Patrick either.

A shallow grave or concrete shoes for my husband wouldn't make me feel any better, or any safer. It would simply be trading one problem for another. I want him in an orange jumpsuit and handcuffs. I want to catch his eye when they hand down his prison sentence. And the next step is the whole trick. Whatever it's going to be, I don't want this happening in our home, behind closed doors and drawn curtains the way everything else has been. But God forbid it should happen out on the front lawn in full view of everyone on our street. That's not normal.

Everything had gone sharp in the details and clear in the colors since I'd pulled my head out and looked at what my life truly was, not what I insisted that it should be. Everything I'd attempted in the last couple of days, from the search of my house, to the folding of my husband's mistress, to the dousing of my brother's interference, had worked like Swiss gears. *Thanks, Mama. But what now?* I've painted myself into a corner. I've assaulted and kidnapped the oddly neutral and very dangerous Jim, rendering myself a felon without a shred of proof against anyone else. Then I've invited the one person in the world who wants me dead out here to confront me in a now-deserted construction yard. Brilliant.

My brother would swing every hammer he had to break me out of this mess, but he is as far away as he can be, and by my own doing, deep in his rum dreams.

If it goes wrong, and I don't even have an idea of what "it" might entail yet, no one will ever know what happened to me. Patrick will probably pay Jim a hazardous-duty bonus and then cash in our Danube cruise or just reissue it in the name of some pretty, sweet woman who cries like a movie star, and I will never know how it all works out in the end.

Well, if I can't prevent it, then I can at least lengthen my reach. Be it alive or dead, I will not be caught without a say in what happens tomorrow, or in the days after, either.

I scrabble through the scraps of paper in my purse and find the card for Hoyle's Compounding Pharmacy & Alternative Medicine Center. I bite my lip and dial. The electronic operator asks me to enter a numeric message or wait for the tone to leave a voice record-ing.

Beep.

"Brian, it's Dee Vess." I drop Aldrich preemptively, but whether in premonition or resolve, I can't tell. "This is the part where I trust you"—I take a big deep breath—"but it's not going to make a lot of sense right now. I'm sorry for that. Maybe you get this kind of thing all the time. I don't know. You probably have a weird life. I'm sort of counting on it, to be honest.

"Anyway, my husband, Patrick, is coming out to a place called Carlisle Inc. He doesn't know I'm here. This is not a good thing. If I don't leave another message for you in the next two hours, please find a way to lead my brother to this place, he'll know where it is. Please help him to look into what happened." I chew the inside of my cheek and slide a look at the regagged Jim. "There's a guy with me named Jim who knows what's going on. He works here. But I don't have solid proof of anything, and I can't exactly speak to where he'll end up." Jim's eyebrows lift in interest.

I blow out the next breath and wonder if this is a time-limited recording. "I'm sorry to drag you into this. Whatever it is." I laugh, tickled in the absurdity of it all. "I can't imagine what the hell I'll say to try to explain all of this if I get to call you back. How un-Spider am I?" My finger hovers over the End button. "Thank you, though, for being out there, for having that weird life so that you can even take this call. I don't know that it's going to do any good, but it was at least nice to have a number to dial. I get it now."

I hit the call dead and wipe my eyes.

30

There was one of my mother's lessons I had never needed to revisit—until today. I'd manhandled Jim like a champ. I had put my hands on him with authority and no hesitation. I hadn't faltered when I felt the warm and unfamiliar bulk of his body, a stranger's body, sliding under his nylon jacket and twill trousers as I pulled and shoved him across the front seats. Even as I noted the slight, dewy catch of his bare skin where it crossed mine when I tied him, I didn't flinch away.

This was her guidance. This is what she had told me to do.

Simon had been an athlete from toddlerhood. Not of the all-star or Olympic-hopeful breed, but he knew innately how his body worked. He trusted his balance enviably and frolicked in the automatic calculations of his height and long reach. Our mother encouraged his bounce and dash and tamed it with sports lessons and strict rules in the house.

But my dexterity was mostly between the ears, and she never let me feel less for it.

Some people live here. She playfully pinched Simon's solid, little biceps. *And some people live up here.* Her hand coursed over the dome of my head. *The luckiest ones have a good balance of both, but it's always slanted at least a little bit one way or the other.*

When I didn't blossom under karate instruction, track and field, or tennis clinics, my mother found a way to stoke my strengths. My advantage was that I could talk myself into (or out of) almost any mind-set. My mother called it *self-possession* or *pluck* on the good days, and *a vacation on Planet Dee* in the times when it was less than admirable.

She, never in denial, used the world as it was, and our natures as they were, to train us. This was often at some odds to what we were learning elsewhere.

We're all taught, from preschool on up, to keep our hands to ourselves. We're flogged with the idea that it is not okay to touch other people. So the good guys mostly don't.

Civilization is a conflicted dance of cooperative intimacy and guarded personal space. We'll drive a bayonet into the enemy's guts, or put our hands, side by side, on a car's bumper to help push a stranded motorist out of a ditch, but still recoil from a fellow commuter's heat or even the errant brush of his arm on a crowded train.

The villains of the world aren't as confined by this inhibition. Someone else's neck isn't all that different from a doorknob for them. If it's an obstacle, they grab it and pull.

My mother coaxed from my tenacity this very trait, the stubborn ability to get past anything obvious, including the ingrained reluctance to put my hands, if need be, on someone I didn't know. She sent me swimming and steered me into lifeguarding at the YMCA. I took lessons until I was good enough to give lessons, and over the years I saved seven people from drowning.

I'd wrangled every age, gender, and body shape, nearly naked, in the water. The ease of the expertise never left me. In my time, I'd felt smooth, taut muscle under my hands, and aged flab, tired and almost weightless, as it sagged into my arms. I'd hauled grown men to safety and taught little kids to punch a panicked swimmer square in the face to subdue his thrashing.

On the day the topic of self-defense came up in our household, only a few weeks after my mother had returned from the Long Trip, the ambient air of the living room warmed and bristled.

Best-laid plans, Plucky—martial arts, role-playing exercises, defense drills. All those self-disciplines are good. They're good for confidence and fitness. They're good practice for feeling how your body moves in space. But the real world isn't choreographed. And reality has teeth and spikes in all the wrong places. The universe doesn't know what it can't do.

You have to know, baby, that I want you to fight. If you're ever in danger, fight like hell. But if you find that you can't for some reason, or if it goes wrong—a little or a lot wrong—I would never blame you. You're pre-forgiven for whatever doesn't work. Disappointing things happen, but you could never be a disappointment.

Across from where we sat, I looked at the patched hole in our foyer wall. Her eyes followed mine. The plasterers had been good at their job. The casual observer wouldn't have noticed the expertly feathered border of fresh drywall and paint, blending new over ruined old.

Besides, I'm not worried about you. She talked over my attention's drift to the wall and its forever untold story. *You know what to do, Dee. My lovely girl, you do it four times a week at the Y. You just pull them in close and save them from hurting you.*

No one had ever before tried to hurt me. I almost felt sorry for Jim. I'd jumped him before he'd got the chance.

Forty minutes later, a few deep breaths are the only preparation I'm going to get. I know what I *will* do once Patrick arrives, which is not even close to the same thing as knowing what I *should* do. I certainly can't call it a fully realized design certified for the best possible outcome.

I'm waiting and rehearsing. The roar of blood in my ears is a soaring music, scoring the scene I've planned out for Patrick and me. The symphonic ringing in my eardrums vies for authority over the doom-drumming of my heartbeat. And Jim's fussing is simply knee-capping the grandeur of the moment. I have already had to threaten him twice with the paintball gun to stop his squirming and mewling, but he's started it up again anyway. Maybe he has to pee.

"What?" I hook a finger under the tight gag and pry it out, dragging it partway down his chin.

Jim smacks and purses his lips to get them working again. The corners of his mouth are raw and glossy where the skin has rubbed down, and the left side has chafed all the way to bleeding a little. Why would I even feel a twinge at that? But I do. Please tell me there is not an *I'm sorry, Jim* anywhere in my script. I will turn this gun on my own eyeball if I'm that beatable. I swear I will.

Jim clears his throat. "I just thought you might want to consider the fact that all your husband is going to find when he gets here is a chained-up gate. The last of the crew will have locked it up when they left."

"What? Son of a bitch. Are you serious? We're locked in? And Patrick is locked out?"

"Look. This could be a blessing in disguise. Are you sure you want to go through with this?"

"Pffft. Did you double-check with Patrick when I was the target?"

"Of course I did. Many times."

"And that's supposed to give me the warm fuzzies?"

"I'm not in the business of warm fuzzies, but I only sell what a very few people are absolutely sure they want to buy."

"Great. They'll probably put that on your tombstone. What the hell am I going to do now?" I scan the horizon as if it might offer up an answer.

"I have a key."

"Well, why didn't you say so?"

"I hadn't gotten around to it. And speaking of, when are you going to untie me? I can't stink-eye him to death, and not to point out the obvious, but the job isn't going to get done with that." Jim nods at the paintball pistol. "You'll have to let me get my big-boy gun."

"We'll get to that." I let the elastic in the socks snap the knot back into place over his teeth.

He patiently planks himself, bracing rigid between the floorboards and the headrest while I wrestle his work keys from his pants' front pocket. My grand scenario doesn't include Patrick's driving up while I'm in mid-fiddle with the padlock on the gate. My heart pummels its pulse into my vision, banging out of rhythm in its suddenly too-tight slot under my sternum as I drive us back to the front gate. I shoot desperate looks down the dusty road. I need more time, whether he's coming right this second or not. I can hardly breathe.

I shake out the tangle on the key ring to find the right one. It sinks home on the first try, and the shank pops free without a protest. The tiny victory lets me take in a steady inhale and send it out through a smile. I feel better. I'll take every little sign that I should be here, in this place, right now, doing what I'm doing. I give a hard yank and the chain clatters through the wide mesh of the fence on the weight of the dangling padlock. I drag the gate wide and run for Jim's car.

Not more than a minute later, a faint dust cloud rises above the crest of the hill just ahead of Patrick's car sweeping into view around the ridge. I drive Jim's car a short way into the compound and stop it on a slant, slightly uphill from the entrance. The last of the molten light pours over us, hopefully dazzling away the specific details of Jim's front seat and how many passengers it holds, and what they look like.

I've figured out the difference between getting low and what would be getting too low. I can't risk drawing Patrick's notice. I need him feeling free to come close. I slouch down in the driver's seat to the least suspicious end of the scale. I motion Jim down lower than me.

I set the paintball gun once more into his crotch. "Now, Jim, I've changed my mind."

His eyes spark bright and worried.

"What I'm buying now is your silence. Same price. Not a peep from you. No matter what happens. Do you understand?"

He nods.

"This might not be a big-boy gun, but you can either be just a failure at killing me tomorrow or you can be a permanent failure at peeing standing up for the rest of your life. Not—a—sound. No matter what. Okay?"

I don't bother to read his face for compliance. I ready my phone in my hand and snug the gun deeper into the crook of Jim's legs. Patrick pulls up close to Jim's car. I hit the Call button and immediately mute the speaker when a woman answers. "Please just listen," I say into the silenced phone, praying for an ally on the other end of the line. "Don't hang up. I only have one chance. Please stay with me. This isn't a joke." I check the icon. The call is still live, the timer rolling off the seconds since I've added her to my team. With the speaker off, I can't hear her reply. But Patrick won't be able to hear her either, if he ever gets out of the car. I have to make him talk, and it has to be over here. Please let him be loud enough.

I wait in Jim's car. Patrick waits in his. The palms of my hands are tingling, and restless needles dance over the back of my neck.

Patrick finally gets out of the car, squinting into the sun. I let him come on.

"Here he comes," I say to Jim, and also to our other silent partner, still waiting, the timer marking the seconds on the phone. One step. Two steps. Three. Then I loosen the reins off my twitching foot. The tires of Jim's borrowed sedan churn up a fog of orange dust as I wheel the car around to block the open path behind Pat's parking job. I clamp my hand down over my purse to keep it and my phone from launching into the footwell. I stop behind Patrick's car, blocking the easy path back to the gate. I buzz down the window.

He gapes at the roar and dust of the gambit, Jim's blue sedan now freshly spun around behind him, but Patrick's expression fades to loose, blank confusion at seeing me behind the wheel instead of its usual driver.

"Jim's over here." I tick my head to the right.

"What the hell? How did . . ."

We stare at each other and the weight of the day rams the foundations of my detachment. I see Patrick, the boy at the front of the class, now thinned and changed under almost fifteen years of too much I haven't known. Until it was too late, I hadn't known on purpose, and it's left me stranded here in this impossible moment, trembling between a long-ago transformed man who wants me dead, and an indifferent man who would have done it without cringing for a cut of my mother's money.

My voice whispers over my suddenly dry tongue. "Why?"

I follow Patrick's gaze as it drifts beyond me. Jim's eyes flash bright warnings at Patrick, while Patrick scans the pathetic state of his hired murderer. "Why is he all green?"

"Pat . . ."

He flinches, and his attention scalds back onto me. His mouth works for some time, his jaw grinding side to side before he speaks. "You don't know anything, Dee."

"Well *he* certainly does," I shout. "A hit man? Really? What movie do you live in? Who does that?"

Jim's bound legs twitch in the footwell, his eyes bulging from his red face.

"The money's all legit. There's paperwork. I'm careful. There's nothing to be able to prove it was for that." Patrick's words are more confident than his knees and he braces himself against the open window frame between us. His composure wavers and he struggles to keep his anger and amazement at just under a scream into my face. "I'm not stupid, you know!"

"Is that what it was all about, Pat? Is that why you were so worried that I might have my own lawyer. Someone who knew we were a wreck? All that smiling, the kissing, the fucking trip to Europe? What was that? So that when I was dead, they wouldn't automatically look to you, except to say, 'Poor Patrick, you loved her *so* much. Anyone could see . . .'"

He laughed at me. It actually straightened him up from using the car as a crutch. "I knew trying to be happy would feel like a trick to you, Dee. It's just not your thing, is it? So I just didn't bother at home."

"You could have just divorced me!" I yell back.

"And what? Started over again? With no money, no credit, staring down middle age with nothing to show for it? Or were you just going to give me everything—*since you're not using it!*" He scrubs his hands over his red face and forces down a breath. "When I wanted to go off with someone who could actually make a real life, would you have given it to me? There's not enough there for *my* half to pay for an entire reboot. My whole life was wasted on you. You don't even care what I do. Right or wrong, I'm nothing. I'm a prop. An inanimate, goddamned fixture in your *Still Life with Attached Garage.* Half of all of the savings we've got isn't worth it, if I'd even get half. I was at least as kind to your mother as you ever were. And I put up with your shit on top of it all. I earned that money, Dee."

"My mother earned that money."

He sneers and spits his accusations into my face. The words are almost hot in the air. "What difference would it make? Huh, Dee? What are you fighting for? You don't even live a real life. You just bide your time trying to be part of the goddamned wallpaper when you're not pouting on a barstool next to your loser brother. Your mother must have been so proud of you two. Small-time cop and small-time—what? Nothing. You shun anything that remotely hints at living. Deep down you know those pills weren't even about me. You knew not to trust your own body with any more life."

"You can't kill me because I was a disappointment."

"It'll never stick. I was careful."

"It's over, Pat."

"Not yet, it's not."

Patrick bolts off around the front of the car, hurling abuse at Jim. "You stupid shit. How did she get you . . ." His voice goes muffled through the distance and the glass of windshield as he hurtles past the front bumper. I can barely scramble out of the driver's side before Patrick has already ripped open the passenger door and taken up handfuls of Jim's jacket to haul him out.

I know I won't stand the odds of me against Patrick's full fury plus Jim untied.

Jim had righted himself higher in the seat. His mutely jerking head draws Patrick's eyes again, signposting as best he can to the center console, where my cell phone sits, propped in the folds of my handbag. I stop my fingers just short of Patrick's collar. I don't pull him back, don't try to prevent him from leaning in past Jim and snatching up the phone. He stabs at the home button. The screen lights up and 911 stares back at him, at us, from the display, just atop the speakerphone icon and the counter showing that the call has been running for more than three minutes.

Patrick spins to face me and our eyes meet. I watch his fall out of focus as he plays back what he's just said, searching for any hope that he's left himself an out when he's inevitably faced with explaining away this recorded conversation. He drops the phone into the footwell of the car.

"No," he says. Just no.

He reaches for me, his voice full of tears and rage. "No, no, no." Over and over. He flails for my face, lunging with open hands, pawing, scratching at my neck, slapping my eyes. He's gasping and grabbing, choking, twisting, blind with pitch and yaw. He is a drowning man.

I know this one.

My eyes are streaming and I taste blood from where his loose fist has crushed my lip against my front teeth. I sweep my left arm in a wide circle and drag Patrick's thrashing arms down, away from my face. I step in close and reverse the arc of my swing, slamming my forearm against Patrick's jaw and ear. His struggling stops instantly in the shock of the strike.

I wrap my other arm around him and draw him in close. I feel his heart banging against his chest. In a single second I meet the forward edge of disaster, the wave of sorrow that is surely coming. The people who loved him will have to find a new way to see him now—the criminal, the cheat, the face on the news, someone they didn't know and would have sworn didn't exist.

Except I am the only one who knows that neither of us has ever existed. Not the us we've shown to the world, or to each other.

I hear the rumble of an approaching car engine.

Patrick rears back to drive his head down into mine. I don't give him the chance. I widen my stance and twist around, driving his off-balance weight over my right thigh. He clamps down and drags me over with him.

The engine roars louder, then there's a bang behind us, but I can't look away from Patrick's teeth snapping at my face, snarling like a dog. A screech of metal-on-metal sings out in the haze. Out of the far corner of my eye, I see Jim's car jolt out of its position next to our sprawl and realize it's been hit. Two points for me for multitasking.

Patrick lands hard and I knock the air out of him, crashing down on his chest. I roll away and he grabs for purchase, any handhold to reel me back. Grit stings my palm as I slap the ground and I scrabble for any inches I can get with my left arm. Patrick's fury holds my right arm useless. I thrash away from his pull, but it's not working. He's dragging me to him. I heave in mouthfuls of air and dust, which melts into metallic panic down my throat. I try to scream it out, but the bitter-tasting, strangled bawl I manage doesn't match the effort. My throat clicks shut, the fear of Patrick's gripping progress up my arm is winning an edge, drawing me in from the only advantage I've had.

I quit fighting, on the outside at least. I fall completely limp to sell defeat. A tidal wave of silvery terror rolls through me while Patrick takes the slack bait. He grunts his effort to haul me in, but he has to loosen his grip to get a better one. He doesn't have the best hold. He's got half a hand's worth of sleeve and I'm deadweight to drag now. I have to get the timing right. There won't be another free second.

His hand opens. I launch myself through the dirt.

My wrist, then pants leg, then knee, then ankle, slip out of his grip. I kick him in the face and struggle away, an ungainly roll of elbows and toes. I look up to see the new car coming on. Patrick scrambles after me.

31

had heard the other car coming. I had heard it hit as it forced its way past the loose barricade I'd made of Jim's car. But only now does the first glimmer of wonder over who might be driving it spark in my mind. Police? A Carlisle employee? Please, not a partner of Jim's. I have some fight left in me, but not three grown men's worth.

I regain my feet.

And Patrick gains his.

We run.

The driver guns the car, swerving toward us, but then it turns at a sharper angle to herd Patrick wide of my path.

Well beyond any guess I had in queue to entertain, Brian Menary runs down the driver's window.

"Dee!"

"Don't let him get away!" I point at Patrick ducking in behind the wheel of his own car. "Please. I need him! Go!"

Patrick wrenches his driver's-side door shut. The engine catches and the whole car bucks as the transmission knocks into drive. Patrick shoots off down the track that leads deeper into Carlisle.

Brian follows.

I run behind them both, falling exponentially farther behind with every half second.

The dirt road churns up a spray of clay and dust-smoke. I tear through the haze as best I can and find that the road splinters, opening up into a rough wagon-wheel array of sheds and equipment with cleared, truckwide paths between them. I see Patrick's car disappear, sliding into a turn behind one of the larger barns. Brian drifts in behind him. The clamor rings off the metal buildings, disorienting the sound trails, the only clues I have to track their race through the complex.

An engine howls close by and I swivel my head to the nearest alley. But Patrick doesn't break from the nearest alley. He plows past a wall of stacked gutters and crates directly across from where I stand. Then he buries the pedal into the floorboards. The overtaxed machine bellows and heaves and rips fresh tracks through the weeds as it chews toward me over the raw ground.

I break left, but so does he. I lower my head and run past the math that's laughing at me. I will never make the shelter of the nearest building in time.

Brian's car shoots from the nearest lane and clips Patrick's bumper, spinning him off my position. Patrick catches the circle almost on the opposite side and disappears between two long ranks of lumber bins. Brian turns his car around and vanishes down the same chute.

The nudge Brian had given to Jim's car at the gate had been a hearty thump and a growl of denting steel panels. The tap to Pat's bumper just now had been one quick, heart-jolting clang.

The crash that rings out ahead of me now is a protracted groan of crumpling bodywork and exploding glass. I sprint toward the echo.

Patrick had hurtled unheeding through the maze of sheds and pallets with Brian's tires eating up the road behind him. They hadn't got far from the hub when Patrick had tried a tricky right turn, sharp and too fast.

The movable platform at the top of the turn is slightly less than a barge on wheels. Its payload of concrete blocks and wooden slats is also bristling with a haul of long metal struts. Patrick has plowed the nose of his car up under the base, between the wheels. Smoke is billowing from under the crumpled hood. A bundle of rods has speared through the windshield.

The accident has sheared off most of Patrick's jaw and troweled a spurting, red furrow from the side of his neck. A few of the rails must have been launched off their pile, and they struck wider, nailing him to his seat through his chest and shoulder. His life is raining down from every spear.

Brian is already tearing at the caved-in door of Patrick's car.

"Brian, be careful!" I run to his side. "Oh, God. Oh, look at him. My God. It's too late."

"Oh, shit." Brian grips the door handle and the bent door and shakes it with all his strength, but he thrashes with no payoff. Patrick's car rocks mildly, mockingly, under Brian's desperate pulling. But the door won't let go.

"I'm so sorry. Dee, he cut that turn so hard. He couldn't control it. What the hell was that? What is going on?" Brian looks at Patrick, but I look only to Brian and leave my husband in the peripheral vision, a red-and-white blur at the corner of my eye. So much howling red.

The meat state of him is a bland fact, a sudden, plain subtraction from the universe. No shrieking whirlwind marks the rip in the bubble of my little world. The supply yard is quiet now and golden, all the same as it was only a few minutes ago. The same, minus one. Birds are chattering on the wire overhead in the quickly cooling vanguard breeze of twilight. And my husband is gone, lifeless in seconds when he'd been seething with every human desperation only a handful of minutes ago, over the short, but vastly deep chasm of the time in between.

"We have to get some help," Brian says.

"No one can help." My numbed lips barely work. "You know that. You can see it, same as me. There's nothing anyone can do."

Brian ignores me and rocks the door into its bent frame again, yanking the door handle to force it to release the latch.

"Don't touch him," I scream, and startle up a flock of sparrows that had taken up the balcony seats for the show. Patrick is dead, immediately and permanently in the past tense. I am alive, but everything I was, or insisted that I was, has slipped away into the same past tense. So what am I, if not Patrick's wife or Jim's target?

That Patrick wasn't wrong isn't the same thing as his being right, but the shame still burns. He flayed the lie off me with all that he'd said, everything recorded for whoever will hear it. It will damn me right along with him. They'll put the blame on him, he'll be the bad guy. But they'll still know about me, that I had never been straight with him, that I had never been straight with myself. What kind of person does that? And what does she deserve?

But I am alive. *Breath and hope go together, baby girl.*

I have to get out of this day.

"You can't be here," I say to Brian.

The horror rolls over me. My knees go soft. Brian catches me up.

"What is going on? I'm so sorry, Dee. I didn't mean for him—"

"You don't need to be sorry. Everything's ruined. He did it to himself."

"What just happened?"

"Why are you even here?"

"You called me!"

"But how did you get here so fast?"

"You have no idea where I was," he says.

"But—" No fully formed question is there. Not a quick one at least. "You have to get out of here." I shove him back toward his car.

"Dee, what the hell is happening?"

"I can't, Brian. There's no time."

"You have to tell me at least this—what have I done?"

"There's no time. They must have sent someone by now. They'll be here any minute. Will you trust me?"

"I don't know what that means." He searches my face, working his stare deep into my eyes.

"Are you looking for my mother in there?"

"No. Not at all." He decides something about me that I don't have time to decode.

I'm surprised that anything can add to the tidal ache in me. He has to leave now. "Brian, can you get to 911 records?"

"Sure."

"Do that, then. I called them. Just before you came. Find the call. Then you'll see. I'm so sorry. Go, hurry."

The first distant wail of sirens floats from far away through the dusty air.

"But, there's a guy in that other car. . . . What are you going to do? Are you okay?"

"Brian, unless you want your early retirement blown all to hell and your whole life to be about this mess for the foreseeable future, just go. Go now. I've got this. I'll talk to you soon. I'll explain everything. It's fine. I promise. You didn't do anything wrong. Go!"

He does. I run back to Jim.

"Ma'am! Ma'am!" The emergency dispatcher calls to me from the open line as I jam my thumb against the speaker volume.

"I'm here!" I let the power of the last few minutes surge into my throat and carry my voice up into the manic ranges. Method acting, for sure. "He drove into some beams! Oh, God! His face. It's Patrick. He's killed himself."

"Ma'am, emergency services are en route. And an ambulance. Stay where you—"

"The guy is here with me. The guy he hired to kill me. The hit man."

Jim's eyes blaze with terror and questions.

"Wha—" The dispatcher sounds as confused as Jim looks.

"I can hear the sirens. Thank you!"

"No! Ma'am, stay on the line. Keep this li—"

I disconnect the call and drop out of hot drama into ice-cold anger. I scrabble over Jim, yanking at his bindings. "They're going to catch you. I'm going to tell them that you ran, but they'll be right on you. I don't think you've got even that snowball's chance in hell, but if you've got one, it's right now." I pull the knotted socks from his mouth and lower my face into his, gritting my teeth over having to talk to him at all. "And you might remember that I'm the one that gave it to you, you son of a bitch."

"What the hell is this? What are you doing?"

"You have no idea how much I'd rather shoot you in the face until you're all the way stupid and ugly"—I snatch up the paintball pistol from the seat and toss it through the still open driver's-side window, into the shrubs—"but I don't feel like being arrested for kidnapping today. Patrick's dead. So is your contract. No payday for you. You've got a head start of maybe two minutes. Merry fucking Christmas. I suggest you get your ass in gear."

Jim rubs at the chafed corners of his mouth. "Thank you."

"Don't thank me, you asshole. You'd just better be glad I'm not my mother."

I scramble out of the car. The other door opens and closes, then another. Then Jim's car roars to life and runs over my long shadow as I sprint for the front gate, scripting my story with the wind dragging the sound of sirens over me.

32

almost had Patrick cremated, even though I knew he had wanted to be buried. With Jim on the run and a tinny 911 recording that is only slightly better than flimsy evidence, and not nearly as much of a smoking gun as I would have liked, I feel cheated. On the heels of that, I feel vengeful and mean. But Patrick's parents have always been kind to me. I changed my mind at the ragged end of the window for him to be embalmed and left a check and a note under my mother-in-law's windshield wiper instead.

The news coverage of the showdown at Carlisle Inc. isn't what I'd braced myself for. The story has been downplayed, almost grayed out for maximum blandness. I waver between grateful and suspicious.

Our friends have been artless in their comforting, dancing with the two left feet of curiosity and unease. I have enough frozen casseroles to get me through an apocalypse, but they all came in disposable pans. No one wants any jinxed thing back from me. I can hardly blame them. My brother is furious with me. The neighbors stare while trying to look like they aren't staring. I float through a life I don't recognize.

Today, I've come to lunch at the food court. I've come every day for a week, scanning the crowd while trying hard to be like my normal neighbors and not look overmuch as if I am scanning the crowd. I've held a book the whole time, each time, and have got not a lot of words off the page and not a lot of food down my throat either. Wavy, dark hair always tugs at my peripheral vision. So do well-cut jackets and tall men in jeans.

It's Tuesday and chilly. I get up from my chair, annoyed with myself in a way that is growing less vague. I've lost weight that I can't afford to. I'm not sleeping well. I flick my long sweater from off the back of the chair and notice an envelope sticking up from the gaping front pocket of my purse.

It's unaddressed and nearly flat. A single sheet of paper is trifolded inside.

I heard the recording. You didn't do anything wrong either. Well played. And thank you. If you ever need anything . . .

Then along came a spider. Most literally. A light brown spider just rappelled from the ceiling and landed on my desk next to my right hand. I'd listlessly been clicking through this and that on the Internet with no direction beyond the stupid pull of whatever caught my eye next. I meant to be here for fifteen minutes. I've been scrolling for an hour and fifty. That spider just scared the hell out of me.

I clap my empty teacup over it and fish out one of the sturdier card-stock flyers from the recycle bin to slide under the whole works. I take my catch to the door, balancing it in my less than reliable left hand, and imagining the cascade of wobble-crash-scream that is going to send this harmless creature running up my arm and probably to its death by flail.

"Freer than me," I say, crouched on the stoop. Predictably, I burst into tears. The spider flees.

My mother's phrase plays through my mind in some of the languages she'd taught us to recognize. *Freier als ich. Plus libre que moi. Friare än mig. Svobodnejší než jsem já.*

Back at the computer, a new tab brings up an appealingly empty search bar. There is no need to type her name. I've done that before, so many times, and all I've ever got in return was a lovely pain in the ass from the past, who also happened to be a hero.

Why not this?

I type, *Freer than me.* Google coughs up nearly 7 million hits of, as far as I can tell, nothing I care about.

I put quotation marks around it and scan a narrowed-down list for a few pages. Still, it goes on forever. That phrase was particular to my mother and to our family, and in more ways than I had known just a few short weeks ago, but "freer than me" isn't an impossibly unusual concept. Other people sigh over what is fair between the haves and the have-nots in everything, surely also in the freedom department.

Everyone weighs everything in the scales of covet, sometimes most particularly the idea of being free. There is certainly freedom in all the things that everyone wants, all the things they tell us we should be. Who is smarter than me, who is prettier than me, faster than me, richer than me? And then my peculiar jealous question: Who is more normal than me?

But not all that many people were ever balancing themselves against a spider.

So I slide the arrow up to the search field and roll it to the inside of the end quotation mark. Click. I type, + *Spider.*

I hit Enter.

There's one result.

I read the preview on the search page and break into a cool sweat.

Once upon a time . . .

The website is an anonymous, leave-a-message, confessional bulletin board, a place to purge a secret or to declare a truth—a love, a fault, an apology. It's a forum to make any of these things feel a little more real than it did when it was only a silent something jailed inside your head. It's an ocean of electronic letters in bottles.

The link on the search page zips to a post, a quarter of the way down the screen, buried in the pages upon pages that make up the site. The username was simply AV. Annette Vess. I close my eyes. The message is a few paragraphs long. I don't want to start it because I don't want it to be over. Whatever it says, I can only read it for the first time once.

I open my eyes.

Once upon a time . . .

There was a girl of pluck and a boy of sixes who grew up to be extraordinary people. If either of them ever reads this, then it means they've gone looking.

And if you've come looking, either of you or both, I hope it doesn't mean you're troubled, but I'm thinking that you might be. And if so, I'm sorry for that. I'm sorry if whatever is wrong has you thinking of me because I'm the cause of your concern. But, I'm even sorrier if it has nothing to do with me at all, and that you've come looking for me out here in the pixels only because I'm not there with you now.

Sadly, I know that there is plenty in this world that you can't handle. But it's really not all that sad, because if you can't handle it, then nobody could have. I lasted long enough to know that. You are both so capable and beautiful, you made it easy to do the best I could. If you could know how grateful I am for that . . .

For the problem at hand, try this: You know what to do, my darlings. And if you don't, do what you think you'd do if you were exactly the person you wanted to be.

Take care of each other and be happy, not sad, when you set a spider freer than me. My love for you is here, it's there, it's everywhere. . . .

I click her username without hope. There are no other messages.

33

Our house, or my house, I suppose, sold quickly. I've just returned to my office from the closing, and Jill rings my desk from her office up front before I can get settled in.

"Um, your uncle's here to see you?" Her voice is full of doubt.

"Terrific. Can you just direct him back here, please?"

He bulks up the doorway a few seconds later.

"Hi, Dee."

"Hello, Paul." I don't like his towering over me in my seat, so I stand and offer my hand for a strictly business greeting, but he twists it over and kisses my knuckles before I can pull away. It wouldn't have been easy anyway; his grip is a vise. "Security let you right up here, huh, just like that?"

"I'm good with security guards."

"I imagine you are."

"I'm sorry I haven't been by sooner. I mean, I heard what happened later that same day."

"Well, there's a surprise." I resist the urge to scrub the back of my hand against my slacks to be rid of the vaguely cool spot his lips have left.

"But I wanted to give it some time. Give *you* some time."

"How unexpectedly thoughtful of you. Are you going soft in your old age?"

"You're never going give me a break, are you, Dee?" He laughs. "Or the benefit of the doubt?"

"I don't know what you mean."

"Okay, well, here's a softball then, just to get into your good graces and to prove that I come in peace. I'd like to help you in this tough, confusing time. You must be rattled. What can I do for you? Do you have any questions for me? Can I help you with anything that you need to know to settle your mind?"

"Fine. I'll bite. Did you massage the media after Patrick died? After what he was accused of?"

"I like that word *massage*."

"So you did."

"I just said it was a nice word."

I sigh. "You know what? Never mind. I'm just going to go with that you did and made it all go away, and I'll say, in hindsight, thank you. I think it would have shattered my nerves."

"Well, it wouldn't do to have your name splashed all over the papers, now would it? Is that all the questions you've got?"

"No, but it seems kind of pointless."

"Do you want to try me?"

"Oh, sure. Why not? I've got nothing better to do all day. Did you know that Patrick was looking into having me killed?"

"No. That sort of thing is not really our pond. That's just freshwater and we're more, um, what you might call deep-sea fisherman."

"Oh my God. That sounded like almost a straight answer, Paul. Bravo. I didn't know you had it in you."

"Brian doesn't know I'm here, by the way. He says he doesn't know about any of this either, in case you were wondering."

"I wasn't wondering." I approve of my cool, unquavery delivery after he zapped me with news of Brian, now obviously a known mutual acquaintance somehow.

Paul laughs. "You are almost an excellent liar. But try not to work a hole into your head, having to believe your own bullshit. It makes the whole thing feel too much like work."

"So, what is it for you, then, Paul, all the lying? Sport?"

"Exercise."

I say nothing.

"Ah, come on, Dee. You're allowed to be in cahoots with your own tongue. It could save your life someday. You never know."

Deep and well out of sight, which was the only place I'd allow it, a chill chases a dread between my shoulder blades. That sounded like something my mother would have said.

"Brian sends his love."

"Not by way of you, he didn't."

Paul drops his gaze and smirks at the crease cresting the knee of his trouser leg. "Well, I'm sure he meant to."

The lull is uncomfortable and pointless. So I throw myself into it just to get it all over with. "I'm guessing you came here for a reason, Paul. And I'm almost thinking I know what that reason might be."

"Oh, do tell."

"Not a chance. Speak now or change your mind. Of course, you can always just take the high road and say you stopped by to tell me how sorry you are for my loss. Either way, let's wrap this up. I am actually a little bit busy. I'm meeting Simon in an hour and twenty minutes, and I have a few things to do before that."

"Yeah, when your brother finds out, he's not going to be all that pleased that I've come to see you."

I roll my eyes and chuckle through my nose. "Simon hates your guts. So I won't tell him if you don't."

"He is really good at singing that tune, isn't he? Do you ever think maybe it's so he doesn't have to talk about me at all?"

"I know my brother. Nice try, though."

Paul stares at me long enough to raise the fine hairs on my arm. His smirk shows that he knows it, too. "If you say so."

He sits down in the guest chair opposite my desk without having been offered the ease. "Well, I'll get to it then. They picked up some guy named Jim. I think you're acquainted with the fellow? Anyway, they caught him trying to get out of the country on a fake passport. I read his interview transcripts. Hell of a story he told. Hell of a story. Then, wouldn't you know it, somehow he escaped custody during a routine transfer. It was the darnedest thing. His whereabouts are unknown."

"Is he coming for me?"

"Absolutely not."

"Is he dead?"

"Um"—Paul punctuates the delay with a small, satisfied smile— "not as such."

"But you know where he is."

"We're in touch."

"I see."

"Fascinating guy, that Jim."

"I don't want to know."

"If his story is to be believed, you broke up a murder-for-hire ring with just an afternoon of poking around and a paintball gun. All with zero training."

"Shhh. Will you please keep your voice down?" I close the door to my office. "I am trying to get things back to normal around here. I still have to live in this town, you know."

"No, you don't."

"And I thought you said this pond wasn't salty enough for you."

"It wasn't until you went swimming in it. Vess is a particular name with particular connotations. I got curious."

I ignore him. "And anyway, you and I both know I've had plenty of *training*."

Paul grips the armrests and heaves the chair a half turn from the front of my desk and stretches his legs out, ankles crossed. "Do you know they've tied fourteen hits on the Atlantic coast to this ring already?"

"No. They won't tell me anything." He's gained advantage again, lolling in my guest chair as I stand off to the side not knowing what to do with myself. I take my seat again and enjoy the span of my desk between us.

"Well, it's big. There's even a ruckus at the phone companies. Until the 'special projects' department over at Carlisle had the clever idea to give each of their 'special' customers one of their own phones, for the duration of said 'special project,' they were paying techs to delete records in the databases. Ergo, a whole new branch of charges and red tape. It's a mess." Paul leans in on the too-polished wood of the armrest.

My desk, my whole office even, suddenly seems fussy and prim. I nudge a short stack of papers out of its finicky geometry, peering over it as if there were something urgent for me printed on its top sheet.

Paul pays no attention to my pretend distraction. "You could have access to whatever you wanted to know if you came to work for me." He's struck a tone without trying, at once flattering, con-spiratorial, and with more than a hint of a dare. The snake in Eden probably had a dose of the same schooling. "You could use a fresh start, Dee. Get out of this silly place, for one thing."

"It's not happening, Paul."

"You'd have access to your mother's files."

"No, I wouldn't." Then a cool echo in my head: *You don't need them, Plucky. Truth be told, you don't need me either.*

Don't say that.

"Why not, Dee? Why shouldn't I say it? That's the beauty of being me. I can say what I like and offer up what I like, all to get what I like. I've been around a long time. I've earned it."

Shit. I had said that out loud. *I really am losing it.* "I'm sure you'd show me a bunch of files that had my mother's name on them, but I wouldn't want to have to bank on what brand of bullshit would be inside."

"You've really got your cloak-and-dagger play all scripted out, haven't you? It's not like that, Dee. We're not that complicated. I would show them to you. Whatever you wanted to know. None of it is that big of a deal anymore. Nothing stays top secret forever. Just the same, it'd be a bit of a Faustian thing." He smiles sunnily. "You'd certainly owe me."

Another long stare off, but this time he can't get my hackles up. He smiles into my eyes as he fishes in his pocket. He hands me a flimsy business card. The ink is thin, the graphic slightly off center. I know full well he could afford better. "If you change your mind, give me a call. I know it says Swan's Dry Cleaner's, but if you leave a message for me, I'll get it."

"I'm sure."

He doesn't turn around, and his parting comment comes from halfway out the door. "If you're curious, ask Simon where he gets his uniforms laundered."

Paul's baiting me about my brother, and even if he isn't, Simon's life is his own. I had point-blank asked him about Paul in the bar on the day Patrick died. But if I was honest, I could play back that conversation verbatim. I had asked him in the present tense. *Does he try to get to you, too?* He could easily have answered no and let it stand as the truth on a technicality.

On the recording, my mother had only asked Brian to steer Paul away from me. She never mentioned Simon, and I burned with private shame that I hadn't wondered why. *Stable full of Vesses,* she'd said it, but I hadn't realized all that it meant. Did Brian know? Simon had said his job made it difficult to have a relationship, and that he'd wanted to rain down special trouble on Patrick. *Once upon a time . . .*

And he'd always known what our mother was, far more and much sooner than I ever had. He'd been her coworker.

He had told me over and over, but I'd never heard him.

I start to tear the business card straight down the middle, intending to turn it into a ragged pile of wastebasket confetti, which is all it deserves. My mother stares saucily at me over her shoulder from the silver frame on the corner of my desk. One of her loves had been a photographer, and a good one. I had always liked that guy. He'd caught her for me to keep forever in that picture. Her eyes drill into mine, and I kind of forget to finish off the poorly rendered swan. A thin buffer of rinky-dink card stock saves its neck. I set the card aside and pick up the photograph. She all but winks at me.

Turning the frame over, I pry the easel back away from the felt and peel a flap in the facing paper. I wonder about people who can grease the gears of the world with stealth and plots and never let the consequences get under their fingernails. I think of Patrick, his image in my mind already faded pale like overexposed film. I hear the distant echo of brakes screaming and glass breaking. I look at my hand; it's steady. The overhead lights glint in my plain, clear-gloss manicure. I tuck Paul's card inside the little pocket I've made and smooth it down, all but invisible. I smile at Mother and she smirks at me.

"It doesn't matter about the stupid card," I say aloud. I'll never look at it again. I'm almost positive.

ACKNOWLEDGMENTS

In Acknowledgment writing, the greatest blessing is a cast of usual suspects. I'm in a fortress of familiar support and never for a moment am I not aware of, and grateful for, how wonderful these people are.

Atop the list are my fantastic husband and the ridiculously awesome daughters we discovered under some rare and magical cabbage leaves way back when. There are three things I prize above all others—intelligence, humor, and kindness. I live a daily jackpot, up to my neck in gold tokens of insight, laughter, and love because of Art, Julia, and Rianne.

My agent, Amy Moore-Benson, well, I hope she knows how much I appreciate her. I tell her often, but I love telling everyone else, too. She's tremendous in all the ways there are to be tremendous. The team at Simon & Schuster/Gallery Books makes the insecure, nerve-racking bits of this business brief and bearable, and they make the fun parts a full-on party. Thank you Karen Kosztolnyik, for your wisdom, encouragement, and patience, and also Paige Cohen, Stephanie DeLuca, Steve Boldt, Jen Bergstrom, and the ghosts of Alexandra Lewis and Heather Hunt (no, no, they're not dead—just off on other parts of life, but newly enough so that they still haunt the business end of this work; they're still mine—if only just a little).

Mike Breedlove (hopefully Sheriff Mike Breedlove by the time this goes to print) is still my go-to guy for police work and crime information. If I asked him more, I'd get less wrong. Thank you, Mike, always.

A writer's writer-friends can do for her what regular friends cannot. That's neither an endorsement nor an indictment. It's just the way it is. Graeme Cameron, my most trusted nay-and-yea-sayer, you're brilliant and thanks for existing. And an avalanche of thank-yous to Tana French, Mark Pryor, William Haskins, Chris Pavone, Brad Parks, Reed Farrell Coleman, Butch Wilson, Sylvia Harmon, Carole Oldroyd, Kim Michele Richardson, and Jane Smith for being writers and for being there for me. You people are absolute stars.

A writer's regular friends are what everyone's friends are: the best thing that life ever invented. Some of these are my patient early readers like Jessica Coffey, Katie Delgado, Mary Rollins, and Simone Kaiser, and some of them would have been if I'd gotten my act together sooner this time—I'm looking at you Kelly Coffey Colvin, Lisa Fitchett, Kristi McCullough, and Cindy Dearman. A little special thank-you goes to Tamsin Moore, a new friend, however far away, a reader and a person who could give lessons in enthusiastic encouragement. I could not leave out Tim Dearman, who is not only a wonderful friend but a master craftsman. He made for me the best place I could ever want for getting my work done. I love my office probably more than he even knows. I can think in here.

And love to my mother and sisters, Jeanne Miller-Mason, Carmen Mason, and Natalie Sherwood, who never are far from my thoughts, no matter how much map we cover.

All these people deserve my love and thanks, and I give them a dose here, gladly.

But it's the reader I don't know who is back here with me now, at the very end—the end that's just slightly after The End, who I want to thank especially. It doesn't matter that I wrote this in my office, all through a morning that is threatening a storm that I'm now starting to doubt is ever going to do its thing. Through the art and science of words and publishing, the real *now* is the now of you reading this, the now of you having given this book a slice of your time, wherever and whenever you did it, and whatever the season and the weather where you are. Thank you for doing that.

I hope we meet on the page again someday, and maybe even become each other's usual suspects for stories.

—Jamie Mason, June 2014

Get email updates on

JAMIE MASON,

exclusive offers,

and other great book recommendations

from Simon & Schuster.

Visit **newsletters.simonandschuster.com**

or

scan below to sign up: